"I don't give guarantees to hellspawn, Rutger.

"You tell me about Perry's new houseguest, and I may decide to be charitable and overlook your Trader's stepping outside the bounds."

As soon as I said it, I knew I'd guessed right. Rutger stiffened, and the ratty gleam intensified. He telegraphed like a four-year-old reaching for candy. As soon as he twitched he knew he'd made a mistake, too, and I lowered the gun. The silver in my hair shifted, rattling. A blue spark popped from my apprentice-ring, and the hellbreed actually flinched. The scarves tied to the bar in front of me lay dead and dark now, bleeding clear fluid across the mirror-polished surface. A ripple ran through the assembled 'breed, and the Traders moved back in one clockwork motion.

"Oh, hit a nerve there, did I? Thank you." I sounded completely insincere. "Pleasant dreams, hellspawn."

When I hopped down from the bar, I expected him to jump me. Instead, he stepped min̄ ___ ide. His shoes clicked like a woman's he__ ___ llbreed footsteps do not sound t__ ___ nt. They're too light, or t__ ___ producing something ___ ___ess.

"He said ___ ___ through the assembled 'br___ ___ e words. Rutger tried out a smile, lig___ ___ dly over his skin. The black bulged and ripp___ ddly, trying to contain whatever lived under the shell of human seeming. "And he said to tell you this: *he cannot hold back the tide forever.*"

BOOKS BY LILITH SAINTCROW

JILL KISMET NOVELS

Night Shift

Hunter's Prayer

Redemption Alley

Flesh Circus

Heaven's Spite

DANTE VALENTINE NOVELS

Working for the Devil

Dead Man Rising

The Devil's Right Hand

Saint City Sinners

To Hell and Back

Dark Watcher

Storm Watcher

Fire Watcher

Cloud Watcher

The Society

Hunter, Healer

Steelflower

HEAVEN'S SPITE

LILITH SAINTCROW

www.orbitbooks.net

This book is a work of fiction. Names, characters, places, and incidents are the product of the author's imagination or are used fictitiously. Any resemblance to actual events, locales, or persons, living or dead, is coincidental.

Copyright © 2010 by Lilith Saintcrow
Excerpt from *Angel Town* copyright © 2010 by Lilith Saintcrow
All rights reserved. Except as permitted under the U.S. Copyright Act of 1976, no part of this publication may be reproduced, distributed, or transmitted in any form or by any means, or stored in a database or retrieval system, without the prior written permission of the publisher.

Orbit
Hachette Book Group
237 Park Avenue
New York, NY 10017
Visit our website at www.orbitbooks.net

Orbit is an imprint of Hachette Book Group. The Orbit name and logo are trademarks of Little, Brown Book Group Limited.

Printed in the United States of America

First edition: November 2010

10 9 8 7 6 5 4 3 2 1

For L.I.
Soon enough.

What like a bullet can undeceive!
　　—Herman Melville

1

*H*ow fast does a man run, when Death is after him?

The Trader clambered up the rickety fire escape and I was right behind. If I'd had my whip I could have yanked his feet out from under him and had him down in a heartbeat. No use lamenting, had to work with what I had.

He was going too fast for me to just shoot him at the moment.

Didn't matter. I knew where he was headed. And though I hoped Saul would be quick enough to get her out of the way, it would be better if I killed him now.

Or got there first. And *then* killed him.

He went over the edge of the wall in one quick spiderlike scuttle and I flung myself up, the silver charms tied in my hair buzzing like a rattler's tail. The scar on my right wrist burned like a live coal pressed against my skin as I *pulled* etheric force through it. A sick tide of burning delight poured up my arm, I reached the top and was up and over so fast I collided with the Trader, my hellbreed-strong right fist jabbing forward to get him a good shot in the kidneys while my left hand tangled in his dark, dirty hair.

We rolled across the rooftop in a tangle of arms and legs, my leather trench coat snapping once and fluttering raggedly. It was singed and peppered with holes from the shotgun blast, where I'd lost my whip. I was covered in drying blood and very, *very* pissed off.

Just another night on the job.

Oh no you don't, fuckwad. One hand in his hair, the other one now full of knife hilt. The silver-loaded blade ran with crackling blue light as the blessing on it reacted to the breath of contamination wavering around the Trader's writhing. I caught an elbow in the face, my eye smarting and watering immediately, and slid the knife in up to the guard.

The Trader bucked. He was thin but strong. My fingers slipped, greasy with blood. I got a knee in, wrestled him down as he twisted—

—and he shot me four times.

They were just lead, not silverjacket slugs. Still, the violent shock of agony as four of them slammed through my torso was enough to throw me down for a few moments, stunned and gasping, the scar chuckling to itself as it flooded me with crackling etheric force. My body convulsed, stupid meat freaking out over a little thing like bullets. A curtain of red closed over my vision, and I heard retreating footsteps.

Get up, Jill. Get up now.

Another convulsion running through me, locking down every single muscle. I rolled onto my side as lung fluid and blood jetted from my mouth and nose. The contraction was so intense even my eyes watered, and I whooped in a deep breath. My hands scrabbled uselessly against dirty rooftop. My nails were bitten down to the quick; if they hadn't been I would've splintered them on tarpaper.

Get UP, you bitch!

My feet found the floor, the rest of me hauled itself upright, and I heard my voice from a dim, faraway place. I was cursing like a sailor who just found out shore leave was canceled. Etheric force crackled around me like heat lightning. I took stock of myself and took a single step.

So far so good.

Now go get him. Get him before he gets there.

I stumbled, almost fell flat on my face. Getting peppered with plain lead won't kill me, but if it hits a lot of vitals it's pretty damn uncomfortable. My flesh twitched, expelling bits and chunks of bullet, and I coughed again rackingly, got my passages clear. More stumbling steps, my right bootsole squeaking because it was blood-wet. The knife spun, blade reversed against my forearm, and I blinked. Took off again, because the Trader's matted black hair puffed up as he dropped over the side of the building.

Now I was mad.

Go get him, Jill. Get him quick and get him hard.

A waxing half moon hung overhead, Santa Luz shuddered underneath its glow, and I hurled myself forward again, going over the edge of the building with arms and legs pulled in just in case. The drop wasn't bad, and I had some luck—the stupid bastard decided to stand and fight rather than run off toward the civilian he'd marked for death.

He hit me hard, ramming us both into the brick wall

of the building we'd just been tangling on top of. This rooftop was a chaos of girders and support structure for the water tank looming above us. I got my left arm free, flipped my wrist so the knife blade angled in, and stabbed.

Another piece of luck—his arm was up, and my aim was good. The knife sank in at a weird angle, the axillary region exposed and vulnerable and now full of silver-loaded steel. My knee came up so hard something in his groin popped like bubble gum, and I clocked him a good one with my hellbreed-strong right fist.

Stupid fuck. While he was running, or at least just trying to get *away*, he had a chance. But fighting a pitched battle with an angry helltainted hunter? Not a good idea.

He folded, keening, and I coughed up more blood. A hot sheen of it slicked my chin, splashed on my chest. I pitched forward, following him down. My knee hit, a jolt of silvery pain up my femur; I braced myself and yanked his head back. His scream turned into a harsh rasping as the neck extended, vocal cords suddenly stressed.

Another knife hilt slapped my palm and I jerked it free of the sheath. My right hand cramped, he made a whining noise as I bore down, my body weight pinning him. I'm tall for a female but still small when compared to most hellbreed, Traders, or what-have-you. The scar helps, gives me denser muscle and bone, but when it comes right down to it my only hope is leverage. I had some, but not enough.

Which meant I had to kill him quick.

The silver-loaded blade dragged across easily, parting helltainted flesh. A gush of hot, black-tinged blood sprayed out. Human blood looks black at night, but the darkness of hellbreed ichor tainting a Trader's vital fluids is in a class all its own.

Arterial spray goes amazingly far, especially when you have the rest of the body under tension and the head wrenched all the way back. The body slumped in my hands, a gurgle echoing against rooftop and girders, twitches racing through as corruption claimed the flesh. I used to think that if Traders could see one of them biting it and the St. Vitus's dance of contagion that eats up their tissues, they might think twice about making a bargain with hellbreed.

I don't think that anymore. Because really, what Trader thinks they're going to die? That's why they Trade—they think the rules don't apply to them. Every single one of them, you see, is *special*. A special little snowflake, entitled to kill, rape, terrify, and use whoever and whatever they want.

They think they can escape consequences. Sometimes they do.

But not while I'm around.

My legs didn't work too well. I scrabbled back from the body, a knife hilt in either fist. Fetched up against the brick wall, right next to the indent from earlier. Sobbing breaths as my own body struggled for oxygen, my eyes locked to the Trader's form as it disappeared into a slick of bubbling black grease starred with scorched, twisting bones.

Watch, milaya. My teacher's voice, quietly, inside my head. *You watch the death you make. Is only way.*

I watched until there was nothing recognizably human left. Even the bones dissolved, and by daybreak there would be only a lingering foulness to the air up here.

I checked the angle of the building—any sunlight that came through the network of girders would take care of the rest. If the bones had remained I would've had to call up some banefire, to deny whatever hellbreed he'd Traded with the use of a nice fresh zombie corpse.

But no. He'd Traded hard, and he'd used his bargain recklessly, burning up whatever remained of his humanity. I coughed again, shuddered as the adrenaline dump poured through me with a taste like bitter copper. Training clamped down on the chemical soup, my pulse evening out and my ribs bringing down their heaving.

Just another day on the job. And we were three scant blocks from Molly Watling, his last planned victim. Who was probably scared out of her mind right now, even if Saul had shown up to get her out of the way.

It's not every day your ex-husband Trades with a hellbreed and shows up with a thirst for human flesh, hot blood, and terror. Trevor Watling had worked through his current wife, three strippers, and two ex-girlfriends, not to mention a mistress and another woman grabbed at a bus stop. His sole victim of opportunity, his practice run for the others.

Even killers start out small.

I blew out between my teeth. The reek was amazing, and I was covered in goop, guck, and blood. The night was young, and I had a line on the hellbreed Trevor Watling had Traded with. A hellbreed I was going to talk to, up close and personal, hopefully with some silverjacket lead, because that was my job.

Time to get back to work.

But I just stood there for a few more moments, staring blankly at the smear on the rooftop. I've given up wondering why some men think they own women enough to beat and kill them. It used to be like a natural disaster—just get out of the way and hope it doesn't get you. Then I thought about it until it threatened to drive me batshit, chewing over the incomprehensible over and over again.

Now it was enough just to stop what I could. But, Jesus, I'm so tired of it.

A vibrating buzz almost startled me. It was the pager in its padded pocket. I dug it out and glanced at it, and my entire body went cold.

What the fuck is he doing calling me?

I tested my legs. They were willing, capable little soldiers now that the crisis was over. My shirt was ruined, and my leather pants weren't far behind. Still, all my bits were covered, and my trench coat was ripped and tattered but still usable.

I got going.

My pager went off again, and when I slid it out of my pocket Concepción, the Filipina ER nurse, looked at me funny. But they're used to me at Mercy General, and Saul made soothing noises at the sobbing, red-haired almost-victim.

"Montaigne at the precinct will have details," I told the ER nurse, who nodded, making a notation on her clipboard. "She'll probably need sedation, I don't blame her."

The stolid motherly woman in neatly pressed scrubs nodded. "Rape kit?"

I shook my head. "No." *Thank God. I got there in time.*

Of course, if I hadn't, Molly Watling would be carted to the morgue, instead of driven to the ER or even forced to endure a rape exam. Small mercy, but I'd take it. Connie's expression said she'd take it, too; her relief was palpable.

"It's all right," Saul said soothingly. The silver tied in his hair with red thread gleamed under the fluorescents, and he didn't look washed out in the slightest. But then, Weres usually look good in any lighting. "You're safe now. Everything's okay."

The slim red-haired woman nodded. Fat tears trickled down her damp cheeks. She flinched whenever I looked at her.

"*Bueno*." Connie patted the woman's arm. "Any injuries?"

I shook my head again. "Nope. Shock, though. Ex-husband."

Comprehension spread over Connie's face. No more needed to be said.

I rolled my shoulders back once, dispelling the aches settling in them. "So, sedation. Call Montaigne, get a trauma counselor over here, and Monty'll take care of the paperwork." County Health has counselors on standby, and so does the police department. *Especially* in cases like this. "I've got to get going."

Connie nodded and deftly subtracted Molly from Saul. The redhead didn't want to let go of his arm, and I completely understood. A big guy who looks like Native American romance-novel cheesecake, red warpaint on his high cheekbones? I'd be clinging too.

"Th-thank you." The almost-victim didn't even look at me. "F-for everything. I didn't th-think anyone would b-believe me."

Considering that her ex-husband had terrorized every

woman before he'd killed them, and he'd been a real winner even *before* Trading, it made sense. If I'd been a little quicker on the uptake, I might've been able to save some of the other women as well.

But I couldn't think like that. I'd done what I could, right?

That never helps. Ever.

"He's not going to hurt you anymore." I sounded harsher than I needed to, and she actually jumped. "He's not going to hurt *anyone* anymore."

I expected her to flinch and cower again. God knows I'm hardly ever a comforting sight.

But she surprised me—lifting her chin, pushing her shoulders back. "I sh-should thank you t-too." She swallowed hard, forced herself to meet my eyes. It was probably uncomfortable—a lot of people have trouble with my mismatched gaze. One eye brown, one blue—it just seems to offend people on a deep nonverbal level when I stare them down.

And like every other hunter, I don't look away. It's disconcerting to civilians.

I nodded. "It's my job, Ms. Watling. I'm glad we got there in time." *Too late for those other women. But take what you can get, Jill.* I shifted my attention to Connie. "I need a phone."

"*Si, señora.* Use the one at the desk." And just like that, I was dismissed. Connie bustled the woman away out of the curtained enclosure, and the regular sounds of a Tuesday night on the front lines swallowed the sharper refrain of a terrified, relieved woman dissolving into fresh sobs. The smell of Lysol and human pain stung my nose almost as much as the dissolving reek of a Trader's death.

Saul let out a sigh. He reached out, his hand cupping my shoulder. "Hello, kitten."

I leaned into the touch. The smile spreading over my face felt unnatural, until my heart made the funny jigging movement it usually did when he was around and a wave of relief caught up with me. "Hey, catkin. Good work."

"I knew he wouldn't get there before you." His own smile was a balm against my jagged nerves. He'd put on some weight, and the shadows under his eyes weren't so dark anymore. The grief wasn't hanging on him quite so heavily. "What's the next emergency?"

I shrugged, held up the pager. "Gilberto paged from home."

He absorbed this. "Not like him," he finally said. Which was as close as he would get to grudgingly admitting my apprentice was doing well.

"That's what I thought." I reached up with my left hand, squeezed his fingers where they rested against my shoulder. His skin was warm, but mine left a smudge of filth and blood on him.

He never seemed to mind, but I took my hand away and swallowed hard.

Saul examined me. "Well, let's see what he wants. And then, lunch?" Meaning the night was still young, and he'd like a slice of time alone with me.

It's kind of hard to roll around with your favorite Were when you've got a kid living with you, after all. I was about ready to start suggesting the car's backseat, but—how's this for irony—I hadn't had time yet. One thing after another, that's a hunter's life. "I don't see why not. I've got a line on the hellbreed Watling Traded with, too."

He nodded. The fringe on his jacket trembled, and he turned on one heel. "Sounds like a busy night."

"Aren't they all." I followed him out, past other curtained enclosures. Some were open, the machinery of saving lives standing by for the next high-adrenaline emergency. Some were closed, the curtains drawn to grant a sliver of privacy. Someone groaned from one, and a murmur of doctor's voices came from another. Mercy General's ER was always hopping.

The nurse at the desk just gave me a nod and pushed the phone over, then went back to questioning a blank-eyed man in Spanish through the sheet of bulletproof glass as she filled out a sheet of paperwork with neat precise scratches. The patient swayed and cradled his swollen, messily bandaged hand; he was pale under his coloring and smelled of burnt metal and cocaine. I kept half an eye on him while I punched 9 and my own number.

He picked up on the first ring. Slightly nasal boy's voice. *"Bruja?"*

"Gilberto. This better be good." I regretted it as soon as I said it. He wasn't the type to call me for nothing.

As usual, he didn't take it personally. A slight, wheezing laugh. "Package for you, *mi profesora*. Wrapped up with a pretty bow."

What? "A package?" My mouth went dry. "Gilberto—"

"Man who delivered it still here. *Uno rubio*, in a suit. Says he'll wait for you."

A blond, in a suit? The dryness poured down, invaded my throat. "Gilberto, listen to me very carefully—"

A slight sound as the phone was taken from my apprentice. I knew, from the very first breath, who was waiting for me at home.

"My darling Kiss." Perry's voice was smooth as silk, and full of nasty amusement. "He's quite a winning elf, your new houseboy. And *so* polite."

Think fast, Jill. My heart leapt nastily. The scar on my wrist turned hot and hard, swollen with corruption. As if he had just pressed his lips against my flesh again. "Pericles."

Saul went stiff next to me, his dark eyes flashing orange for a moment.

The hellbreed on the other end of the line laughed. "I have a gift for you, my darling. Come home and see it. I will be content with the boy until then."

He dropped the phone down into the cradle. The sound of the connection breaking was like the click of a bullet into the chamber.

I slammed my receiver down, pulling it at the last moment so I wouldn't break the rest of the phone. The man on the other side of the glass jumped, and the nurse twisted in her chair to look at me. I didn't bother to give a glance of apology, just looked at my Were.

Saul's eyes met mine, and I didn't have to explain a single thing. He turned so fast the fringe on his jacket flared, and he headed with long strides for the door that would take us out toward the exit. I was right behind him. The scar twitched under the flayed cuff of my trench coat. Saul's stride lengthened into a run.

So did mine.

2

Sarvedo Street was dark and deserted this time of night. I didn't pull into the garage. I bailed out in front of my warehouse, barked a "Stay in the car!" at Saul, and hauled ass for the door. Steel-clad boot heels struck sparks from the concrete, the front door was open a crack, and I barreled through, rolling and coming up to sweep the front hall and wide-open space of the living room. The charms tied in my hair buzzed, a warning.

Gilberto was on the couch, dark eyes wide and thin sallow face almost bleached. His knees poked through the holes in his jeans and his red T-shirt glared against the couch's slipcover. He looked cheesy-sick, and I didn't blame him. Because on the other side of the coffee table, looking down at my apprentice like he was choosing bonbons out of a box, was a bland-faced, pale-haired hellbreed in a white linen suit.

My apprentice had Jack Karma's Bowie knife out, the silver loaded along the blade's flat running with blue light. He held the knife up, a tiny bar between him and the slender shape of the hellbreed, who was leaning forward, weight on his toes. Highly polished wingtips placed just so on the hardwood floor, his expensively cut platinum hair ruffled on a breeze that came from nowhere, Perry smiled a shark's smile. His chin jerked to the side and he almost moved before I was on him.

The shock grated through me, my aura fluorescing into the visible. Hard little sparks of blue crackled off sea-urchin spikes, an exorcist's aura hard and disciplined— and reacting to the soup of baneful intent in the air.

Gilberto let out a harsh yell, his voice breaking. Perry didn't speak, but that could have been because I had him on the floor, arm twisted up so far behind his back that whatever he had serving him for bones crackled, the gun pressed to the back of his shiny blond head. One of my boots was on his other wrist, flexing down until something else made a creaking, almost-snapping sound.

He gave a token heave or two and went still, the scar turning to soft velvet fire, sliding up my arm.

I would have preferred pain. Either way, the gun didn't waver. All of a sudden I understood why Mikhail had almost drawn on him the first time he'd shown up at the bar, sniffing around me. A million years ago, back when I was the apprentice and Mikhail was the hunter.

The longer I live, the more things just seem to repeat themselves.

Perry chuckled. "Kisssssss." Subvocal rumbling slid under the surface of the word, trailing away on a long hiss like a freight train's brakes failing on a long sharp hill. "*Darling.* So rough."

"Shut. Up." My knee dug into his back. I made sure I was braced, *watched* him. "Gil?"

A long, tense-ticking two seconds. My apprentice gulped. "*Si, señora?*" No trace of sarcasm or machismo. That was either good...or very bad.

"Go out the front door. Saul's in the car. You two are going to have some lunch. I'll catch up with you." A nice even tone, but I did not relax. Perry didn't move, his body loose and unjointed against the floor. As if I was kneeling on a sack of loosely threaded bones in a bag of noisome fluid.

"*Si, señora.*" He got up, slowly, like an old man. The Bowie knife boiled with blue light, and my finger tensed on the trigger.

It was time to make it very clear to a certain hellbreed that my apprentice was off-fucking-limits. If you give 'breed an inch, they *will* take twenty miles. Your only hope is to make it clear the first time.

And God help me, I liked making things violently clear to this particular 'breed. "Let's start at the beginning, Perry. *You do not threaten my apprentice.*"

He said nothing, just hissed. Which meant I wasn't getting through.

So I pistol-whipped him twice, bouncing his head off the floor. He hissed again and surged up, I shoved him back *down* and snapped a glance at Gilberto, who was stumbling in slow motion, a sleepwalker in a nightmare. But he was heading the right way, toward the front door. Saul would take care of him.

"Sweet nothings." The sibilants dragged out over the rumble of Helletöng. "Oh, my *darling*. I've missed you."

I stuck with the safest response possible. "You do not threaten my apprentice." And I was so close to blowing his head all over my living room floor. So, so close.

Not only because of the scar, rubbing against itself

and moaning on my wrist. Not only because of Gilberto's cheese-sick cheeks or the fact that Perry was here, inside the house I slept in.

No. Because it would feel good. Too good. I hadn't seen Perry since the circus came to town, and that wasn't as long ago as I liked.

It would *never* be long enough.

"Of course not." Now he sounded irritated. "I came to bring you a gift. He was *entertainment*. Thoughtfully provided by—"

I hit him again. One more time, because it felt necessary. And another for luck. Once more because by then, I wanted to so bad I couldn't stop myself.

Hunters live on the ragged edge of adrenaline and violence. When all your problems are hellbreed, all your solutions start to look like murder. The trouble isn't that you're tempted to do it.

The trouble is that it feels so goddamn good.

Perry screamed, an inarticulate howl of rage and pain. I bore down as he tried to heave up, and the scar turned into barbwire instead of velvet, sawing against the nerves in my arm.

It was a physical effort to stop hitting him. I could have turned his head into hamburger, I had the firepower, but then I would have had to burn him and scatter the parts and ashes as far apart as possible. And what would the scar do if I killed him?

I just didn't know. But oh, God, I was getting so close to not caring.

It almost made me sweat. Threads of black ichor crawled through his hair. I settled the end of the gun barrel against his skull again and he went still.

Bingo, Jill. Even he isn't sure what you'll do.

It's nice when a hellbreed considers you unpredictable.

"Now." The sudden calm was a warning, just like the thunder of my pulse smoothing out, dropping into the steadiness of action. "Let me hear you say it, Pericles, so I know you *understand*."

"Dearest one." It must have been hard to talk with his face in the floor, but he managed. He even managed to sound cheerful, if you could call a tone like a razor slipping under cold flesh cheerful. "I was pulling your chain, Kiss. Such a nice chain it is, too. Attached to the wall of that conscience of yours."

I said nothing, but my hand tensed again. Such a little squeeze, and a .45 bullet would frag his head all to pieces. And then I'd find out what the scar would do without him behind it.

"I do not threaten your apprentice." A singsong, over a deep well of roaring Helletöng. The speech of the damned rattled the walls, made the floor groan.

"English, motherfucker." My throat had locked up, so it was a whisper. "You speak *English only* to me."

"Bigot." A soft, hurtful laugh. He had frozen under me, waiting. "Your maternal instincts are fetching, darling."

"Give me a reason, Perry." A certain amount of threatening theater is necessary to work this job. You stop the threats and the bitches start getting uppity.

But I meant it. I was begging him for a reason. To give me that opening. I could not just kill him out of hand.

That would make me just like him. Just like the things I hunted.

"Two gifts in one day? Woman, thy nature is greed."

He laughed, the sound bubbling in a pool of black ichor. "Look on the table, Kiss."

I didn't. I looked down at the seeping mess of his head. The urge to slam him down a few more times trembled in my bones. My heel flexed down on his stretched-out wrist, and he made a squirming, uncomfortable movement.

Like a worm on a hook.

"Say it again." This time I sounded almost normal. A huge relief threatened to descend on me. If he mouthed off one more time, it was good enough provocation to shoot him. My conscience wouldn't raise a peep, that was the important thing.

"I do not threaten your apprentice." Level and bland. Like he'd gotten what he wanted.

Every muscle in my body tensed. I lunged aside, my heel grinding down sharply once more. I skipped back, and he rose in a black-spattered wave, shaking out his hands and turning to face me. His wrists crackled, and he made a queer sideways movement with his head, crunching noises inside his neck as he resettled himself inside his shell of normality.

Under the streaks and spatters of hellbreed gore, his face was...normal. No scrim of hurtful beauty, no sharp handsomeness. Even a hunter has to look closer than usual to see the *twisting* on him, the worm in the apple. I've given up wondering if the lack of beauty in his disguise makes him more scary, or less. It's one of those questions that will keep you from sleeping, and I need my sleep more than ever these days.

My gun was level, my aim settling right between his eyebrows. The scar turned back to velvet. My arm was straight, though. It did not waver. The silver in my hair rattled, and the chain at my throat holding the carved ruby warmed. So did my apprentice-ring, snug against my third left finger. The heat prickled and teased at my skin.

My peripheral vision snagged on a flicker of silver and white. A plain white paper box, tied with silver ribbon. A pretty, professionally made bow.

A present from a hellbreed is never a pleasant thing. And the more attractive the package, the less likely you're going to get something nice out of it.

My mouth was dry. "Take it away and go crawl back into your hole. I accept no gifts from you."

Not when he was looking to get me back into our bad old cycle. The scar and its attendant power for a slice of my time each month, that was the original deal—until he welshed and I got the scar's power for nothing.

Because I'd survived. And because I called his bluff. Yet another question that would keep me from sleeping— how deep had his tentacles been inside Inez Germaine's little operation? How much had he lost, gambling for the chance that he could make me damn myself? Once I did that, once I stepped into the abyss, I had a sneaking suspicion that he would own me.

He had been gambling for nothing less than my soul. And he was still looking to hook me.

The warehouse creaked around us, its usual nightly song as the wind came up off the river, whistling through the trainyards and the industrial section. Not all the noise was from the pressure of air outside, though. Some of the groaning and creaking was the strings under the physical world being plucked, both by my will and by flabby-corrupting hellbreed fingers. I met Perry's blue, blue stare and thought longingly of having him on the floor again and this time pulling the goddamn trigger.

"This gift you'll accept. It's more in the nature of recovered property." He stepped to the side, easily and slowly, I tracked him with the gun's snout. My left fingers dropped to my whip, and he grinned. White teeth flashed through the mask of thin viscous black dripping on his face. His suit would be ruined, a dark stain all the way down the front. His tie was steaming as polyester fibers reacted with hellbreed ichor. The rest of the fabric had to be natural—silk and cotton don't react the same way. They get eaten away, but they don't steam or smoke.

Just like a hellbreed to wear a polyester tie. A snorting sarcasm threatened to reach my lips. I killed it.

His gaze dropped to my left hand. "I'm not about to make trouble, my dear. I just want to see your face when you open my present. The boy's no challenge. You'll have your work cut out for you, making *him* into one of your kind."

That's none of your business, hellspawn. My blue eye was hot and dry, watching for a shiver of baneful intent. When I didn't respond, he chuckled softly as if I had.

The ribbon unfolded under his clever fingers. I tensed. It fell aside, and he opened the box with a quick flick, pulling his hand back and inhaling, shaking his long, elegant fingers as if they'd been singed.

"There." A sidelong glance at me. "Come and see, Kiss. And tell me what a good little hellspawn I am, bringing you what belongs to you. Scratch behind my ears, who's a good boy." A flicker between his lips—a wet, cherry-red tongue, scaled and supple. The flash of color was obscene against his bloodless pallor.

I ran through everything he could possibly mean with

that statement, came up with nothing good. "Step back. Over there." I indicated a spot on the hardwood floor with my chin. Waited while he minced a bare foot, then two. "Further, Perry."

His mouth turned down, but he did mince back a few more steps. "Your mistrust wounds me. It really does. Here I've gone to all this *trouble*—"

"Shut up." I glanced down into the box, my whole body expecting him to jump me. The longer this went on, the more I expected something like that from him.

Hellbreed and Traders aren't known for impulse control.

Inside the box were glinting shapes that refused to make sense for a moment. I exhaled, hard, as if I'd been punched.

Mikhail's voice, from the secret space inside my head he always occupied. *Sekhmet is Eye of Ra, and this is Eye of Sekhmet. Been passed down*, milaya, *from hunter to hunter in Jack Karma's lineage. Before the first Karma we know little. But this is Talisman he had, for whatever reason. Is for my little snake when I am gone, no?*

And then I was there in that shitty little hotel room, Mikhail's life gurgling out through the hole in his throat and Melisande Belisa's tinkling laugh echoing as she fled. With this Talisman clutched in her spidery little fingers. It had probably bought her up quite a few ranks in the Sorrows' arcane and crowded hierarchy.

My shot went wide. Perry rammed into me, we slammed into the wall across the living room. Drywall dust puffed out. His fingers closed around my right wrist, *squeezing*. Bones ground together and the scar sent a sick wave of hot delight up to my shoulder, his fingertips plucking as if my arm was a string instrument. He pressed against me, his other hand worming at my hip, looking for my whip handle. And there was something hard in his pants, too. Shoved right up against me as if I wasn't a hunter.

As if I was what I had been before Mikhail plucked me out of that snowbank.

A knife handle smacked into my left palm. I jerked it free and *cut*, the blade going in with little resistance. Silver in my hair and at my throat rattled and crackled, spitting blue sparks showering his marred, ichor-streaked face. He was grinning madly, and I didn't dare blink while I sheared through whatever served him as stomach muscle, finishing with a twist, and brought my knee up.

He recoiled, I heaved him away. The gun came down, but he knocked the barrel aside as I squeezed the trigger again. The bullet whined, dug a furrow out of the floor, and buried itself in the wall between living room and my bedroom. The scar shrieked with pain, napalm rubbed burning into skin.

My leg came up. I *kicked*, the blow unreeling, boot smashing solidly into his belly. A gush of black ichor pattered free. He folded over, arms wrapped over his stomach, and hissed, baring his teeth. The mask of bland normality slipped for a moment, and troubled air swirled in two points behind him, above his shoulders. The buzz of flies rattled everything in my living room, and the etheric protections laid in the walls tolled once like a bell.

It was a shame I couldn't consecrate the warehouse's grounds and keep him out of here permanently. I'd give up my monthly municipal check for that. But no—I'm a hunter, not a priest.

He fled, and I tracked him with the gun. My aim

wasn't off—I plugged him twice in the back before he nipped smartly down the hall, footsteps too light to be human, hitting the ground oddly.

It was only after the front door banged closed and the sound of him running—northward, toward the meat-packing district and the Monde Nuit—faded too much even for my hellbreed-jacked hearing that I slumped against the hole in the wall. I tore my gaze away from the hall and stared at the box on the table.

Hard darts of silver glitter spiked up from the Talisman. My legs were unsteady. I made it, step by uncertain step, across what seemed like acres of floor, my boots gripping through a thin stinking scrim of hellbreed ichor. When I could look into the box fully, my smart eye watering and hot tears slicking that one cheek, I saw that it was, indeed, the Eye.

The ruby at my throat was a pale imitation of this barbaric red gem in its rough silver-claw setting. It glowed fierce crimson, darts of light shimmering into white glow at the edges. Its chain, large silver links that looked sharp enough to cut, was broken. Spilling out of the box, vibrating in place, the Talisman rattled as I drew closer.

I halted. But the necklace just vibrated more intensely on my coffee table, next to the stack of *Home Beautiful* and *Cook's Illustrated* Saul was always reading. A thin curl of smoke rose from the paper of the box.

Is it going to burn me? I was acutely aware of sweat touching the curve of my lower back, blood and hellbreed contamination all over my clothes, the scar humming a soft little chortle of corruption on my right wrist. And who was I kidding? *Both* my cheeks were wet, because my eyes were brimming with tears.

My throat clicked as I swallowed drily and blinked away the water, looking for traps. He'd had plenty of time to lay them, but I saw nothing except the burning etheric smear of an angry and awake Talisman. The smell of burning intensified.

The Talisman hummed, plucking at the strings under the world's surface. But not like a hellbreed. No, this was music. It was humming along with the song that naturally unmade things. The same music that triggered landslides and catastrophes, a great harmonic resonance instead of the crashing discordance of hellbreed corruption.

I don't even believe in Sekhmet, I'd told Mikhail.

And his response? *I don't either,* milaya. *But never hurts. Don't have to believe to do job. Just have to do.*

It took more courage than I thought I had left to take the final five steps to the table and reach down. I was prepared for sparks, or for a backlash of etheric energy to knock me away. Prepared for anything, actually, other than the thing that actually happened.

My fingers touched cool metal. The thready curls of smoke evaporated, leaving behind the smell of burning and the reek of rotting hellbreed. I found I was holding the Talisman, and the sharp edges of the chain brushed lovingly against my hand. They didn't cut, they just scratched a little.

Like fingernails against a lover's skin.

Oh, my God. The gem nestled in my palm and thrummed at me. When I lifted it to my throat, the broken links of the chain slid across my skin and melted together as if they'd never been ripped from a hunter's chest. The Talisman settled against my breastbone, its low humming note disappearing into the sound of wind touching the walls and the etheric protections settling back down.

And I knew, miserably, that I should have shot Perry when I had the chance. Because sooner or later I was going to have to go back to the Monde Nuit and ask him how he got his hellspawn hands on the gem my teacher's killer stole.

3

Mickey's on Mayfair Hill is the kind of restaurant locals like to keep to themselves. Good food, a full bar down two steps in the back, pictures of film stars decking every wall, and a strict policy of toleration. It helps that Mayfair is the part of town where you can see same-sex couples walking hand in hand more often than not—the churches have rainbows on their signs, most of them stating unequivocally ALL ARE WELCOME!

The nightclubs are wildly popular, too. I'd call it a cliché, but that might get me in trouble.

It also helps that Mickey's is completely owned and mostly staffed by Weres. When you have claws and superstrength, tolerance takes on a whole new meaning.

Lean dark Theron met me at the door. The Werepanther's face was unusually solemn, and his shoulders came up a fraction as I swept the door closed. "Kid looks shaken up."

Not even a greeting. Weres are normally so polite, too.

"He should be." I glanced past him, saw Saul in our

regular booth. Across from him, Gilberto slumped, staring at his beer bottle. The bottle's label was half picked off.

The kid wasn't old enough to drink, but that didn't matter in the barrio. It doesn't matter on the nightside, either. I turned a blind eye—God knows an apprentice is kept on a short enough leash otherwise.

Theron didn't move. The front of Mickey's is a narrow tiled foyer, a half wall holding back the tables to your left and the kitchen directly in front of you, with all its steam and heat. One of the cooks, a slim dark bird Were, was tossing a spatula, plucking it out of the air with graceful dexterity while he stared back at the freezer, tossing it again.

I finally looked up, met Theron's steady gaze. "What? Am I not allowed to come in?"

"I'd tell you to be gentle." Theron folded his arms. "But that's so not you."

I had washed my face, smearing my eyeliner and putting fresh on. But I hadn't bothered to change. I could spare the time to rinse my face, and I like to do it. The rest of me doesn't matter so much.

The Talisman hummed low on my breastbone, beneath the ruin of my black T-shirt. The shirt still covered all my bits, but I wished suddenly that I'd stopped to grab a new one. I used to wear shirts with witty sayings, but now I bought them—black, V-neck, three-quarter sleeve, slightly fitted—in job lots. Saul sometimes found nice ones at Goodwill, especially old concert shirts, but I bleed all over them so often I feel kind of bad about it. There's only so much he can do with a sewing machine and a T-shirt.

"Theron." I tried very hard for what could be

considered a gentle tone. It sounded like I had something dry stuck in my throat, or like I'd been smoking a pack a day. "Why are you standing in my way?"

He leaned forward a little, on the balls of his feet. "You smell like burn—" Then his eyes dropped to my chest.

If I'd had any breasts to speak of after the workout I get all night, I might've been insulted. As it is, I'm scrawny in that department. Sometimes I wished I was a little more feminine, a little curvier, for Saul's sake. But no, a B cup is about all I get. The rest of me is packed tight with muscle and crisscrossed with scars.

Saul doesn't seem to mind. He traces some of the scars with his fingertips, gently. I usually let him.

Sometimes he even kisses them.

"Ah." Theron actually backed up, palms out as if he wanted to tell me to take it easy. "Sorry. My mistake."

I stalked past him. He actually skipped back out of my way as I hopped up the stairs to the tables. We were a regular dance team.

"Jill."

I didn't turn around. But I stopped, one hand light on the half wall. My nerves were twitching raw, and taking it out on a Were wasn't a good idea. He didn't deserve it.

"You smell like Mikhail," he said quietly. "I'll bring you a beer."

In other words, a peace offering. Not like he needed to. But goddamn Weres, they notice the damndest things. I did *not* raise a hand to the Talisman's lump under the ragged T-shirt.

Instead, I just braced myself and headed for the table, the flayed edges of my leather trench flapping a bit around my ankles.

Gilberto's color was better, but he would never be a prize. Sallow even on the best of days, with lank dark hair and a nose that belonged on an Aztec codex, acne scars pitting his cheeks, dead eyes. His long fingers played with the beer bottle, and as I approached he slid down further in the bench and took a long, throat-working draft.

I did not blame him at all.

I stopped and checked him, smart and dumb eye working together. Having an apprentice is like that—you add up everything you see, no matter how small. Constantly weighing. Not *judging*, because that implies they won't make it. *Weighing* in order to give them the best chance to make it.

After they show up on your doorstep and refuse to go home, that distinction is the least you can give them.

Gilberto's hands looked too big for his wrists, like a puppy's paws. He hadn't even finished growing yet, and you could tell it from the way he ate—hunched over the plate, as if someone or something would snatch it from him, shoveling the food down in great gulps.

That's the way kids in juvie eat, too. And prisoners.

He wasn't old enough to drink *or* vote. But those flat dark eyes belonged in a killer's face. Even in the ferment of the barrio, that kind of gaze makes people step back and reconsider, some without knowing quite why. He'd just graduated to being able to hold his own for thirty seconds in the sparring room against Saul. I watched, and weighed, while they went at it.

Gilberto did not give up. He kept getting up long past the moment when any rational person would have decided it wasn't worth it.

He had potential.

Right now he was still shaking a little. The fume of emotion on him was complex fear and shame, as well as defiance. Still just right. Of all the people I'd run across in my city, he was the only one who had even an inkling of what it takes to be a hunter. There had been a girl—Hope—not too long ago...but she hadn't lasted two weeks.

Sometimes they don't.

We're rare. It's probably a good thing. Without training we could end up worse than the things we hunt. Even with training, we're no picnic.

Saul glanced at me. His dark eyes widened a little, but he said nothing as I finished my once-over and strode up to the table.

I slid in next to my apprentice, bumping him with my hip as he scrambled to crowd up onto the wall. "Thought I'd find you here."

"*Bruja.*" Gilberto, getting the first shot in. He was actually sweating, and his pulse thudded along like he'd just run a marathon. "He was just there. One minute I'm sittin' on the couch, the next, *chingada*, there he is. He's *el Diablo*, right?"

Not quite. "Or so close it makes no difference. But he's just hellbreed, Gilberto. Relax, you did okay. Take a deep breath and get your pulse down; it's loud."

He gulped down a breath and concentrated. I waited as if we had all the time in the world. Saul studied me, a line between his dark eyebrows. The paint on his cheeks was still fresh, two bars of vivid red. I never asked why he did that. It just seemed fitting. And, well, I don't need to offer a comment on any Were's sartorial choices.

Not when I walk around in leather, silver, and increasingly heavy eyeliner. The leather is so my skin doesn't get erased when I land on concrete. The silver is a mark of what I am, a bulwark against Hell's legions.

The eyeliner? Well...Saul isn't the only one who needs war paint.

Finally, Gilberto's pulse smoothed out. His eyelids fluttered, and I could almost *feel* him making that subconscious little *click*, shifting over into the place of calm. It was getting easier for him.

Saul was still watching me. I pulled the neck of my T-shirt down so he could see the barbaric, sharp-looking silver links. The top edge of the Talisman peeked out.

"Smells like a forest fire." His eyebrows came up slightly. "What is it?"

"The Eye of Sekhmet." It was hard work to keep my tone level. "What Belisa stole. When she..."

The unreality of it hit me sideways. I put my hands on the table, flat, and had to inhale deeply as well. The scar was dissatisfied, puckering against itself; I'd taken a spare leather cuff from the dish on the counter and buckled it on before I left. The relief from hellbreed-jacked sensory acuity was as intense as the new feeling now squirming around inside my uneasy belly.

That feeling was something suspiciously like fear.

"Oh." Saul absorbed this. Then, as usual, he gave me the right question. "How the hell did *he* get hold of it?"

I watched my left hand make a gun of thumb and index finger, cocked it, and shot at him. "Bang. Dead on, squire."

And then the next question: "What are you going to do?" His expression didn't change. Thoughtful, and worried.

I let out a sigh that was only half annoyance. It had taken me the whole trip down here to come up with what I *should* do instead of what I *wanted* to do. "I'm not going to do *anything*. Perry wants me down at the Monde. That's one place I'm not going. I have the Talisman, fine. It was mine in the first place, Belisa stole it, I'm not goddamn going to dance to his tune and come asking questions."

"Unless that's what he expects, you avoiding him."

Good point.

I snorted. Then shut my mouth, because Theron was back, setting two cold bottles of beer down for me, one dark microbrew for Saul, and a plate of cheese blintzes and hash browns, with a small dish of fresh strawberries on the side for my apprentice. That was worth a raised eyebrow, but Saul's twitch of a smile told me the Weres here were feeding Gilberto what they thought he *should* be eating, not anything he'd order.

Gilberto opened his eyes, stared at his plate, and shut his mouth before a word could escape.

He caught on quick.

Theron paused, dangling his tray in long, expressive fingers. "Other food'll be just a second. You want some water or something?"

Another peace offering. Was I really looking that temperamental tonight?

I shook my head, watching my fingers against the tabletop. Bitten-down nails, tendons standing out under fishbelly-white skin—I don't tan, I'm never up during the day—and a healing scrape across my left knuckles. The skin was repairing itself as I watched, the scar on my right wrist humming a dissatisfied little song. "No thanks." My lips felt a little numb, and the Eye was warm against my chest.

It was surreal. I never thought I'd be wearing Mikhail's greatest treasure. Not even while he was training me and saying, *Some day this will be yours.* I'd never thought that far ahead.

He'd seemed eternal to me. I guess your parents— or those you choose as your parents—always do. Until they're not.

Theron lingered a little longer, then left as one of the cooks swore. There was a hiss of something hitting the grill, and I looked up to find Saul watching me.

"*Chingada,*" Gilberto mumbled. "No *frijoles.*"

The laugh caught me by surprise. I bit it in half, swallowed it, and Saul's expression went from thoughtful to outright concerned.

"Do you think..." he began, but left the sentence hanging.

"I think I'm safer staying out of the Monde." Each word carefully held back from a sharp edge. "I think whatever Perry expects me to do, me ignoring this is not in his plan. Therefore, I am going to do what is *not* in his plan."

Saul nodded. Thought it over. "And the fact that he's fooling around with the Sorrows again?"

I took a long pull off one of my beer bottles. It hit the spot. There's nothing quite like a beer to bolster you in a situation like this. "That's why you're taking my apprentice to Galina's."

"Oh, man," aforesaid apprentice piped up. "*Again?* She just makes me take care of her plants."

"You have to be alive to be trained, Gil. And if the

Sorrows grab you, you'll wish very hard you were dead."
I kept my gaze steady, locked with Saul's.

My Were's dark eyes did not waver. "Where should I
meet you after that?" Careful, tactful, and to the point.

In other words, *You're not leaving me behind, Jill.
Don't even think about it.*

"I'm going to be visiting the son of a bitch who Traded
with Watling." I set the bottle down with a click. Bacon
was frying, and it smelled good. "I want that sewn up
tonight."

But I didn't tell him where, even though I knew. I
couldn't say what I suspected, but I did know I wanted
Saul nowhere near where I was going tonight. Full 'breed
nightclubs aren't healthy for Weres.

A short, sharp nod, his hair falling across his forehead.
It had grown out, and he could tie charms to match mine
in it now. A silver wheel gleamed near his left ear, knotted
in with red thread. "So I'll just follow the screaming."

"Unless she decide to blow something up, man. Then
you can follow the fire *and* screaming." Gilberto was
looking down when I glanced at him, my mouth set in
a straight line. He forked up a gigantic mouthful of hash
browns, his arm curled around the plate. Shielding it.

I decided I wouldn't really take him to task, because
it was true. "Gil, *poquito*, the adults are talking. *Cierra
el pico.*"

He mumbled something impolite. I let it go. Picked up
the bottle again and drained it. It went down easy, but it
didn't quite get rid of the bitter taste in my mouth.

Saul tapped once on the tabletop, twice. Thinking. "I
don't like this. It's not like one of his kind to give anything away."

"He needs something out of me, or he has a plan." I shrugged. Silver in my hair jangled a bit, restless. "Like every single other time he has a plan or wants something out of me. He'll have to deal with disappointment."

We looked at each other, Saul and I, and both of us knew it was pure bravado. I hadn't gone over the edge yet, even with Perry pushing and cajoling. I'd stood there and watched the abyss yawn right next to my toes, and the only thing that kept me from going down into damnation was...

...what?

Was sitting right across from me, playing with his beer bottle and looking worried, the way a Were almost never looked worried.

They don't usually date hunters. And I was helltainted to boot. We were an exception all over, Saul and me.

I slid out of the booth, pushed myself upright. "Get to Galina's. If all else fails I'll see you at home, at dawn." A judicious pause. "There's a mess there. Sorry about that."

"Jill—"

I shook my head. Silver clashed and chimed. A small sickle-shaped charm dangled in front of my eye for a moment, I tossed it back. "Got work to do, Saul. Depending on you to get my apprentice under cover. My instincts are tingling."

"I hear they have a cream for that. Jill—"

"The cream's for burning. Not for an unpleasant tingle. Give my apologies to Theron." I turned, sharply, and strode away. Made it outside without anything else happening, and let out a deep, dissatisfied breath. It was rude to leave before they fed me, but the night was wearing away and I wanted to get this wrapped up.

The Talisman's warm weight against my chest throbbed like a second heartbeat. Sooner or later Perry would come back, and I'd find out what he was dabbling in now.

But that didn't mean I couldn't question other hell-breed. And I knew exactly where to start.

With the hellspawn who was eyeing the number two position in Santa Luz's 'breed hierarchy. Who just happened to be the same spawn who had Traded with Trevor Watling.

What a coincidence.

4

The Kat Klub was closed for good, Shen An Dua—the 'breed who ran it—dead in a stinking cellar room way back last year. But hellspawn are like pimps. There's always someone lower on the food chain willing to step up, if profit's to be had.

Down at First and Alohambra the granite bulk of the Piers Tower rises, one of the oldest skyscrapers in Santa Luz. Mikhail told me once that the property had been a mission long ago—before the town got big enough to attract hellbreed.

In other words, back when it was just the mission and a couple of chicken coops. And maybe a pig trough if the padres were lucky.

A gaudy sign shouting UNDER NEW MANAGEMENT had glared across the street for a couple weeks while the infighting went on. When the dust settled, I'd walked in and found that bastard Rutger supervising a small horde of contractors.

He'd gotten sassy. I shot him two or three times just

to make him sit down and listen. Shen had been the *eminence grise* of Santa Luz, the only serious contender for Perry's position and a thorn in Perry's side. Rutger had big dreams, but that didn't mean I wasn't going to teach him who was boss. It was either that or have to kill him later and play roulette with whoever *his* replacement was.

So the Kat Klub was now the Folly. It kept the same hours—a cabaret changing to a nightclub at about midnight, rollicking along until dawn in defiance of the liquor laws. Which is no big deal; most nightside places wink at those kind of regulations. Cash changes hands, and the authorities wink, too. Of course, the cash mostly goes toward a hunter's salary. The municipal check every month, in fact.

I think that's called *irony.*

Instead of the stuffed cats and opium den vibe Shen An Dua had gone for, the Folly's décor was choke-a-baroque French bordello, with a side of lace and fringe.

It was just before midnight, so the cabaret was winding down. A female Trader in a painted-on latex outfit brought the cat-o'-ninetails up. Fluid spattered under the pulsing red lights. The cat's tails were wire, studded with barbs. Whatever she was whipping had six misshapen limbs and was the size of a tall man, stretched on an iron rack. It whimpered as the cat came down again with a sound like dissonant wind chimes.

The wires and barbs bit deep. The thing opened a hole at the top of its vague mass and howled. Hellbreed tittered. The Trader pivoted on her stiletto heels, brought the whip back and down again with an expert flick. There was a ripping sound as wet, pulsing flesh parted. A long vertical tear opened in the thing on the rack, and something white showed.

The collected 'breed and Traders stilled, expectantly.

A slender white hand rose. More wet sounds. A thin, curving arm. A knob of a shoulder. The Trader in black vinyl reached forward, the cat dangling in her other hand, and laced her fingers through the questing white hand like a girl grabbing a basket. She leaned back, hip jutting out, and pulled.

More wet tearing sounds, and a pale nakedness rose from the pile of steaming, lacerated flesh. High shallow breasts, wide dark eyes with the flat shine of the dusted, a cherry mouth, long wet strings of hair. Another Trader. Markings that could have been scars, tiger stripes on that dead-white, waxen flesh.

Polite applause. I had my back to the bar, a monstrous thing of mahogany and curlicued iron, silk scarves tied into the grillwork and fluttering upward in merry defiance of gravity. Sorcery and contamination crawled over the cloth, dripping onto the slowly corroding iron. The seaweed scarves flinched away from me, as every piece of silver I carried ran with blue light. Sparks didn't break free of the metal, but it was close.

The Talisman was still on my chest, like an alert little animal, frozen into immobility. I'd only seen Mikhail use it once or twice, when the situation was desperate. It was like the long, slim shape under its fall of amber silk in the sparring room—not to be touched until the need was dire.

But he'd *worn* the Eye everywhere.

Talismans are like that. You can't just leave them in a box. They get irritable, and then you have an even bigger mess to clean up. I'd heard of a hunter in Kansas who had left a Talisman at home for too long and got three tornados in one day to show for it. At the same time he was working a string of disappearances and almost got his ass blown off by a Middle Way adept.

Embarrassing. I'm pretty sure he hasn't lived that one down yet. Still, considering the Talisman *he'd* been left with, I didn't blame him for thinking that maybe he shouldn't touch the damn thing any more than absolutely necessary.

The bartender was another Trader, tall and big-eyed, broad-shouldered—and with a messy line of vertical stitches closing his lips together. One of Rutger's little jokes.

Two vodkas, brief stings relished but gone by the time they hit the back of my throat, and I waited. Rutger was up in his office, probably watching the closed-circuit television. I could go up there and drag him out, but what would be the point?

No. I wanted this public, but I also wanted him to come to me. That would make the game mine, on my terms.

Admit it, Jill. You want to beat the shit out of someone. That's what you're aching to do, and if you do it in public you might not go over the edge. That edge that gets closer every time you do this.

Philosophizing in the middle of a hellbreed bar is a dangerous occupation. The risk of getting distracted is high. Still, I didn't jump when he appeared out of thin air with a sound like little voices tittering.

They like doing that.

"Ah, Kismet." Rutger's oily tenor, dripping with saccharine. "An honor to see you again. Enjoying the show?"

He was lean, and had a full head and a half on me. His skin was spilled ink. Not human-dark, or ethnic. No, his skin was literally *black*. It swallowed light with no sheen of human at all on its surface. A pointed chin, wide cheekbones, the slightly yellow cast of his too-sharp-to-be-human teeth, and a fluff of white thistledown hair all competed to add creepiness. The final touch was his irises. A deep throbbing hurtful magenta, the pupils X-shaped. In the crux of the X lurked a leering, sterile point of red-purple light.

He liked velvet coats and ruffled-front shirts, breeches in odd gemlike colors, and high-heeled, shiny-buckled, pointy-toed shoes that should have looked absolutely ridiculous.

On this hellbreed, they looked very sharp. You could just imagine the edges of those shoes, heel or toe, slicing flesh. While he grinned with that V-shaped mouth, showing those shark-row teeth.

"No." I eyed his bodyguards—slabs of Trader muscle almost too dumb to be breathing. They looked like Frankenstein's monster crossed with a steroid burner's dream—even their muscles had lumps of muscle on top, like overyeasted bread.

And they were too far away, hanging back and staring at me with little piggy flat-shining eyes. I could have killed him twice before they got to me.

I bared my teeth, a bright sunny approximation of a smile. My left hand rested on the whip handle, and Rutger's eyes blinked—first one, then the other. Just like a lizard.

There was a crack of bone and a scream from the stage. It sounded like a peacock's cry, or a sexless being in fullthroated orgasm. Then it shaded up into agony before it was cut short on a gurgle.

Everyone else let out their breath. One Trader whistled,

a keen piercing note that belonged more in a strip club than a murder cabaret.

Some people have no couth.

"Trevor Watling." The name fell into a well of silence. A single spark cracked from the carved ruby at my throat, and one of the bodyguards flinched. My smile widened just a trifle. It felt unnatural, a layer of paint over my skin.

Rutger shrugged. "Never heard of him."

I was kind of glad we were going to do this the hard way. He might have been, too, because he thought he was fast enough to jump me.

The corruption in them makes them easy to track. That's why hunters are human. We can track what we're akin to.

Quick as they are, a hunter's quicker. Especially with her reflexes amped up by a hellbreed scar. My boots hit the bar's shiny surface, and I pivoted slightly on one foot. My other lashed out, steel-shod heel cracking him square on the chin. The whip flashed, too, catching one of the bodyguards across his wide sweat-greased face. Rutger fell in slow motion, black ichor spraying in a wide perfect arc. I cleared leather, had the gun pointed at the next bodyguard, my foot coming back, touching lightly.

The bartender, down at the other end of the curlicued monstrosity, cowered. He didn't have a gun, but I couldn't bet on it staying that way. On the other hand, here I had the high ground.

And every eye was on me. The seaweed scarves dribbled, streaming away from me as the silver in my hair, at my throat and fingers and weapons, hissed and sparked. Each spark died quickly as it left my aura.

Up on the stage, there was a pool of waxen white

striped with sluggish black, the slim body broken like a flower. The Trader in vinyl crouched, her hand on her cat-o'-nine, in a pool of garish spotlight that turned her eyes into blank holes. Some of the 'breed had half-risen from their seats, the waitstaff all stood, tense and ready. Some of them had hands inside their white jackets.

"Ah-ah-ah." Hard and bright, my voice rang out. Like a teacher admonishing a room full of third graders. "Now, now. Let's not be hasty. That's the penalty of lying a single time to a hunter in Santa Luz. Want to go for more?"

Rutger surged up from the floor. The gun settled on him. At my chest, the Talisman throbbed a little, a sore tooth. A thin curl of smoke rose from my T-shirt. I wasn't imagining it, but there were other things to worry about.

I'd broken the hellbreed's nose. Thin rivulets of black ichor threaded down, glittering against the odder darkness of his skin. His teeth champed. "*Bitch,*" he hissed.

Like I hadn't heard *that* one before. "I repeat. Trevor Watling."

"The Trade was legitimate," he hissed. Ichor bubbled down his chin.

He'd admitted it. Now we got to the fun part. "He stepped outside the rules. You're liable."

A ratlike little gleam surfaced from the center of his pupils. I know that gleam.

The *how can I make this work for me* look. The one my mother had whenever one of her boyfriends got out the belt or the fist. The one in the eyes of the man who put me on a street corner to shiver. The one in the eyes of every single john on that corner, in a car, in an alley or a cheap hotel room.

I *hate* that fucking look.

"Stay still." I didn't have to look at the second body-guard to feel the way he was tensing up, getting ready. "Now, Rutger. Let's just say I don't want to have to train your replacement not to piddle on the floor." I stared at the bridge of his nose, knowing it would make my mis-matched gaze piercing. And that the focus would warn me before he decided to move.

"You want something." It's hard for a hellbreed to look shocked. He managed it. A caricature of a human emo-tion, like every expression on a hellbreed's face. Except greed and sadistic pleasure, I guess.

I made a little beeping noise. Every nerve under my skin dilated, alert and quivering. "Wrong. *You* want something. You want to stay alive and continue your games in this tacky little nest. Now, I'm willing to think that your Trader didn't check in with you before commit-ting his murderous little rampage. The only thing left for you to do is to prove your good faith. Give me a reason to decide your successor would be a bigger problem than you are."

Instinct alerted me. I dropped to one knee and fired in one smooth motion. Recoil jolted up my arm, almost too much for even a measure of superhuman strength. The bartender, a sawed-off shotgun in his stealthy little clawed hands, dropped like a stone. Half his head had evaporated.

Why I didn't switch to the bigger custom guns sooner was *so* beyond me.

Rutger had taken a half step forward. I trained the gun on him again. "See? You're just jumping at the chance to help, aren't you."

Another thin curl of smoke drifted up from my torn T-shirt. Rutger's pupils flared with diseased red-purple light, a bruise on the air. "What guarantee will you give?"

Please, you think I'm new at this game? "I don't give guarantees to hellspawn. You tell me about Perry's new houseguest, and I may decide to be charitable and overlook your Trader's stepping outside the bounds."

As soon as I said it, I knew I'd guessed right. Rutger stiffened, and the ratty gleam intensified. He telegraphed like a four-year-old reaching for candy. As soon as he twitched he knew he'd made a mistake, too, and I lowered the gun. The silver in my hair shifted, rattling. A blue spark popped from my apprentice-ring, and the hellbreed actually flinched. The scarves tied to the bar in front of me lay dead and dark now, bleeding clear fluid across the mirror-polished surface. A ripple ran through the assembled 'breed, and the Traders moved back in one clockwork motion.

"Oh, hit a nerve there, did I? Thank you." I sounded completely insincere. "Pleasant dreams, hellspawn."

When I hopped down from the bar, I expected him to jump me. Instead, he stepped mincingly aside. His shoes clicked like a woman's heels, but oddly. Hellbreed footsteps do not sound the same as human movement. They're too light, or too heavy, different musculature producing something that shivers the skin with its wrongness.

"He said you'd be here." A ripple ran through the assembled 'breed and Traders at the words. Rutger tried out a smile, light dancing oddly over his skin. The black bulged and rippled oddly, trying to contain whatever lived under the shell of human seeming. "And he said to tell you this: *he cannot hold back the tide forever.*"

The gun spoke again. I dropped, rolled, came up and the whip flashed out. The second bodyguard fell like a stalled ox between one step and the next, and Rutger let out a long rumble-roar of Helletöng, glasses chattering on the iron shelves behind the bar. The seaweed scarves, dripping with corruption, flattened and swayed. The ones that had cringed away from me shriveled, blackening afresh. The curse missed, flashing by like a freight train at midnight, and the whip spoke again. I didn't dive *away*, like he was obviously expecting. No, instead I pitched myself straight at the hellbreed and cracked him a good one with the gun butt after the flechettes finished tearing a chunk out of his chest. Blessed silver spat and crackled. Rutger howled, glass shattered from the sound, and while he was on the floor I kicked him twice, both good solid blows.

He curled like a worm on a hook, still screaming. The gun swept the massed ranks of hellbreed and they drew back, eyes shining, lips pulled up in snarls, and the scrim of beauty they wear faltering for a heart-stopping second.

"That makes it three times I've visited here and had to shoot an uppity 'breed or two. I wonder if maybe this place needs to be *cleansed*." I had to raise my voice to be heard over Rutger's yelling. But you learn pretty quick to aim for a tone that slices through noise without seeming like you're yelling. I kicked Rutger again. "Shut *up*."

"Pay." He bubbled and blurbled through ichor. "You'll pay for this, Kismet."

I swept the massed ranks of hellbreed one more time. They made no move. "You are *so* not in the position to be threatening, Rutger. Ta-ta, boys and girls. I'll be back."

When you've just put down the owner of a hellbreed

nightclub, the right kind of exit is a sort of insouciant amble that is much faster than it looks. You don't want to give them time to think. But it is imperative not to look weak.

Or they will be on you in a moment.

"*Kismet!*" Helletöng rumbling under my name. "*I will kill you for this!*"

The Talisman on my chest gave a *thud* like a sledge-hammer hitting the side of a refrigerator, and I turned on my heel. Retraced my steps, and the smoke coming up from my chest wasn't an illusion. It stung my eyes, and I had the sudden lunatic vision of my T-shirt burning off me in the middle of the Folly.

That never happened to Mikhail. What the hell?

The 'breed were all still as death. Bright eyes, painted lips, the shadows of what they really were rippling under their flesh.

I halted. Looked down at Rutger. Painted with hell-breed blood, down there on the floor, sniveling and whining. It wasn't a pretty sight.

Do not ever underestimate, milaya. Mikhail's voice inside my head. *Is fine way to get ass blown off sideways.*

"Come and try it." I didn't have to work to say it flatly. "Anytime, Rutger. That goes for every single Hell-trading one of you in this entire building. Whenever you're brave enough, *come and fucking try it.*"

To really finish it off right I should have kicked him one last time. But it was more of an insult to leave him there and saunter out the front door like I had all night, the smell of burning trailing in my wake.

And a very, very bad feeling starting in the middle of my chest.

5

*B*eaky, skinny Hutch sat up and rubbed at his hazel eyes. He didn't quite squeal, but it was close. "What are you *doing?*"

I hadn't been in here for very long. Maybe twenty seconds, hearing him sleep and regretting that I was going to wake him up. I know what it's like to wake up with someone in the room, when you thought you were alone.

Hutch was lucky, though. It was just me.

"Same thing I do every time I wake you up in the middle of the night. Light." I flipped on the bedside lamp, almost forgetting how I looked. Hutch squeaked and fisted his eyes even harder.

His living quarters were up above the bookstore, and his bedroom was full of extra shelving. Clothes hung next to bits of high-priced computer corpses, ready for him to strip out and use at a moment's notice. He'd just come back from vacation two weeks ago, sunburnt and rested, and I'd met him at the airport with our local FBI liaison, Juan Rujillo. I'd finally gotten everything smoothed over from Hutch's last escapade—the one he wasn't covered for in court, because he hadn't been hacking at my request. No, he'd just been proving he was still bulletproof in cyberspace.

I guess I hadn't been keeping him busy enough. *That* was about to change.

"Jesus!" Hutch grabbed at the blankets. "Is it the cops? I haven't done anything, I *swear*!"

"You know, every time I hear you say that, it fills me with despair. Because I know you're lying or *about* to lie to me." I tried not to sound so grimly amused. "Wake up and get your glasses on, Hutchinson. I need you."

"Why don't you keep normal hours?" He turned even paler than usual the moment it escaped his mouth. I magnanimously refused to comment. Instead, I put my back to the wall near the door—or, if you want to be precise, to the overflowing bookcase right next to the door. "Never mind, forget I asked. What's up?"

"I want you to get on that goddamn computer and find something out for me." I did not tack on a *What did you think, I wanted to sing Christmas carols?* But it was close.

"What something am I finding?" He grabbed his glasses and put them on, blinked frowstily.

Something that will help me avert another fucking apocalypse. "I'll tell you once you're downstairs with some coffee."

"God." He groaned, levering himself up out of bed. "Why don't you pick on someone else?" His threadbare, penguin-covered boxers flapped; he picked them out of his ass crack and yawned. His narrow, sunken chest was sparse with wiry, reddish-dark hair, and you could see the scars up along the right side of his ribcage. Claw marks. You could see clearly where the hellbreed's three fingers had dug in, flexing.

There are reasons why Hutch doesn't ever want to get close to the nightside. He's wiser than most.

"Because I like you so much, sweets." I made a little kissy noise. Under the cuff, the scar was a wet, burning pucker. There was a hole in my T-shirt, and the red gleam of the Eye peered out through it. Above the Eye, the carved ruby—a pale imitation, to be sure—glowed as well. I did *not* reach up to play with it nervously, but my fingers itched.

He grabbed a Santa Luz Wheelwrights T-shirt from a pile of laundry on the floor, pulled it on over his head. "Don't *say* things like that. God. Go make me some coffee. Jesus H."

I slid out of the room and down the hall. The kitchen was as gleaming and shipshape as his room was messy and dusty. He had a state-of-the-art espresso and drip coffeemaker, complex enough to make a cappuccino by itself and pilot a rocket ship at the same time. I poked at it for a few moments, thought longingly of what a great sound it would make if I shot the damn thing, and figured out how to make the drip side work. After a search through every cabinet, I found the coffee canister in the fridge, exactly where Saul would have put it. By the time Hutch shuffled down the hall, reeking of Right Guard and scrubbing under his T-shirt with one hand, there were six cups of coffee and more dribbling out.

"I made a whole pot," I said, and glanced at the window. Night pressed against the bulletproof glass. Each window up here was reinforced with silver-laced chicken wire.

"What am I looking for?" He looked marginally more awake, grabbed a Wheelwrights coffee mug, and yanked the coffeepot out. Thick dark liquid sploshed. "Jesus. You make coffee like my dad did."

If it's not strong, it's not coffee. I shrugged. "I need you to go digging all over. Find me any disaster, anywhere on the globe, in the past six months big enough to let a *talyn* or bigger hellbreed slip through. I want you to cross-reference it with everything you can find on Argoth."

He jerked. Coffee splashed. My hand arrived, caught the mug before it could fall more than a foot, and I straightened, subtracting the pot from him with my other hand. The liquid burned where it hit my hand; it soaked into the tattered sleeve of my coat. Hutch stepped back, barking his hip a good one on the counter. It was anyone's guess whether he was disturbed by Argoth's name or by me moving too quickly to be strictly normal.

"Holy *shit*. No way." He shook his head, his hair standing up in bedhead spikes. "Not that again. Really?"

"I don't know yet. Could be a red herring." I finished pouring, slid the pot back in, and offered him the dripping mug. "But I need everything you can get. If there's *any* breath of that bastard getting out of Hell and making trouble, I want to know where, what, and when. I also need you to brush up your Chaldean and look at the Sorrows calendar. See if there's anything shaking down there." A deep breath. I tried not to notice how he was going whiter than his usual pasty-boy at the thought. "There might be more."

"Sorrows and Argoth? Jesus Christ." He took the cup with shaking fingers. "They're connected?"

"I don't *know*, Hutch. I need you to do these things,

and at noon today you pack everything you need for a siege and go to Galina's." *Because I am not about to lose my apprentice* or *my pet researcher.*

"Goddamn, Kismet. What kind of trouble are we talking about? No, wait. I don't wanna know. I'll get started right now. Anything else I should take to Galina's?"

"Just whatever you'll need to stay there for a while, and to keep up your research. Don't open up today." I cocked my head, listening. The entire neighborhood was quiet, and I'd made sure I was clean before even coming *near* the bookstore.

"Like customers are beating down my door anyway." He blew across the top of his coffee, snagged a pad of paper placed precisely under the yellow phone bolted to the wall at the end of the counter, and looked around for a pen. "Sorrows calendar. Argoth—hey, I thought you barred him from coming through. That time, what, two years ago or something? That case with the scurf."

"I did." *But it was close, Hutch. So close. You don't even want to know.* "But I can't be everywhere."

He gulped. If it was possible to go any paler, he probably would have. "Yeah. I, um, I got that. You okay? You look pretty pissed off. More than usual."

As well as covered in blood and blow-dried. I dredged up what could be called a smile. "Why, Hutch. I didn't know you *cared.*"

He gave me the most evil look a weedy hacker boy I outweighed could possibly give. And to top it all off, my pager buzzed in its padded pocket.

When I dug it out and glanced at the number, I had to suppress the urge to roll my eyes. Never rains but it pours. "Can I use your phone?"

As if he was going to say no.

He backed up a couple more steps, as if I'd moved. "Go for it. As long as something doesn't crawl out of it when you're done. I'm gonna get to work."

"Nothing will crawl out of your phone, Hutch. Promise." I gave him a wide sunny smile, or as close to one as I could get. I even tried to make it unscary.

"That's what *you* say." He reached up, grabbed a box of energy bars from atop the sparkling-white fridge, and retreated with his coffee. I heard him stamp down the stairs, cursing, and picked up the phone.

It rang twice. I stared at the back of my left hand, the scrape across the knuckles healed up and looking weeks old instead of fresh. My fingers drummed on the countertop, bitten nails scratching the cheerful yellow tile. The Talisman was a warm weight against my chest, and a shiver went through me.

I can only hold the tide so long. Perry, standing in the warehouse and snarling at me. That case had almost ended up unleashing utter destruction on my city. The last time this Argoth came through into our world was in 1918, in Europe. The second Jack Karma—the one whose knife my apprentice had taken such a shine to— claimed the dubious honor of sending him back into Hell in Dresden, February 1945.

In the in-between time, Argoth had been a very busy boy. Some parts of the world were still reeling, between that and the great demonic outbreak in '29.

The phone picked up. "Sullivan," he barked.

"It's me. You rang?"

"Yeah. Me and the Badger, we got some live ones. Well, dead ones. But it looks like one of yours."

Jesus. "Where?"

"Cruzada. 153rd and Anita."

Out in the suburbs. "All right. I'm on my way. Hold the scene."

Like he needed me to tell him that. But he just made an affirmative noise and hung up.

There was little I could do until Hutch finished digging. The night was getting older by the second, and it already seemed too long. I drummed my fingertips for another few seconds, as if it would give me something useful.

Then I got going.

6

The Cruzada district is a collection of suburban streets, most of the houses from the seventies and all of them needing to be taken on a street-by-street basis. Some are pretty nice, neat and clean, with hardworking neighbors who look out for each other. Some have crackhouses and shootings. The higher up and farther away from the river, the more likely there are to be bars on the windows and busted-down cars on the lawns.

Anita and 153rd was a buffer zone. Yellow grass slowly dying, bars on the windows that weren't for decoration, but plenty of the houses still had neat fences and all-weather children's toys scattered around. The air was heavy with the promise of spring, though the storms weren't threatening over the river yet and the desert cold had its winter bite. A scrim of snow still clung to the mountains and frost-rimed anywhere the sun didn't reach during the day.

It was three a.m. and dark even through the stain of orange citylight. The drunks would be making their way home, traffic fatalities occurring, the really bad domestic disturbances getting underway. In another couple hours the world would hold its breath for the long, dark shoal before dawn, the time when old people slip under the surface and drift away. But for right now, things would be hopping, one last frenzied burst of activity to take us through the night.

It wasn't hard to find the place. Two black-and-whites, their lights dappling blue and red, and a coroner's van lodged like splinters in the street in front of a trim fake-adobe. The adobe's door was open, a warm yellow block of electric light spilling out. Sullivan, his sparse, coppery hair catching fire under the reflected light, stood there talking to one of the blues. It was Jughead Vanner, the big blond unlucky one. He ran across weird nightside cases with distressing regularity. It was getting to be a joke with the crew of regular exorcists attached to the police department.

Some people are like that—unlucky. At least he knew who to call when things got weird. And he knew what kind of scene not to go barging into. He hadn't expressed any interest in the cases themselves yet, which was a good sign.

If he had, he probably would have ended up as an exorcist himself. Nobody can be unlucky *and* curious, and walk away untouched.

The gate in the chain-link fence was open, I pushed it further and it squawked. Sullivan and Vanner both glanced at me. The other black-and-whites were near the coroner's van; bullshitting since there was nothing for them to do, but they couldn't leave the scene until I cleared them.

"Hey, Kismet," Sullivan called. "Glad you could make it."

He looks like an overexposed photograph of a rumpled, thin man, despite the ruddy tinge to his hair. That washed-out exterior hides a mind so sharp it threatens to cut itself on a daily basis. Word was he'd almost ended up an accountant instead of a cop, and the finicky precision of his reasoning made me believe it. Of all the odd couples in Homicide, Sullivan and the Badger are probably the physically oddest.

He's lanky and almost transparent. She's round and solid-motherly, with a white streak in her iron-gray hair. She doesn't get her nickname from that, though. She gets it from being tenacious as hell. If she and Sullivan ever tangled, she would be the one holding him down and rubbing his face in the gravel.

At least, that's what the betting pool says. Odds are on the Badger any day of the week, and especially once a month.

She was in the hallway, arms crossed, her broad face solemn.

I took in the neatly clipped yellowing grass, touched with frost. People in the Cruzada have better things to spend their money on than astronomical water bills, especially in winter. No bikes or kid's toys, thank God. "I hurried right on over to get a hot date with you, Sullivan. What do we have?"

Vanner, as usual, flushed a bright scarlet and dropped his baby blues to my boots. He was the size of a small mountain, the beefy type that runs to fat early without hard exercise. "Neighbor called from the pay phone two blocks away at the Circle Mart. Said they heard screaming.

Dispatch sent us out with backup. We got here, everything quiet. Except the front door was unlocked. We identified ourselves, went in, and…"

The Badger stepped out, warm yellow electric light painting the stripe down the side of her head. "Hullo, Jill." A soft, unassuming voice that had fooled a lot of perps into thinking she'd be easy to bowl over. "Pretty sure this is one of yours."

I nodded. My earrings swung, and silver shifted, chiming. Vanner flinched a little at the sound, covered it well. "How many?"

"Maybe four. It's…well." Her mouth turned tight, pulled against itself. "Come on in, take a look."

I stepped up onto the porch, sliding past Sullivan, who didn't move. Jughead pressed back against the wall like I had some sort of disease.

"You have the worst luck, Vanner." I tossed the words over my shoulder as the edges of my coat brushed his knee. "Seriously."

He mumbled something. His entire face was crimson now, flags of color spilling down his neck.

Sullivan snorted. "I think Jughead's got a crush on you. He keeps tripping over your kind of cases."

Nobody can taunt like a Homicide detective. It's like some sort of unwritten law. "Maybe that's because he's smart and perceptive. Ever think of that?"

"If he was, he wouldn't be working this job." Sullivan's fingers twitched.

"Exactly." I stepped into the hallway, my eyes roving. "And neither would you, right?"

"Bingo." The Badger let out a soft laugh, pushed her glasses up on the bridge of her nose. Dark circles scored under her eyes, and her shoulders were held stiffly, as if she expected a blow. "Now shut up, Sully. Leave the kid alone."

Sullivan muttered something uncomplimentary. The smile felt tight and unnatural on my face. Because as soon as I passed the threshold, the gassy, ripe smell of violent death filled my nose. It was enough to drive you back on your heels.

Huh. I stopped.

The entry hall was tiled in brick-red, and chilly. If there was any sort of heater or air-conditioning, it had been turned off. The smell should have just about knocked me over halfway up the path from the gate. Instead, it was like stepping through a curtain. One second, nothing but dust and the wind off the river. The next, the reek was so powerful my eyes threatened to water.

Badger was watching my face. She nodded, slightly.

Every nerve suddenly tingling-alert, I stopped dead. "Outside. Get those two off the front porch. Everyone pull back to at least the fence. Don't let anyone go just yet."

She nodded and padded away, shooing the boys in front of her. For such a round little woman, she is amazingly light on her feet. I drew a gun, kept it low and to the side. Didn't ask her where the bodies were.

No use in asking what you're going to find out anyway.

Living room: faded brown couch, camp chairs, dinged-up yardsale coffee table, big but old TV. Kitchen tiled in red, too, large window over the sink looking onto the backyard, clean, dry dishes in a rack. A large stockpot sat in the left-hand sink, full of water and a scrim of pinkish soap bubbles. Looked like someone had been cleaning up after spaghetti. The dining room held a table with six chairs, two places at the end stacked with bills. A whiteboard on the dining-room wall held five columns in black marker, each labeled neatly.

Joan. Elena. Alice. Kendall. LOVE!

Under each woman's name, chores and notes in different handwriting and colors. Things like *Take out garbage* and *Electric bill.* In the LOVE column, two notes.

E, Kenny called. Said to call him back. And *A, picked up your dry cleaning, it's in your room. K.*

Two bathrooms, both clean and neat. One had a Post-it at eye level on the mirror over the antiquated sink—*Have u taken ur pill 2day?* And a smiley face. Three smallish bedrooms, one pin-neat and pink, the other two looking like bombs had hit them.

The master bedroom, at the end of the hall, was a soup of bruised etheric energy. I kept the gun ready as I tapped the door with my foot. Something was wrong with the hinges; the door opened only reluctantly and wanted to swing back closed. Either that, or the pulsating darkness inside the room wanted no witnesses.

Tiny crackles and sparkles of light preceded me, the sea-urchin spikes of my aura. I swept with the gun, my blue eye piercing and untangling a mess of threadlike tangles.

Oh, shit.

They lay on the king-sized bed, all four of them. Packed like sardines: one girl's head on the pillows, the next with her feet at the top of the bed, and so on. All utterly still, when viewed through my dumb eye. Through my blue eye, however, little crackles and twitches tingled through them. Nerve-death, some of it, bits of electricity still trying to connect over synaptic gaps. In most circumstances the body doesn't die all at once. Like living, death—even violent death—is most often a process.

But this cracking and twitching wasn't just nerve-death. It was flat out unnatural.

Sweet-sick corruption filled my nose. Vanner and his partner probably hadn't gone further than the door, and it was a damn good thing, too.

One of the bodies on the left, the one with its head pointing toward the foot of the bed, let out a gassy exhalation. The reek turned thick and clotted, like scabs pressing against the inside of my nostrils.

"*Sssssss...*" one of the bodies hissed, as trapped air escaped. The knotted foulness in the ether pressed *down*, obscenely, and the bodies jerked, writhing together. The scar tingled, and I reached over with my left hand, unsnapped the buckles, and tore the cuff off.

What was going to come next was not going to be pleasant.

If you've never seen a hellbreed reach through a rotting corpse, forcing the decaying meat and violated nerve endings to do its bidding, you're lucky. The body jerks in ways no human joints would, crackling like fat tossed in a fire as cellular reserves are depleted, and they make deep guttural sounds that are the closest frozen human vocal cords can get to Helletöng. It was a good thing Vanner's curiosity was nonexistent, because if he'd stepped over the threshold the way I was stepping now, I would have been looking at dead cops on this scene as well.

And I just hate that.

The four bodies wrenched into motion, squealing eerily with one voice. Every inch of silver on me sparked. I scanned the room one more time to make sure I wasn't missing anything. Then the one on the far right leapt off the bed with the jerky, disconnected speed of the damned, and I had no more time for caution.

If they got out into the front yard we were going to have serious problems.

7

The last one had probably been an athlete, she was strong and quick, as the hellbreed's will cannibalized every scrap of flesh left on the skeleton's frame. My breath came hard and fast, blood slipping down my forehead as I tracked, bullets spattering the wall. Glass shattered, and the unearthly chorus of four corpses singing in hellspeak was reduced to just one guttural chanting.

She jagged for the hall leading to the front door, skin peeling back from wasted muscle and the eyes cloudy with low reddish hellfire. Two of the four had been in sweats and T-shirts with ragged, gaping, bloody holes in the front, one was naked, and this one was in a babydoll nightie of cream-colored material, also torn in the front. The ragged holes in their rib cages and flayed holes in their bellies, splintered white ribs showing and tissue flapping free, spatters of blood and other fluids, told me things I didn't want to know.

But first things first.

Since she was the last one up and moving around, I

leapt on her halfway into the dining room. The impact knocked her down, bits of flesh splashing everywhere and the steady cadence of 'töng breaking for a thin half second before roaring back, like a radio coming in clear and strong through static.

The trick in putting down corpses hellbreed have taken control of is to either cause such massive damage the body can't move anymore, *or* break the etheric connection between 'breed and body. If you're dealing with more than one, you go for damage.

Which is always my favorite option, anyway. Call it a personality quirk.

Tangle of arms and legs. Splatter of stinking foulness, cold smoking fluid splashed in my face and I blew out through both nose and mouth, freeing the passages. I spend an awful lot of time wrestling around on the floor, getting leverage. Jujitsu is a *godsend*.

We rolled, and my right hand thrust into the stinking cavity in her chest.

Even if you suspect something so strongly, it's still a shock to have it confirmed. Her heart had been removed. Gristle scraped my slipping fingers, the body twisted and lurched with inhuman strength. It reminded me of fighting zombies, though zombies are a different proposition. For one thing, they're not impelled by a hellbreed's sheer power and desire to cause hurt. No, zombies are just like maddened animals.

Corpses with a hellbreed pulling their puppet strings, on the other hand, are cunning and ruthless.

The thing that used to be one of the girls on the whiteboard snarled as my fingers closed around something hard and egg-shaped. The tissue around it grabbed with slippery, grasping fingers, and my own voice rose, cutting through the babbling, grinding, tearing sound of Hell's language from a dead throat. I wasn't praying—no, I was cursing, yelling each filthy word I knew and combining them automatically. I dug in its chest, my legs wrapped around it, and my left hand punched the rotting face repeatedly.

The egg-shaped hardness almost squirted free, greased with noisome ick. But I yanked, and meat tore apart. The body spasmed, its hellfire dimming. Shattered wood flew as we struggled.

My fingers crunched down, the scar singing a piercing high note, burrowing hot as a dollop of melted lead into my wrist. The egg slipped free. I wrenched it all the way out of the gaping hole in the body's chest. Muscle and bone sagged aside, its frenetic activity snuffed out.

Harsh, ratcheting breathing filled my ears. It was my own. My pulse pounded. Cold sweat stood out all over me.

I shoved the body aside. Electric light from the fixture overhead was merciless, beating down like desert sun. The dining room was a mess—I'd had to fight while retreating down the hall, keeping them bottled up and away from the civilians out front. One of them could have gone out a window, if they'd gotten lucky. Or if I hadn't kept them bottled so hard. The last one *had* been looking to escape, probably to get out and cause a little havoc for their master, since I'd just come across a huge violation of the rules.

Whoever it was had to know I'd be along sooner or later to check this out. Thoughtful of them to leave a calling card. I lay on the floor, chest heaving to get enough breath in, and lifted the *bezoar*.

It glimmered nastily, a smooth, nacreous gleam from the packed-tight hairthreads it was made of. Pulsing with unnatural life, slippery with a weird clear fluid that dripped upward and vanished into smoke, the thing nestled in my palm.

This little seed, planted in a body, would make controlling easier. It was also something I could use to track the 'breed responsible. You don't see *bezoar* much; the act of destroying the body usually shreds them all to shit. Taking it out while the thing's still wiggling is key.

I swallowed hard, forced down nausea, and gained my feet in a convulsive rush.

The dining-room table was in splinters. One of the chairs was still whole, the others not so lucky. Cold, jelly-thickening blood splattered, already decaying and stinking, on all four walls and the French door.

My left hand was already digging in one of my pockets. Out came a square of white blessed silk, a little dingy from time spent stowed away.

Boy Scouts aren't the only ones who like to be prepared.

"Jesus." My own raw whisper took me by surprise, bounced back from the walls. The whiteboard was cracked, knocked down to the floor and rolled on. I probably had dry-erase marker smeared all over my coat. "Jesus Christ."

The silk went around the pulsing stone. The seeping liquid cringed from the blessing in the cloth. I had to use the breakfast bar between kitchen and dining room, laid the whole thing down and tied it up with quick gestures. Sorcery crackled on my fingertips, intent married to etheric force bleeding into the knots.

Most of the great hunter sorceries are sympathetic, echoes of a time when naked priestesses traced ley lines in dew-wet grass, using the earth's force as the basis for the simple magical theories of attraction and repulsion. And, not so incidentally, using that same force to push the night back from human settlements. To keep the dark at bay. Every hunter is an heir to that time and those sorceries.

"Thou Who," I found myself saying. Licked dry lips, continued. The Hunter's Prayer unreeled, with the ease of so many repetitions: "Thou Who hast given me to fight evil, protect me; keep me from harm." I skipped a bit, got to the important part. "O my Lord God, do not forsake me when I face Hell's legions. In Thy name and with Thy blessing, I go forth to cleanse the night."

A blue spark cracked. Two. The *bezoar* lay inert in a shield of white silk and blessing. A faint scratching sound came from the breakfast bar, and somewhere a hellbreed's rage mounted, but my hands were steady. I finished the last knot. "Amen."

Silence. The entire house was dead still. They were probably out there trying not to wonder what was going on. Sometimes I think it's worse to wait; other times I'm sure it's worse to see and know. After all, one of the more common responses to brushing up against the nightside is suicide.

A sharp pinch under my breastbone. I've lost good cops to the nightside. *My* cops, my eyes and ears, the people I protect. When you get down to it, there's not much difference between the work I do and their jobs. It's just a matter of degree.

Everything these days is just a matter of degree. It didn't used to be that way.

A tiny noise. I whirled, clearing leather, and saw Jughead Vanner in the doorway to the hall. His jaw dropped and his hands were up. He was so pale he was almost transparent, and sweat filmed his skin. His pupils were dilated, and he looked halfway to shock.

I lowered the gun, carefully. Tried to swallow my heart. "What the hell are you doing?"

He blinked. His mouth worked like a fish's. I holstered the gun, slid the wrapped, twitching *bezoar* into a pocket, and crossed the dining room in long swinging strides.

I grabbed his shoulders and *shoved* him all the way through the hall and across the living room. I'd gotten up a good head of steam, too, and when he hit the wall next to the barred window in the living room the impact jarred us both. "What. The *fuck*. Are you *doing*?"

"I…uh, I…" His mouth worked wetly. I shook him, shoved him back against the wall again. A thin thread of smoke teased my nostrils. The Talisman vibrated uneasily, tapping at my breastbone like impatient fingers.

"I said to *stay at the perimeter*! What about that did you not understand? God *damn* you, you could have been hurt!" I was yelling, full throat, and they could probably hear me all the way out by the fence. "When I say you *stay, you motherfucking stay*!"

I ran out of words and glared at him. My blue eye was dry and tingling, and I knew a crimson spark was dancing in the pupil's darkness. His Adam's apple bobbed as he swallowed convulsively. Dots of feverish red stood high up on his cheeks. I took a good look at him and swore, filthily. He shuddered at each word.

"Fucking stay right there, do *not* move," I spat, and checked the house one more time. Forensics was going to hate me for this. The bodies had been all neat in a row, but now the bedroom hall was an abattoir and bits were scattered everywhere.

Unfortunately, you do have to rip them up sometimes. I was lucky to extract the seed of corruption from one of them, something I could use to track the hellbreed responsible. The last body lay tangled on the floor in the dining room, amid the shattered wreckage of the table. Her face was turned to the light, the mouth wrenched open in a long silent scream, and that's the worst thing about corpses hellbreed have been playing with. They look like even death doesn't stop the agony.

This was turning out to be a long goddamn night.

8

The Badger called in paramedics, and they treated Vanner for shock in an ambulance. "We kept hearing noises," she said quietly, watching them. "He just got more and more nervous, then headed in. I had a job to do keeping the rest of them here."

"You did fine." I hung up, handed her cell phone back. "Four bodies. I want a full workup on whatever's left of them. Find out which internal organs are missing. Find out who they are—"

"Already have, at least a bit. Student nurses from Saint Simeon. Pooling their rent, it looks like. Next of kin is going to be a bitch." She looked like she was sucking on something bitter.

Each one of them was probably a parent's pride and joy. The funerals were all going to have to be closed-casket. "Shit." I blew out a long breath between my teeth. "Tell Piper not to release the bodies until I give the okay."

It wasn't going to be pleasant for the families. But that was the way it was.

She nodded. Sullivan stood with the blues in a huddle near the gate. The sound of male bullshitting had a high sharp note it doesn't normally have, and the blues kept glancing at me. Short little nervous glances that skittered off the edge of my consciousness.

Vanner moaned, shapelessly. I looked at the house. A cloud of etheric bruising lingered, intensifying now that I'd unleashed sorcery inside its walls and ripped apart the bodies. One of the regular exorcists was going to have to come out and clean it. Probably Wallace, since Eva was on vacation and Benito was handling part of her caseload. Avery had enough to do keeping up with the police department. "Make sure Jughead gets one of the trauma counselors. And get Wallace out here for cleanup after Forensics is through."

She nodded, digging out one of the tiny pads of paper she was always carrying. A pen appeared, and she made notes. "Jughead, trauma. No release on bodies. Wallace out for cleanups. His number's still good?"

"The 3309? Hasn't changed for eight years." But the Badger's thoroughgoing little heart wouldn't let her take it for granted, and I knew as much. "Have I ever told you how much I love your eye for detail?"

"Don't let Sully hear you say that. He thinks my body's the only thing to love me for." A flash of a grin, but her eyes were dark and grieving. "I tell him the line starts on the left. He thinks I should make exceptions for him."

"Does your husband know Sullivan's desperately in love with you?" I played along. It sounds callous, but when you see lives cut short and bodies strewn in pieces, it's either gallows humor or screaming sobs.

I prefer the humor.

The Badger's smile did not ease. "Oh, no. Frank would kill him. Then I'd have to break in a whole new partner. And I just got this one housebroken—"

"Are you taking my name in vain again?" Sullivan called. He detached himself from the knot of blues and ambled over. He didn't look at my chest, where the Talisman was peeping out through its burnt hole. It was glowing, a fierce reddish gleam strong enough to read by if I was in a dark room.

I should calm down. I took a deep breath. It didn't work.

"Of course not." The Badger gave him a sweet smile. "Just talking about your bathroom habits. Anything else, Jill?"

"Phone records." I stared at the house, my eyebrows drawing together. "See if we can piece together their visitors, or an estimated time of death. I'll need to know what's missing from the bodies before I—" My mouth shut, jaw clenching for a moment before I focused again. *Or what's not missing.* "Have them rape-kitted, too."

"Jesus." Sullivan's lips turned down and he fished out a worn pack of Lucky Strikes.

The Badger was solemn. Jughead moaned again, but quietly. It was anyone's guess what had scared him more—seeing the decaying corpse up and moving around, or seeing me fighting it with inhuman speed.

I checked the sky, shuffled through everything I wanted to do, and got exactly nowhere. We were wearing toward dawn faster and faster, and all I could do was wait for Hutch to pull the references, wait for the autopsy to tell me what I should be suspecting.

Thrashing around without something more definite

would only waste time and resources. Still... "I've got to get going. Buzz me when you've got something."

The Badger nodded, waving me away. Sullvan tipped me a salute. Jughead Vanner made a thin muttering noise, and the EMT in the back of the ambulance with him spoke up. "Blood pressure's fine. You're going to be okay, kiddo."

I wished I was that optimistic.

Mikhail's headstone is on the northern side of Beacon Hill's lush green, overlooking downtown and the mountains in the distance. The whole valley sprawls out, a vista as familiar as my own face in the mirror. I'd known, as soon as I saw the Talisman in the crushed paper box, that I would eventually end up here.

No use putting it off. And besides, better here than Perry's nightclub. If I went into the Monde like this, there was no telling what would happen.

I'd stopped at the edge of the barrio for a bottle of Stolichnaya—have I mentioned how loose the liquor laws are on the nightside?—and when I uncapped it the colorless fume could be an excuse for the prickling behind my eyes. I took a long hit and poured him a good healthy shot. It splashed on the granite stone. A faint whisper of traffic in the distance, the lamps along the periphery and at intervals failing to make any dent in the night. Darkness hugged the ground here, hung between the trees in rubbery sheets. The water they dump all over this place every day is a great psychic conductor. Grief and longing roiled under the surface of the neatly clipped grass.

I crouched easily, took another mouthful from the

bottle. Swallowed, relished the brief sting. "Hi." A thin, breathy sound. "It's me." As if he wouldn't know.

Here was one place I still felt young. I knew his ashes were carefully scraped up from the pyre the Weres built him, safe in an alabaster jar in Galina's vault. But it was here at the gravestone that I felt his presence. I didn't think he'd be a stickler for tradition and only hang around his ashes. Or maybe it was just that I needed him here, out on a hillside with the whole city spread beneath us and the vast dark sky above. At Galina's, someone would be trying not to listen. And what could I do, wake her up in the middle of the night every time I wanted to talk to him?

I poured him another shot. The thin sound of the liquid hitting the stone vanished into the breeze, the river inhaling as dawn approached. I let out a long breath, my shoulders slumping a bit. A red gleam touched the puddle, hot and baleful even when reflected.

"So, yeah. I guess you've noticed the Eye. Perry dropped it off." It didn't sound like much when I said it out loud. But the night tensed around me. I glanced up. All quiet, trees standing watch over the soundly sleeping dead. "I've got a bad feeling about this, Misha."

I could almost hear him. *Bad feeling every day on this job,* milaya. *Is part of contract.*

Well, yeah, I knew that. Jeez. What would he *really* say to me?

It's one of the hardest things to get used to. No matter how well you know someone, when they die you will never know exactly what they'd say. Especially if you loved them.

Especially if you *still* love them, deep in that room in your heart where you keep the only things that truly matter. The baggage you take to your own personal desert island, the exile called life all of us are born into.

The Church holds it as a point of doctrine that hunters don't go to Heaven. Mikhail had been nominally Eastern Orthodox, with a few significant exceptions. *I go to Valhalla,* he had told me more than once. *Where the fight is the play, like movie.*

I'd only asked him once why someone from his part of the world would pick a Viking afterlife. *Because,* was his answer. *Now stop the asking stupid question,* milaya, *and do your kata.*

I found my free fingers were touching the Talisman's sharp-scratching edges. The gem thrummed, the carved ruby at my throat warming as well. The Eye purred like a kitten under my touch.

I put my hand down with an effort.

"I never got to ask you why you did it. Why you fell for that Sorrows bitch." I swallowed the rest of the question—*why you didn't stay with me. Why I wasn't enough.* Yet another thing I would never know.

The scar puckered and twitched, tasting the misery in the air. I hadn't bothered to cover it again. "I guess it doesn't matter." The words were ashes. "Not like any answer's gonna bring you back. But still."

A rustle of movement. I was up, the bottle hitting the ground and my right-hand gun free, before the shape resolved out of the darkness and I recognized him. I reholstered the gun and waited while he came up the hill. It was a courtesy to make noise while approaching.

When his deeper shadow finally detached itself from the rest of the night, I pitched the words to carry. "I thought you were going to wait for me at home."

Saul tilted his head slightly. Glitter of eyes, the silver in his hair glinting. "It smelled bad. And I knew you'd come up here." He avoided the headstone with respectful ease, striding around to the right, and stopped a couple feet away from me.

"Sorry." I could have been apologizing for both things. "I, uh. Well. It got messy in there. I busted Perry up a bit." I was suddenly aware of the rags of my T-shirt, rips in my leather pants, the reek of rotting corpse, the ick stiffening in my hair and the mess I'd left behind me just about everywhere tonight. Some days are like that. You just break everything as soon as you drag yourself up out of bed.

My trench coat fluttered. The wind was rising, and it was cold.

He bent and scooped up the bottle. It had landed on its bottom, fortunately. "What else did Perry say?"

"He hinted that a big-time 'breed was looking to come through." *Again,* I added silently. *Since I only narrowly slammed the door on him the last time.* It wasn't technically a lie, but the less Saul knew about that case the better. He worried enough as it was. "A 'breed with a big reason to hate any hunter of Jack Karma's lineage."

"Oh." He touched the bottle's open mouth to his lips, then handed it to me. A graceful gesture, like all Were movements. Polite, tactful, expressing everything. "Which is why you're going to invent some reason to ask me to stay at Galina's."

My face froze into a mask. *I didn't think I was that obvious.*

But who else knew me the way he did? "It crossed my mind," I admitted. Then, because it was dark and we were at my teacher's grave, because the Talisman throbbed like a sore tooth on my chest and I ached all over, especially with the heavy weight of the *bezoar* in my pocket, I told him the truth. "It would kill me to lose you, Saul."

He turned his head. Clean, beautiful profile presented as he looked down at the city. "I've done all right so far."

Damn touchy Weres. But at least he wasn't assuming I didn't need him around and clamming up. *That* was no good. "I'm not implying you can't take care of yourself. I just...Jesus, Saul. Please."

"Look." He pointed, a swift gesture taking in the lights huddled in the valley, cuddled against the blackness of the river's flow and the bulk of the looming mountains. The stars were hard, cold diamonds scattered over dirty velvet. "That's Santa Luz."

I know that. I lifted the bottle to my mouth, waited for him to make his point.

He waited a beat, as if he'd expected me to say something, then went on. "Every single innocent soul down in that valley is pulling on you from one direction. And I'm pulling from the other. How long is it going to be before we tear you in half?"

Is that what you think? That you're on different sides? The vodka burned my mouth. I swallowed. Dried blood crackled on my skin. "You're wrong. You both pull me in the same direction, Saul. The only thing pulling on the other side is...this. The things I'm trained to do. I commit murder every night. Several times, if everything's hopping and the 'breed are uppity." It was a night for uncomfortable truths. I would have expected us to be halfway to a screaming match by now. "Sometimes I wonder what makes me different from them." It was my turn to wait before giving him the answer. "Then I realize it's you."

"Jill—"

I wanted to get it all out. "I'm scared, Saul. I can't retire. This is the only thing I know how to do. The only thing I'm *capable* of. And if something happens to you, I am going to end up worse than the hellspawn. Because I won't care."

Silence, then, between us. I lifted the bottle, let a thin stream dip from it and plash on the headstone. None of us would get drunk—my helltainted metabolism ran too fast, and Weres burn through alcohol like it's sugar.

And Mikhail? He wasn't even here. It was just a stone I poured hooch on to make myself feel better.

Most of the time I was glad he was sleeping soundly. Because if he wasn't I would have to *make* him. Then there were the other times, when I almost didn't care.

I wanted him *back*.

Saul was very still, the charms in his hair glinting. "I wouldn't take the Long Road without you, Jill." Quietly, stubbornly. "Not even you could make me do that."

Sometimes talking to him felt like a cardiac arrest, like my heart was literally stopping. Or just hurting. What do you do when you love someone so much your body does that? You can't fight it, you can't shoot it, you can't do anything but let it happen. "I don't want to push my luck."

He stepped close. Paused. Stepped closer. His arm came over my shoulders, and the tension went out of me. I leaned into him, filth and dried blood making small crinkling sounds as my head dropped down. Silver chimed as charms hit each other, and I saw the red glow of the Talisman on my chest had muted to a glimmer. It faded as I leaned into him.

He let out a soft sigh. "It's not luck. I *chose* this, and so did you. We made a decision. Even if you let go, kitten, I'm still holding on."

A hot bubble rose up in my chest. It was a scream. I had to work to keep it locked down, swallowing several times. "Saul?" Again, the high, breathless voice. I sounded fifteen again. And scared.

"Shhh. Listen."

I did. Heard nothing but the breeze in the trees, whispering over the well-watered grass. Traffic in the distance. My heartbeat, a song in my ears. Silver clinking a little as Saul moved, lifting his chin.

"I'll go to Galina's." Quietly. His arm tightened around me.

Oh, thank God. "Thank—"

"Someone has to look after Gilberto. You've sent Hutch there too, I presume?"

I nodded. He could feel the movement against his shoulder. I reeked. He smelled of healthy cat Were, the dry-oily, slightly spicy tang of a brunet male. "Saul—"

"Don't thank me, Jill. I'm doing this for your peace of mind. I'll stay there for a day or so, but then I'm back on the job with you. It's a compromise."

Compromise, consensus, cooperation. It's how Weres work. It's also goddamn annoying. "You mean you're just staying there long enough for it to get dangerous."

"You see? A compromise." He even, damn him, sounded amused. "So Perry's hinting about a hellbreed coming through. What makes you believe him?"

"Besides the fact that he brought me a present?" I sounded as snide as Gilberto. "Nothing. He wants something, I'm going to hang back and make him work until I figure out *exactly* what's going on." The *bezoar* twitched in my pocket—another task to finish, before dawn if I could. "Then I'll start shooting. This may be the game that ends up with me killing him."

"Can't happen too soon," Saul murmured, and we were in wholehearted agreement on *that* score. "What are you doing tonight? Or this morning?"

The thing I wished I could say—*having some quality time with my favorite Were*—was tempting. It stuck in my throat like the lie it was, because I knew I was going to jump the gun and go hunting. "Tracking down a hell-breed who killed four student nurses over in Cruzada. When I'm done I'll come by Galina's. You can make me breakfast."

"And Hutch. And Gilberto. And Galina. We'll be a happy merry crowd." His arm squeezed gently, half a hug. "Come soon, huh? I know, I know. As soon as you can."

Another nod. "If I don't track this 'breed down by dawn I'll come by for breakfast. Promise."

"Good." He let go of me and stepped away. The wind touched where he used to be down the side of my body. A hunter doesn't care about external temperatures, but I felt abruptly cold.

But he cupped my chin in his hand. Warm skin, a Were's metabolism radiating heat. I leaned forward, he bent down, and our mouths met.

It should have been uncomfortable, kissing in front of Mikhail's gravestone. I had the oddest sense that Misha wouldn't mind. And then there was the hot, nasty feeling squirming under my breastbone for just a moment—*look, here's someone who wants me. Someone who hasn't run off with a Sorrow and ended up dead in a filthy hotel room.*

It wasn't fair. I didn't know why Mikhail had done... what he'd done. I just wanted him back. And the sex, I understood now, had just been another way to tie us together. High pressure and availability instead of... what I had here and now in front of me, his fingers on my face and his purr thrumming through me, loosening my bones.

I didn't want to let him go, my dirty fingers twining in his growing-out hair. But we both had to breathe more deeply after a bit, so we stood, foreheads together, my eyes closed. His purr, a Were's response to a mate's distress, settled into a subliminal pressure. Minutes ticked by.

It was no use. I had work to do. Even if I knew I was going out looking for a fight when I should be waiting for Hutch or Forensics to get back to me.

The vision of the last corpse's face, screaming silently and forever under the glare of the dining-room light fixture, printed itself inside my eyelids. I didn't flinch, but I did make a small sound. Immediately clamped my lips together.

I am about to do something stupid.

He let go of me, one finger at a time. Kissed my forehead, a gentle pressure of lips. Then he was gone, boots just touching the fresh, juicy grass. I listened as long as I could to the sound of his footsteps, light and graceful-quick. They shifted as he blurred into muscled, four-footed cougar form, still running faster than anything normal could.

Super-acute hellbreed-jacked hearing was good for something.

I found I was still clutching the bottle of Stoli. It made a thin musical sound as I upended it, washing Mikhail's headstone. Alcohol fume wafted up, whisked away on a brisk breeze. The river's inhale sped up as dawn approached. If I was going to find—and serve bloody, screaming vengeance on—the 'breed who had killed those girls, now was the time.

I won't lie. I wanted to kill something else tonight. And it scared me even as I turned on my heel and vanished into the darkness.

9

The thinnest tendril of gray false dawn was touching the eastern horizon as I halted, the *bezoar* straining and writhing against blessed silk. I'd had to tighten the knots two or three times now. My apprentice-ring crackled with blue light, sparks under the surface of the metal occasionally breaking free with tiny snapping sounds, like itty-bitty razor teeth clicking together.

An iron gate stood ajar; the chain supposed to hold it broken and useless. They sometimes try to replace the padlock, but all it takes is dark falling for it to be burst into jagged metal shrapnel and the gate to drift open just a bit. Inviting.

The colorless, crumbling concrete wall is topped with razor wire. Behind it, the old Henderson Hill rises. The grass is long and always yellow now, clinging to life and sandy soil. Its buildings huddle together, spindly weeds forcing up through the cracks in the pavement squares and walkways. Several windows are broken, and no matter what time it is, it always seems a little darker the closer you get to the buildings. The wind makes odd sounds against every edge, even if no air is moving.

Sounds like faraway cries, or soft sobs. Or nasty, tittering laughter.

In 1927, construction on the new Henderson Hill was begun. It was almost finished when the great demonic outbreak of 1929 occurred.

That was too late for the inmates. They, like a lot of hunters we couldn't afford to lose, died in the first wave of attacks. They don't just call it Black Thursday because of the stock market, you know.

When some things come out of Hell, they come hungry. And the asylum, its physical structure impregnated with suffering from years of insanity and the torture that passed for treatment inside its walls, was a buffet.

The carnage here was blamed on a gas leak. Santa Luz's hunter at the time, Emerson Sloane, was still trying desperately to get a handle on things when he was ambushed and went on to whatever afterlife he'd chosen. The city went without a hunter until Mikhail showed up, fresh from postwar Europe and trained by one of the best—the second Jack Karma. Mikhail brought peace of a sort to the streets—or at least forced a lot of the stuff still running around to keep a low profile. It would take a long time and more hunters to truly tame the nightside.

We are so few. The Church—and other churches— tries to make sure we're funded and trained, and we have better firepower than ever, but even the best firepower is useless without someone capable of using it. I'd been at this for a while, and Gilberto was the only one out of plenty of candidates who even came close to measuring up.

Go figure. A murderous ex-gangbanger with a sarcasm habit and yours truly, the only help Santa Luz had against the nightside. Then there was Leon. I heard he'd been in the Army, in some South American country or something. And Anya Devi over the mountains, God alone knew where she came from.

No hunter likes to talk about what they were *before*.

I eased out of the shadows across the street from the gate. Psychic darkness swirled, coalesced between the posts. The *bezoar* twitched in my pocket, and my fingers made sure the knots were tight one more time.

The closer to dawn, the harder the fight. But any traces the 'breed who murdered those four girls had left would be fresh. That is, if they were smart enough to just leave, not stupid enough to stick around and wait for me.

Jill, you're lying. You need another fight the way a junkie needs another fix. That's why you're doing this.

I tried to tell myself one reason didn't cancel out the other. It didn't matter. I knew I was lying.

It's hard to look everywhere at once, especially when adrenaline is dumping into your bloodstream and nasty little flickering things are showing up in your peripheral vision. My blue eye turned hot and dry, untangling layer after layer of misery, agony, ill intent, cruelty—if ever a place deserved the name "haunted," the old Henderson Hill did. It was so bad up here, the psychic soup so thick, that even a lot of the nightside stayed away. I'd chased a not-quite-physical *arkeus* or two up into those chilly-thick halls. But the more physical 'breed and nightsiders give this place a wide berth.

The nastiness in Henderson Hill can hurt them, too. It doesn't care much *who* it hurts.

The gate let out a long moan as I approached. Nobody came down this part of Henderson Road, and there was a pocket of abandoned buildings washing up around the concrete walls. Before 1950, the entire complex had been loosely fenced; the public works department had put the walls up ostensibly to keep teenagers and hobos out. That was after the Carolyn Sparks incident, which you can find wildly varying descriptions of in the Noches County and Santa Luz Municipal library systems' microfiche. What you won't find is what really happened.

Trust me, you don't want to know. Suffice to say the boyfriend Miss Sparks thought loved her so much turned out to be a Middle Way adept just looking for someone to use as a gate. He'd talked her into coming out to the old spooky Hill on a dare.

There's no better gateway for some of the Abyssals than a gifted, untrained psychic, and the one who had come through... well, he ate Sparks's boyfriend and settled down inside the psychic's skin like a hand in a comfortable glove. It *almost* managed to raise another gate to bring a whole mess of its friends through. By *almost*, I mean it did for a split second, and released three more of them, before Mikhail could get out here to shut it down.

It took him a month to track all of them down. They went through civilians like a hot knife through butter. Misha never mentioned it directly. The notes he'd made in the file for the incident were gruesome enough.

The gate moaned even harder as I elbowed it. I knew better than to touch the metal with bare skin. Little sparks were visible all around me, the sea-urchin spikes of my aura crackling. There was enough ambient light for my hellbreed-jacked vision to have no trouble, but it was paired with a thick psychic darkness, a wet oppressive blanket almost blinding my smart eye's capability to look *between*, beneath, around.

The scar puckered wetly, chilled as if someone had licked the ridged tissue and blown on it. A shiver of sick delight spilled up the nerves of my right arm. Tasting the misery in the air, the scar pulsed as if it would swell.

I stepped over the threshold, Henderson Hill closing around me like a toothless, decaying mouth. The temperature dropped a good five degrees. A shiver passed through me, crown to soles, and my blue eye was suddenly alive with phantom images. Ghost faces, each one contorted in a rictus of terror or awful pleasure, swirled like smoke. Screams eddied soundlessly around me, moans and cries just at the edge of hearing. My skin was suddenly alive with little needling pinstrokes as insubstantial fingers brushed my shoulders, touched my hip, flinched away from the silver I carried.

It was getting bad up here. The spirits were almost visible, cheesecloth veils fluttering as the breeze veered. For an instant I smelled smoke, and the screams mounted, winding closer and closer. Etheric force crackled as I *pushed* outward, sweat springing up on my skin the way it never does unless I'm in a hard fight. Gravel scattered across the cracked driveway rattled like dry bones, pebbles lifting and dropping in place.

It's always that way—the first few seconds are the time when most trips to Henderson go wrong. The world rippled around me, and normality reasserted itself. The shades retreated to the edges of my vision, flickering in the corners. The sounds drew back, too. Having an exorcist's aura, hard and disciplined, is far from the worst ally when you're stepping on ground that's been unhallowed with a vengeance.

I let out a soft breath. Everything calmed down.

An untrained psychic might be drawn into the labyrinth of buildings and passages, deeper and deeper, until they ended up as a meal or one of the shades swirling around. Thank God most psychics, untrained or not, kept well away from this slice of real estate. Even normal people could get caught in the spider web of misery this place had become. Most of them had sense enough to stay clear.

The local exorcists called me instead of following if a victim headed for the Hill. There was a mute, scarred caretaker—the only person I'd ever seen here. He sat in the boiler room most of the time with a quart of rye, and I'd never figured out exactly *what* he was. Once, and only once, he'd appeared out of nowhere and walloped a writhing possession victim on the head with a shovel. The Possessor had been strong and wiry, using its victim's body recklessly, and the caretaker's appearance had given me a precious few seconds to get the vic down and mostly trussed up. The resultant quick and dirty exorcism had almost killed the victim, but I'd ripped the little bastard of a demon out and smashed it into screaming flinders.

The caretaker had merely shuffled off with his shovel. I felt bad about not thanking him, but with an unconscious human woman shivering and moaning in my arms, her blood pressure and pulse dropping fast, my options had been limited. And he'd never shown up again when I chased an *arkeus* or two around the halls. If I wanted to see him, I had to go around the corner of the building and penetrate the maze that used to be a quad for the inmates to shuffle around.

And I did not want to see that imitation of a garden again unless I absolutely had to.

I set off up the driveway. Pebbles shifted and clicked as I walked, the edges of my aura like a storm front setting off waves of disturbance. It was like walking under a blanket of something a little less heavy than water. Setting each foot carefully, every inch of me quivering with alertness.

"*Kisssssssssmet...*" A faint, faraway giggle. "*Kissssss-met, come closssser.*"

You bet I could. But not in a way they would like. I kept my mouth shut.

The main building loomed up the hill, all its windows dead eyes. The *bezoar* twitched, and I stopped. Slid my hand into my pocket and made sure the knots were tight one more time. Before carefully, gently, drawing it out.

A soundless buzz almost made me jump. It was my pager, silent in its padded pocket, vibrating insistently. *Not right now, dammit.* I promptly shut the sensation out and yanked the *bezoar* back as it tried to squirt free of my fingers.

A sick green light flashed in one of the upper windows. Third floor, fifth from the left. Odd that it was up there, instead of in the basement—hellbreed usually like dark holes. The darker, the better. But the Hill's basement is someplace not even a 'breed might want to be.

What the hell was a physical 'breed doing here? *Arkeus* don't murder so directly; they usually gain substantiality a little at a time by stealing it from Traders. It's a long process, and I usually kill them before they get halfway.

I leaned forward, each boot landing softly and rolling through, ready for any sudden movement.

None of the buildings were locked. There was no need, and in any case the locks went the same way the padlock on the front gate did. Boards were nailed up over random windows, as if the caretaker just came out and put a couple up for the hell of it every once in a while, a token show. It was like Band-Aids over leprosy.

As soon as the light flashed it was gone. My right hand curled around a gun butt as I stuffed the silk-wrapped lump back in my pocket. Seaweed-shifts of etheric interference blurred my smart eye, threatening to give me a headache.

That was the least of my problems. At least, if I couldn't get a lock through this static on the disturbance in the ether a hellbreed represented, they couldn't get a lock on *me*. Which meant I could come out of nowhere and knock them on their ass.

The steps were wide and oddly bleached. I went up them cautiously, eased across the wide porch, its columns cracked and dripping scabrous paint. A chorus of children's voices, screaming, roared between them. Echoes bounced, ruffling my hair and bowing the world in concentric ripples.

The scar turned hot and hard as it pumped etheric energy through me. *Now. Do it now.*

I uncoiled from the porch, one boot thudding home on the left-hand door. Cold air closed over me—outside on the grounds it's just cooler than normal. Inside, it's frigid, and my breath turned to steam. I hit the ground, rolled, and was upright again in time to see the short 'breed hanging in the air over me, lit by the weird, faint illumination filling the entire building. My pager was going crazy in my pocket again, but I didn't care, because I was in deep fucking shit.

It was the masked 'breed who does assassinations and dirty work all through Santa Luz. I say *masked* because he is, and "he" because it moves like a boy. The mask was a half veil, fluttering at the edges, and he wore loose-fitting black silk. He looked like a ninja in pajamas, complete with slippered tabi feet, except for the orange hellfire dripping from his black, black eyes. It crackled on his high cheekbones as it smeared, drops flying upward in merry defiance of gravity.

My arm jerked up, the gun spoke. Bullets spattered behind him as I tracked, rolling to the side. Henderson Hill rocked on its foundations, each silverjacketed round blowing a hole in the sweeping staircase's wall and puffing out dust. He was fast, even for a 'breed. I'd never gone up against him, because he confined himself to killing his fellow hellspawn and Traders.

I like to encourage that sort of behavior. As long as it makes *my* job easier.

He hit where I had been lying bare fractions of a second ago. My left hand jerked the whip free, it struck like a snake and missed, flechettes jangling. The sparks—sterile orange from him, cold blue from me—were photo flashes etching shadows on the rotting walls and ceiling. I skipped back, footsteps grinding in dirt and trash against the scarred ancient linoleum of what used to be the reception foyer.

On all fours, the assassin snarled behind his veil. His breath didn't paint the air with vapor. Mine swirled around my head like cigarette smoke.

Where plenty of them are tall packages of bad news, this 'breed is compact and skinny, almost childlike because of the weird proportion of the head to the limbs.

White skin showed above the mask's sheen, pallid and waxy like a maggot's sides. Orange hellfire crawled and dripped, each droplet snapping out of existence as it rode the updraft of the hellspawn's fury.

I shook the whip, calculated the ammo I had left in the gun, squeezed off a shot. He lunged aside, but it clipped him low on the left. Black ichor sprayed. It wasn't a critical enough hit to put him down or slow him, but a few more like that and I'd send him back to Hell.

If I could stay alive long enough.

Still skipping back, the intake desk looming behind me under its drift of nameless, shapeless trash. Shadows spasmed and danced. Streaking with inhuman speed, he left a smear of fluorescent spangled hate behind him, each drop of hellbreed blood hissing as it hit turbulent air. I leapt, getting the high ground of the counter. It lurched under me like a living thing, rotting wood splintering, but I had my balance. The gun spoke again, its muzzle flash etching every line and angle for a brief instant as the whip cracked. My arm came down hard, leather singing as it stretched. My pager still buzzed, I ignored it.

Hit him now, hit him hard, *goddamn you Jill, hit him—*

The flechettes struck home, chiming, and the hellbreed howled. But he was so ungodly *fast*; he hit the desk and splinters smashed up in a wave. I was already airborne again, a tight-curled ball as my coat snapped once like wet laundry shaken before you put it on the line. Every muscle in my body straining against gravity, I *twisted* in midair and thumped down near the stairs, whirling and dropping to one knee, pointing the gun as the whip landed in a soft slithering coil...

...and the foyer was empty, from sagging walls to

damaged ceiling. Thin curls of steam lifted from splattered hellbreed ichor, decaying rapidly. My ribs heaved; flickering with deep, harsh breaths that flashed into ice at the edges and fell in spatters of diamond frost. Dirty cheesecloth veils pressed close, tangling like wet weeds. The scar burned, throbbing, obscenely full.

Movement. The gun jerked, but it was just a twist of paper on a stray breath of air. The hellbreed's footsteps retreated, faltering. I'd hit him but good. I didn't have to chase him now—I knew who it was, and I could afford to go after him during the day when I'd have more of an edge.

I was beginning to think I'd need it.

I rose slowly. *Could be a trick. What's a 'breed doing here, though? Not an* arkeus, *either, a fully physical spawn.* Intuition tingled as Henderson Hill breathed around me. A whole cavalcade of little sounds—an old building creaking and ticking as dawn approached, rustles and half-heard cries as the spirits crowded around me, drawn by violence—

—and the thump-shuffle of halting footsteps.

I crouched easily, the whip dropped, and my hands reloading my right-hand gun with the speed of long habit. The *bezoar* twitched spastically in my pocket and my pager just would not stop vibrating. I was about to pull the damn thing out and shoot it.

My bitten-down fingernails scraped in dust and cold grime as I felt for the whip handle, grabbed it. Shook it a little, testing. I did not rise—if something jumped me, I was a smaller target and better off having my balance, even if every fiber of my body was screaming at me to move. To face whatever was coming at me standing up.

That's what training is for. To make sure you don't do something stupid. At least, to *help* you not do something stupid. The fine hairs on my neck and back and arms stood up, quivering like sea anemones, searching for danger.

A shadow moved in the hall to my left. I had a split second to decide whether it was real, unreal, or a threat either way. The gun pointed itself, my finger tightened on the trigger. I kept breathing, smooth swells as my body recovered from the tendon-popping strain of superhuman speed. My shoulders were bridge cables, the need to move drawing down tighter and tighter inside me.

Darkness swirled. My shot went wide, blowing out the doorjamb above his head, and a mild blue, cataract-clouded gaze met mine.

The caretaker pursed his scarred lips. The lower half of his face was a runnel of broken and battered tissue, parts of his cheeks and jaw suppurating under a shield of startlingly white gauze. No matter how many times I see it, I still feel the urge to flinch.

I lowered the gun. Tried not to look like I was gasping for breath. Stared at him.

The caretaker is scarecrow-thin, in a gray coverall with a name embroidered on the left breast pocket. The embroidery is just a mass of snarled stitches now, and the coverall washed so many times it's almost worn through at knees and elbows. Lines fan out from the corners of his eyes. His hair is indeterminate, somewhere between blond and dishwater. The only saving grace is those blue eyes, intelligent and mild even if they are filmed with gray. They looked at me, sad and wide, and I promptly mostly-dismissed him as a threat.

At least, he'd never been a threat before.

The masked 'breed was gone. Now I knew, or at least could assume with a degree of certainty, who had killed those girls. But Jesus Christ, if he was killing *humans*...

...something was very wrong here.

The idea that maybe it was related to Perry's little present and dark hints was enough to break me out in a cold sweat.

I stayed crouched, every nerve alert and the scar humming as it sipped at the foulness in the air. The caretaker stopped, his hands hanging loose at his sides. A brief unease ran through me—not too long ago the circus had been in town and there had been a Trader with big paddlefish strangler's hands.

That case is over, Jill. Deal with what you got in front of you.

Nothing. The world was creeping closer to dawn, and I had a lead. I could track down the masked 'breed without too much trouble, and find out why he was killing humans. *After* I found out what he was doing here at Henderson Hill.

I straightened, slowly, my knees creaking. The caretaker was staring at me. As soon as I was fully upright, he nodded and pointed up the stairs.

Behind me.

I threw myself down and aside, both guns slapped out now and the whip discarded. It hit the ground with a soft slithering just as I felt like an idiot.

There was nothing there.

He shuffled forward, his ruined face coming into view. There was now amusement sparkling in those filmed-but-piercing eyes. His breath turned into a cloud, just like mine.

"Jesus," I said shakily. "Go ahead, laugh. I know you want to."

The sound of a living voice echoed oddly. The crowding spirits flinched away. I got to my feet, shaking dust and sand out of my hair. The caretaker shrugged, spreading those long fingers. An odd kind of clarity lingered around him, none of the ghosts playing tricks or pressing close to probe for openings. He didn't *look* like an exorcist. To my blue eye, he just looked . . . solid. And normal, but without the shifting fields of color that most often clung to living things.

Still, he breathed. And he was physical enough to hold a shovel. You learn to take what you can get on the nightside.

Again, he pointed at the stairs.

I holstered my guns, picked my whip up. "All right, all right. I'm going. I don't suppose you're coming with me."

But I was surprised again. He edged past me, carefully, his back to the bullet-scarred wall. I'd done a fair bit of damage; the desk still quivered with the dregs of violence. There was a hall in the east building, second floor, that was probably still reverberating from my *last* visit here.

I didn't like thinking about that. It was *freezing* in here, and even though temperature matters very little to a fully trained hunter this wasn't a physical cold. It was far worse. A soft rustling scraped through the foyer. The chairs tumbled along the far side, swept there and jumbled together, creaked sharply once. Like a shot, or a leather strap cracking down on unprotected flesh.

I stepped back. I didn't blame him for keeping his

distance. He smiled very gently, his ruined mouth twisting against itself, and turned. He tested each step with a scarred work boot before committing his weight to it, and after he'd gone up four or five I moved to do the same.

The fifth floor had been a maximum-security ward. Some of the rooms were windowless, padding hanging in strangling, sticky scarves from the ceiling and walls. Others had bars and chicken wire holding glass that by some miracle hadn't broken, or else crystalline shards held in by wire. My pager kept going off, frantic in its padded pocket like a small bird's heartbeat. The *bezoar* twitched, too. My coat was beginning to feel like a live thing.

The caretaker kept to the middle of the hall, an exact distance away from either side. The heavy, reinforced doors occasionally twitched, each one ajar just a little.

Except for one most of the way down the hall. That one switched back and forth lazily, like a cat's tail as it contemplates a mouse. Nasty little titters hovered around us, the spike tips of my aura glittering sharp and the clarity around the caretaker moving with him, a double sphere of normalcy. A soft chill breeze full of medical antiseptic touched my face, shuffled through my dirty hair.

I couldn't wait to clean up. Soon enough.

I kept my right hand on a gun, and my left, deep in another pocket, tightened the knots on the silk. I had a visual on the 'breed I was going to be questioning about this, but it would be silly to let the *bezoar* out of my grasp. Galina would have something to lock it down further, and as long as I had it there was nowhere the masked 'breed could go to escape me.

Not like he could escape me anywhere in Santa Luz anyway. When I get a real hard-on for a 'breed they don't stay hidden long. And it's not like he blends in.

The caretaker paused. Half-turned, and I saw his profile as he laid a finger against his mutilated lips. The bandaging on the bottom part of his face still startlingly white, even if crusted with seepage, and I wondered, just like I did every time, just what exactly he *was*. There was no sick-sweet perfume of hellish corruption hanging on him, and none of the other classifications of night-side or nonhuman seemed to fit him. The only place in this whole heap that wouldn't give someone the heebie-jeebies was his dark, dirty, *normal* boiler room, where he sat sucking on his bottle and staring at the walls.

I nodded and drew the gun. Kept it pointed at the floor, nice and easy. He set off again down the hall, and I found myself stepping only where he did. As if he was Mikhail and I was still an apprentice.

The Talisman sighed on my chest. No matter how much time goes by, missing someone never gets any better. You just learn to work around it.

The door's twitching motion sped up, imperceptibly. The hallway rippled like a funhouse mirror, the floor rumbling as if we were above a subway.

He stepped wide of the door, carefully turning himself. Moved sideways, crablike, to give me room. Pointed, with one long pale finger.

I edged around the door, trying to stay away from it and not get too close to the opposite wall. The door stopped twitching. Now it just quivered a little, jabbing out into the hall like an accusing finger.

Inside the room, the disturbance was so bad I had

to shut my smart eye. For a moment the pictures didn't make sense, then they snapped together behind my eyes and bile rose in my throat. I backed up a half step, instinctively retreating, and a hand closed around my upper arm.

I almost punched him. Jumpy, jumpy.

The caretaker shook his head, and those sad eyes stopped me. He pointed again, and his ruined mouth opened. I waited for him to speak for the first time ever, but he just gave me the saddest look imaginable, closed his lips tightly, and pointed inside the room again.

This time I steeled myself, and looked with both smart and dumb eye. My pager quit buzzing, blessedly.

A misshapen hunk sat in the middle of the gouged linoleum, dripping with corruption. It was veiled with a fall of black cloth, but it was almost certainly a chunk of a hangman's tree. Various shapes squatted on its surface—a chalice of clotted scum, a claw from no creature that walked under the sun, other things whose intent was only to maim and harm. The altar wasn't finished, but the atmosphere here was already so poisoned they probably wouldn't need much. All it would take is the slightest push to gap the borders between *here* and *somewhere else* the smallest bit, and something could step through.

There were no vulnerable victims waiting in here, but the febrile boiling of agony, misery, hatred, and just plain nastiness here would be snack enough to feed something fresh out of Hell. There was no scoring on the walls, no drawn circle, and no parchment candles on wrought-iron pillars yet.

But there were four lumps of meat on the black material draped over the block. Small lumps, each about the size of a woman's fist.

I knew what they were. The rest of the organs missing from the student nurses would be at other evocation sites.

I cannot hold back the tide forever.

There's nothing that can tear down the walls between here and Hell like innocent flesh. I knew what the important part of the autopsy would say. I'd even bet my next municipal check that the four student nurses were all virgins, too.

My city was in deep trouble.

10

I couldn't get out of Henderson Hill fast enough. The caretaker shuffled away, his thin shoulders slumped under his coveralls, and I'd spent a few minutes of effort to coax whispering-blue banefire off my fingers. The last time I'd seen an altar like this, I'd been flinging yellow hellfire around, razing an entire airfield. It had taken a long time and concerted effort to call out the banefire instead.

Hellfire near an evocation altar is *such* a bad idea, there are barely words for it. The banefire struggled under the weight of contamination in the air, but finally I coaxed a wisp of blue up from my right-hand fingers. Once it had a good foothold, wreathing my hand in pale blue flames, singing in their hissing little whispers, I cast it at the altar. A blue streak roared foaming from my fingers and hit the nastiness squarely. It would burn clean and leave a thin layer of blessing in its wake, and if it spread to the surrounding rooms, so much the better.

I was seriously considering, like I did each time,

burning down the entire goddamn place. But there was no way of doing it without hellfire, and like I said, bad *bad* idea.

Hellfire feeds on rage. It would be the psychic equivalent of a nuclear weapon, and it would leave even worse fallout.

I got out through the gate and stood for a moment, head down, listening to the chatters and whispers fading behind me. My skin crawled, not just from the dried blood, hellbreed ick, and other gunk coating me. The Talisman was quiescent, nestling under the rags of my shirt. Dawn was underway, the sky lightening to gray in the east and the first flush of color in a thin line along the horizon.

My pager went off again. I almost swore, checked the *bezoar* one more time, and dug the little electronic gadget out. Clicked back through the calls, once more wishing I could carry a cell phone. But no dice—pagers have a greater tolerance for sorcery, and with as much as I'm half-drowned, electrocuted, or other fun things, replacing a cell is a prohibitive expense. Especially since it's the police department that pays for it. Monty would have a cow if this one didn't last more than two weeks; I'd been having a bad run of it lately.

Montaigne was, in fact, calling me right now. Twice. I had a bad feeling about this.

I frowned. Galina, calling me. Several times. The pager quit vibrating, but immediately lit up again.

I juggled priorities for a moment. The autopsies wouldn't be done for hours, even with a rush on them. I had the *bezoar* and the capability of tracking that masked 'breed, plus I could figure out where he'd gone to ground without too much trouble. I needed to start digging to find out where the other evocation sites were, because bringing a high-class hellbreed through isn't something you undertake without a few planned backups.

I'd promised Saul breakfast. And if Galina was spamming my pager, something big was happening.

But first, I had to check in with Monty.

It never rains but it pours.

I cursed internally. Made a note to pick up my car from Galina's this morning, no matter what else was going on. And picked myself up into a weary run.

I must know where every working pay phone in the entire city is. When that infrastructure goes the way of the dodo, I'm either going to have to start carrying a cell and eat the cost of constantly replacing it, or I'm going to have to figure *something* out. Breaking and entering to use people's phones was the option I was most sneakingly in favor of, but one I suspected I'd never actually engage in. There are enough places open even in the dead time of early morning that I'd probably have no problem.

The closest phone was on Henderson after it jagged past Marivala Boulevard, in the corner of a stop-and-rob's cracked, dirty parking lot. The entire city had gone still, Santa Luz sinking into weariness before false dawn started coloring the eastern horizon and the nightside retreated glaring to its holes and burrows. I was hoping this wasn't going to be too complex, that Monty was just catching me up on forensics or something . . . but intuition as well as logic told me I was just trying to make myself feel better.

Oh, Jillybean, you are having one hell of a night, aren't you?

I had to stop and breathe before I plugged in my calling-card number, then dialed Montaigne.

"*What?*" he barked right after the second ring. He must've been sitting on the damn thing.

"It's me." I didn't have to work to sound tired. "What've you got?"

"Jesus Christ." Click of a lighter, a puffing inhale-exhale. He was smoking a cigarillo, dammit. In his office, despite the fact that all public buildings were supposed to be tobacco-free as of two months ago. And despite the doctor telling him to lay off.

I couldn't help myself. "Your wife's not going to like you smoking, Monty."

"Stay out of my marriage, Kismet." And boy, did he sound grim. I checked the sky again, decided it was about four in the morning, and winced inwardly. "Got a mass grave just outside the city limits. At least seven contenders, probably more. Weird work."

Crap. I thought about it for a second. "Bodies ripped up, some organs missing?"

"Oh yeah. They're crispy, too. Parks & Rec guy stumbled over it; Rosie and Paloma are out there. Rosie called in, said to get you on the wire and send her some fucking backup."

Jesus. I should've expected this. "Where?"

"Follow the Strip south and stop when you see the flashing lights. Do it as fast as you can, Channel Four's not there yet, but it's only a matter of time. Jesus." Another pause, and I heard him swallow. Probably coffee. At least, I hoped it was coffee. "Rosie says it's fragrant, too. Just a barrel of roses to start the day with."

"So you're in early, instead of late? When did that start?"

"I ain't got home yet, Kismet. Go take a look at this so I can fucking get there, okay?"

"Temper, temper." But he had a point, for something like this he was in his office playing central control until I got there and cleared the scene. "Cheer up, Montaigne. It could be a serial killer. A *normal* one."

His reply was unrepeatable, and he banged the phone down.

I set the receiver down with a grimace. Rubbed at my forehead, dried blood and gunk crackling off my skin. "Goddammit." It was just a whisper. Dawn was coming up fast.

I was going to have to catch a cab.

11

The driver—a placid, tired, middle-aged Chicano I'd flagged down on Marivala—pulled over onto the shoulder, coming to a neat stop just behind a black-and-white with flashers lit up. They had two of the four lanes going south out of town blocked off, and it looked like Christmas had come early. His license said *Paloulian*, and I didn't ask how he'd ended up with a Greek surname. In return, he barely even looked at me. Relying on sheer outrageousness to slide under the notice of normal people has its benefits. Besides, any cabdriver on shift long enough to greet false dawn sees a *lot* of weird.

Paloulian threw his smoking Camel butt out the window as soon as I closed the back door. His tires chirped as he took off, and the IN SERVICE bar on top of his cab flicked out. He slewed left to get through the empty lanes and took the exit for the industrial park, probably meaning to turn around and head back north.

Thank God there was no traffic just yet, at least not going this direction. And people complain about *my* driving.

There were at least six black-and-whites, a couple of nondescripts with bubble lights going, and yellow tape fluttering. A Parks & Rec truck sat in the middle, a big white goose among the flock.

All the activity was past the ditch, in a stand of trash-wood serving as a modesty screen. The Strip is pretty lonely right here, for all that a regular patrol goes through on the freeway to discourage drag racers. It doesn't work; pretty much twice a month in summer there's a bad bustup right where the freeway curves after coming out of downtown.

This part of the Strip was past where the races usually end. The city limit's about a half mile back, the freeway arrowing for the desert and the steadily lightening horizon in a straight gray line. There are still exits for fast food, industrial parks, or tiny suburbs, but right here there was nothing but concrete, the divider between northbound and southbound, and a strip of greenery on either side surviving on periodic runoff from uphill, where blank fences stood scrawled with graffiti. *Greenery* is a deceptive term; it's mostly low slashwood and yellow weeds. Life clings to every breath of water out here, and clings *hard*.

I cocked my head. Dawn was coming fast, like a brass bell ringing along the eastern horizon. I'd be late for breakfast.

The question was, just how late?

I stalked for the carnival lights. The blue standing guard stiffened. It was "Crosseye" Garcia, so called to differentiate him from the twenty or so other Garcias on the force. Squat and balding, he didn't quite have a lazy eye, but it was close. If my own mismatched gaze makes people nervous, Crosseye's just makes them inclined to take him less seriously.

He doesn't quite have something to prove, but it's close.

"Hey, Garcia." I settled for a closed-mouth smile. "Where's Rosie?"

He jerked a thumb over his shoulder. "That way, with fuckin' Paloma. Take a barf bag. It's nice an' juicy."

"I heard they were crisped."

"Some. Go take a look, freakshow."

Considering Crosseye was only slightly less foul-mouthed than "Fuckitall" Ramon, who never opened his mouth without an obscenity of breathtaking creativity slipping loose, I suppose I should've taken it as a compliment. I skirted the closest car and headed down the shoulder. "You've got such a winning personality. Goes with your smile."

His reply was unrepeatable. We were all in such a good mood this morning.

I hopped the ditch and headed into the slashwood. Murmuring, someone's voice raised in an exclamation of disgust. And something else.

A breath of smoky, corruption-laden perfume.

Pulse, respiration, my stride didn't change. But my right hand reached down, drew the gun free. Another high sharp note of disgust, and I heard Rosenfeld, sharp as a new brass tack, saying something about Forensics. Hunter's silence folded over me—the deep cloak of quiet that an apprentice learns early, because moving soundlessly is a survival skill.

There was a screen of brush along the top rim of a declivity. I edged along it to find the right angle. If there was a mass grave down there, I couldn't smell it. Which was bad.

I slid through the brush, following the drift of the

corruption. This was a goddamn fire risk right next to the freeway. Maybe Parks & Rec had been out here on a preliminary sweep before they cleared it.

At the darkest time before dawn? Come on, Jill. Something's wrong here.

I kept the gun low as I stepped out of the brush.

I had a few seconds before they spotted me. Rosenfeld had lost more weight; she was just on the edge between looking good and stick-scary. She was on the far side of the site, her lantern jaw sticking out even more stubbornly than usual. Next to her, Ricky Paloma crouched easily, peering at something. Between us lay a shallow depression full of tangled shapes I didn't look too closely at yet. Blues ringed the scene, all of them recognizable. I spotted the one stranger before he saw me, and the silence over me deepened.

He wore a taupe-and-green Parks & Rec coverall. Weed-thin, a thatch of dark hair—but his shoes were wrong. They were wingtips, not work boots. And the perfume of a hellbreed bargain clung to him.

Luck wasn't with me. He twitched, dark eyes rolling like glass marbles, maybe sensing a current of blood-lust in the predawn quiet. He saw me, but by then I was already moving. I cleared the fresh-scraped hole and twisted charred bodies in one leap, and I would have been on him like white on rice except for his immediate flinching backward leap. As it was, I jerked and my left boot smacked him in the head with a sound like a melon dropped on an icy sidewalk before he landed.

Rosenfeld yelled. Someone else cursed. The Trader went down in a heap, arms and legs bending oddly, and rolled. Dirt exploded up, and I got a stomach-loosening noseful of grave smell and the bad-pork stench of charred bodies before I hit again, just bare inches away from his scrambling.

"*Kismet!*" Rosenfeld yelled, but the cry was choked off midway as the Trader lunged up to kneeling, hands splayed on the ground and knees wide akimbo, his lip lifting and the yellowing stubs of his teeth cracking as he growled.

The gun roared. I had to not only get him down and cuff him for questioning, but I had to keep him away from the cops he had been standing around bullshitting with.

The defenseless mortal cops.

Lured them here, maybe. Or lured me. What the hell?

That's why the whip flashed forward, oddly quiet until it broke the shell of my silence; then silver-laced flechettes didn't jingle but cracked like silver lightning. They tore across his chest, and he howled.

I screamed, too, a short cry like a falcon's, and the gun was tracking him. He scrambled aside, but a single shot forced him into scrabbling to the right and back, *away* from my cops. He'd bargained for speed and probably strength, but I *anticipated*, and he jagged right into my next shot.

Which blew out his knee. The joint evaporated in a smear of red oatmeal flecked with white bone and the black lacing of hellbreed corruption. I was on him in a hot heartbeat, the whip doubled and slipping around his neck like it belonged there, my knee in his back and the other knee on his left arm. He tried to heave up, but when you lock the arm that high up they just have no goddamn leverage.

God bless jujitsu. Leverage is *good*.

"Mother*fucker!*" I yelled, cutting through the noise that was his howling and the screams of several grown men. I yanked back on the whip, twisting it, and choked him off. That brought down the volume somewhat. "Mother*fucking cock*sucking *son* of a *bitch*, what the *fuck* are you doing here? Huh? Having yourself some fun? *Huh? What the fuck are you doing here?*"

Rosie was making a lot of noise. I snapped a glance over my shoulder, just to make sure there wasn't anything nightside-ish to worry about. Nope, she was just getting the boys back, shoving Paloma in front of her and yelling like a battlefield general. She was getting them into a firing line, and while I appreciated that, I was going to have to kick her ass for keeping herself and other cops in danger while I was working.

Just as soon as I took care of this fucker here. Which reminded me: I needed to ease up on the whip, or he was going to collect his eternal reward without telling me what he knew.

And we couldn't have that, now could we.

I untwisted the taut leather a little bit, listened to him wheeze. Snapped another glance back. Rosie had the blues spread out, some of them kneeling, their backs to the brush. "*Rosenfeld!*" I yelled. "*Get them back to the road, goddammit!*"

The Trader was shuddering. It took me a second or two to realize he was *laughing*. Cold fury boiled through me, I choked him a little, and the laughter cut off. Creaking leather loosened when I figured I'd shown him there was nothing funny about the situation.

I heard Rosie and the others moving. Thank God. "Now." I kept my balance. "Tell me what you're doing here, Trader, and I'll grant you a clean death."

Another weird, quacking laugh. Shaking his whole body like a seizure. If he felt his shattered knee, he didn't show it. "Hunter," he crooned, through a mouthful of dirt. I hoped I'd broken a few teeth. "*He* said you'd be here. This is a gift. *His* gift to you."

"Who?" No answer, so I choked up again a little until his body started juddering not with laughter but with panic. He was attached to his skin, this Trader. I let up a little. "*Who?*"

"*Him.*" A retching, he spat dirt and snot and saliva. "The table's laid, the tide is turned. You're dead. You just don't know it."

Oh, please. Like I don't hear that or some variant every day. "The bodies. Who are they? Where are they from? It's not like I won't find out, so buy yourself some time. Make it easier on yourself."

He writhed under me, yellow grass smoking and flattening away as my aura hardened. He was strong, but he had no leverage. What the *hell* was he doing here?

A low creaking *sssssssssss* from behind me jerked my head around. The Trader started laughing again.

A thin line of blue hellfire crawled between the corpses, sharp little fingers poking and prodding. The bodies twisted and jerked, and the curse laid on them triggered with a *fwoosh* of flame. The Trader tried to heave me off, I shoved him back down and twisted the whip again to cut off that goddamn screeching laughter.

What the hell? But I knew. Someone was jerking me around. If I was called out here, something was happening somewhere *else*. Goddammit.

I braced myself, eased up a bit on the whip. "Tell me!" I yelled over the snap-crackle rush of unholy flame. The small clearing leapt with sterile light, shadows dancing like little imps. "Give me a motherfucking name, or I will start cutting!" *And hold bits of you in that goddamn fire over there for good measure.*

The Trader merely writhed. I realized something was wrong right before the secondary part of the curse laid on the bonfire of bodies snapped, a line of force snaking from the pit—

—straight for me. Or more precisely, for the Trader I was perched on top of.

Oh shi—

The world went white and turned over. I flew, weightless, and hit *hard*, snapping through brush and rolling to shed momentum. Thorns and other things tore at my coat, little grasping fingers. All the breath drove out of me in a huff, but no bones broke.

I struggled up to my feet, guns out, sweeping the clearing. The Trader was a twisting, jerking mass of flame and screaming. There was a sickening *crunch*; he fell like a dropped toy and lay in a burning heap. The bodies in the mass grave were writhing shadows, and the stench boiled out now that it was no longer laid under a shell of concealment. I scanned, trying to look everywhere at once, bracing for the attack. If a 'breed was going to hit me, they were going to do it now.

Nothing. The glare of hellfire stripped everything living of its substance, bleached the entire clearing and the bare branches on each trashwood bush. I waited, braced and ready, my pager going buzzwild again in my pocket. The *bezoar* had calmed down, just fluttering a little bit. It was like my coat was full of little animals, shivering away.

I exhaled sharply.

What the flying fuck?

This was a definite trap, but with no hellbreed lying

in wait to kill me. So, the real problem was occurring elsewhere. And if Galina was trying this frantically to get hold of me...

First things first, Jill. Get that hellfire down, and check your cops for damage.

I got moving.

"I should kick your ass." I glared at Rosenfeld, but there was no heat to it. I was too relieved. The pile of bodies behind me smoked and let out a vile reek, the sky was brightening, and a plume of thin, greasy black smoke was rising in the windless hush. Curses and hellfire, what *next*?

"You looked like you could use some backup." Rosie glared back at me, her hands stuffed in the pockets of her leather jacket. She had wrinkled her nose exactly once at the smell. Beside her, Paloma held a snow-white handkerchief to his face. If it was an affectation, it was a useful one.

I could barely believe Rosie had agreed to Paloma. He was a mincing little martinet, and if he hadn't been so good at teasing order out of the chaos of long-cold homicide cases he would probably have been "promoted" into jockeying a desk somewhere Monty and his ilk decided he wouldn't do much harm. As it was, nobody wanted to partner up with the bastard, until Rosie had come back from her vacation ten pounds lighter and with those lines around her mouth, and stepped up to bat.

"Shoes," Paloma said from behind his handkerchief. His small, dark little eyes were avid. "He had the wrong shoes. The bodies were wrong, too. Naked and charred. It had your name all over it."

I nodded. Maybe he was trying to distract me from chewing Rosie a new one. If so, chivalry wasn't dead. But it was far more likely he was looking to get brownie points instead, so I magnanimously ignored him. "Jesus Christ, Rosie. The backup I need is not to worry about some of you catching a severe case of dead from tangling with a bastard Trader." I decided not to get bogged down in that. There was work to be done. "By the time you get Forensics out here the bodies will be cold; get them untangled. If we can identify *any* of them, I need to know yesterday." I'd already pulled out the Trader's wallet; I handed it over after glancing at the driver's license and memorizing the name and address. "Find out everything you can about this guy too, but *don't* go knocking on any doors. Just get me last-knowns. I'll check his truck before I leave; but I want you to go over it with a fine-tooth comb. I don't like the looks of this."

Rosie's jaw was set so hard it looked likely her teeth would shatter. She had to work to get them apart long enough to spit out two words. "What else?"

Jesus, Rosie. But I knew why she was angry. It had to do with a good cop's grave, and the fact that she still blamed herself. Or me. Or both of us.

If I'd just kept better tabs on Carper...but I hadn't. He'd brushed up against the nightside and paid the price, and I still hadn't found the dirty cop who'd pulled the trigger on me outside Galina's shop.

Goddammit, Jill, get back up on the horse. I scrubbed irritably at my forehead, dried blood and other gunk crackling as I worked it free. I'd pulled something in my leg, and it hurt enough that I shifted a little, easing it while the scar hummed wetly, pulling on etheric force.

"Detail one of the black-and-whites to give me a ride. I've got to see what this was a distraction for."

I had a sick feeling beginning right under my breastbone. But *don't assume* is one of the first hunter laws for a reason. I didn't have enough information to guess at the pattern yet.

Paloma let out a whistling little laugh. "Hell of a distraction. Can't they just send you Christmas cards?"

My eyebrows shot up. If he cracked a few more like that I might actually get to like the prissy little bastard.

Rosie's face eased, bit by bit. "Careful, Ricky. That was suspiciously like a joke you just cracked there."

"Fuck you." He turned his nose up—quite a trick with the hankie still clapped against his face—and stepped gingerly away. I noticed, bemused, that he wore wingtips too. His were spitshine-polished, glossy black numbers. Even his socks matched his trousers.

He dug in the pocket of his natty gray suit for a cell phone, and I winced at the thought of whoever was on call for Forensics tonight coming out and getting a load of this. They were just going to love it.

Rosie and I faced each other. There was a lump in my throat and too much work pressing down on me. I settled for clapping her gingerly on the upper arm as I brushed past. My coat flapped a little, a whole new collection of rips and gouges letting air through. "Good work, Rosenfeld. You've got a hell of a battlefield yell."

"Thanks." The compliment apparently gave her no joy. "I suppose I'd better get the psychs out here too to eval everyone. That guy..." She glanced at the still-steaming pile of charred bones that had been the Trader.

Some of the cops were going to have nightmares after

seeing me violate the laws of physics, not to mention the Trader's hellish snarl. The psych boys and girls were going to earn their cookies on this one.

"Yeah. Don't let anyone go home without a session with the counselors. I mean it. Even you, Rosie." *Because I would hate to lose any more cops to the nightside. I really would.*

You could never tell. A few people handled it just fine. Others . . . not so much.

Her lip actually curled. "I don't need a fucking evaluation, Kismet. I've got pills for that."

And a patch of white in your hair you dye out every two weeks, not to mention some scars. You've seen the nightside and survived once. And she'd marched right down to my warehouse afterward to apologize for almost getting herself killed.

But sometimes it's the ones who have seen it before that crumble, too. You just can't ever tell. "Don't get cocky, Rosie. Get your eval and eat something, will you? You're losing your girlish figure."

"Don't you have some more property damage to commit, Kismet? Let me do my *job* here." All her walls up, a scowl to match one of Monty's best on her unpretty face, and she turned away. Paloma had jammed his phone shut and was issuing staccato orders; some of the blues were rolling their eyes. Rosie headed for the pile of charred flesh and stopped at its edge, looking down. Her shoulders were stiff, and her entire body closed in on itself like she wished she could disappear.

I let it go. My pager started buzzing again, and I told myself the prickling in my eyes was from the acrid smoke. The sun lifted above the rim of the earth, and I braced myself for a sleepless day.

12

The Parks & Rec truck reeked of cigarette smoke and the fading perfume of hellbreed, but held nothing out of the ordinary. Vinyl seats, papers scattered everywhere, a plastic coffee cup half-full of ice-cold coffee and the rest filled up with used Camels filters. I glanced through the glove box, checked under the seats, gave the tires and undercarriage an exam.

Except for some fresh scratches on the bed, where something square and goddamn heavy had done a number on the paint job, there was nothing.

For the moment I was going to work on the assumption that the truck was stolen. I made sure there was nothing in there likely to make it blow up and cost me another couple cops, scanned it for any etheric disturbance, and decided to get out to Galina's. Crosseye Garcia was tapped to give me a ride, and the entire way there he kept the scanner turned up to jet-takeoff level.

I guess I made him nervous. At least I kept the window down so he didn't have to smell me.

Golden light was beginning to stretch and lick between buildings by the time we got to the right neighborhood. He let me off a few streets away from Galina's, but before I got out I made sure he knew he wasn't going home until he had a session with the headshrinkers. He cursed me roundly for that, and I replied with a grin and a slam of his cruiser door.

"Fucking freakshow," he snarled before he gunned the engine and sped down the street, lights flashing.

I watched until he was out of sight, then disappeared into an alley, muscled up a fire escape, and cut across the rooftops. I circled Galina's house warily, twice. An exhausted dawn hush clung to concrete, brick, siding, and pavement. The etheric protections on Galina's shop reverberated uneasily, but they weren't tolling like bells.

I sometimes wondered how hunters in other cities functioned without a Sanctuary around. Neutral supply of necessities to all the practitioners and quite a few of the nightsiders in a territory is the least of the services they provide. In Galina's case, she was the closest to a confessor I'd ever have.

The Church doesn't offer hunters Confession or Communion, because we traffic with Hell and commit the sin of murder every night. It was Galina who probably knew or guessed the most about me, with Mikhail dead. Saul didn't ask—he knew everything he needed to. Perry? Don't make me laugh—the more he thinks he knows, the less he actually does, and I want to keep it that way.

A chill finger touched my tired spine. *You're lying, Jill. He knows more than you think he does. You're only a hairsbreadth ahead each time he plays one of his games with you.*

A hairsbreadth was enough, wasn't it? I wasn't damned yet.

That was faint comfort indeed. And this was not a set of events guaranteed to make me feel better.

Ever since I'd gotten filled with plain lead right out in the middle of the street in front of the Sanctuary, I'd felt queasy coming in the front door. So this time, I dropped down soft as a cat from the neighboring rooftop, landing on hers. The greenhouse, its glass rapidly silvering as morning dew caught the dawn light, stood silent. Inside, green growing things breathed and dreamed.

The lock gave under my fingers and a tingle of sorcery. The color of the protections on the walls changed. I froze, and waited.

You do *not* drop in on a Sanctuary when she's upset. You let her know you're there, and you wait for her to let you in. Inside their thick walls, they have near-godlike powers.

I guess it makes up for being a tasty defenseless snack outside, kind of. But it would drive me utterly insane.

The protections calmed, flushing a dusky rose under a flood of mellow morning sunshine. I stepped inside, breathing in the smells of potting soil and fresh oxygen. My shoulders unhitched a little, before my pager buzzed again and cut off midway. Was that her calling again?

A long silver shape lay on a butcher-block table in the south quadrant of the greenhouse, placed for maximum exposure. It had been dead and black, a long time ago. Now the sunsword trembled eagerly against the table, its clawed crossguards chattering against the wood. The carved ruby at my throat woke up, warming, and the Talisman hummed a low, sustained note.

You can't have a sunsword without a key, after all. The

Eye had been the original key, and with it gone, the ruby Mikhail had given me functioned quite handily as a secondary. Wearing both of them while I was worked up was bound to make the sunsword edgy.

The empty place in its clawed pommel held a glimmer of crimson light before I exhaled sharply, my will flexing. The sunsword went back to sleep, I drew in a nice deep breath, and the trapdoor in the floor was thrown open from below, slamming into the chair used to prop it so hard the chair leapt back like a bee-stung dog.

Galina clambered up through the hole. Her marcel waves were disarranged, there were dark circles under her green eyes, and she was in her sleeping gear: boxers and a ragged blue Popfuzz T-shirt. Behind her, Hutch peered up through the trapdoor, his hair sticking up like a bird's nest. He let out an undignified *eep!* and vanished.

"Jill." Galina was breathless. The mark of the Order at her throat—the quartered circle surrounded by a serpent, a solid chunk of silver—glimmered. The walls resounded to her distress, and the morning light was very kind to her. "Jill, be very careful. *Be very careful.*"

I almost rocked back on my heels. *Oh, Jesus.* "I got your pages. What's up?"

"I want you to be calm," she continued, running right over the top of me. "I just want you to be calm. Calm down."

"I'm perfectly calm." I was beginning to get a hell of a bad feeling, but I was nice and chilly. "What the fuck?"

A familiar dark head rose up through the trapdoor. But it wasn't Saul. It was Gilberto, and the instant he looked at me, his dead dark eyes flat and expressionless, I knew.

The world ground to a stop. I actually swayed.

"Oh, Jill." Galina backed up two steps when I looked at her, fetching up against another table, this one holding empty pots and small shovels, twine, bamboo rods for bracing weak plants. Everything jumped, once, like a group of trained dogs twitching in unison. "It was right out in the street. We couldn't—there was *nothing*—"

"Shut. Up." It isn't the sort of thing you say to a Sanctuary in her own home. But she stopped talking, high flags of color in her pale cheeks. My face felt strange, like it didn't belong to me. Lying against my bones like a mask. "Gilberto?"

He finished climbing up, brushed his lean brown hands together as if ridding them of dust. Coppery highlights came out in his lank dark hair as he stepped into a bar of sunshine. "You takin' me with you, *bruja*." Flat and unironic. "We gonna have to burn some fuckers for this, *es verdad*."

I didn't want to ask. My traitorous mouth opened. The most banal thing possible came out. "I'm late. Has Saul finished breakfast?"

Because there was still time for God to see He'd made a mistake, and take it back. I should have known better. God doesn't work that way.

He never has.

"Oh, Jill..." Galina's hand clapped over her mouth.

"They took him," Gilberto said. "They took *el gato hombre, mi profesora*. 'Breed and Traders. He put up a good fight. She"—he jerked his head at Galina, who grabbed the table as if it was driftwood and she was drowning—"knocked me 'cross the fuckin' room, ay? I was gonna go out."

Galina peeled her fingers away from her lips. "You would have gotten killed. Jill left you under *my* care. It was in the street; if he'd just been a little bit closer—"

Is he still alive? Not dead? "Galina." I didn't recognize my own voice. The trembling was in my arms, my legs. "Shut up. Please. Just for five seconds."

She did. If there had been a clock, it would have ticked heavily in the thick silence. The scar burned against my wrist, and the sunsword chattered once more against the table. It was hard work to get it to stay still, with the Eye on my chest and the ruby at my throat spitting sparks. *One, two.* Little crackles of blue electricity.

Three. Four. Five. Then I counted again, because I still couldn't put the words together. Finally, they came.

My throat was full of bitter ash. "Now." I had to work to speak above a whisper. "We're going to go downstairs. I need a new shirt and ammo. And grenades. And while you get those for me you are going to tell me *everything*."

"I go with you." Gilberto's face settled into sallow stubbornness. "You hear me, *bruja*? I go with you."

"Gilberto," I said very softly, "do not fuck with me right now. Tell me everything you remember while I get a clean shirt." I thought for a second. "And for God's sake don't get close to me." It hurt to say it. The sunsword chattered again, and my hands were making fists and uncurling, completely independent of me. "I'm not safe."

13

The Pontiac leapt forward, clearing the slight hill and going airborne. Landed with a jolt. This was not my usual intuition-tingling run through the streets, threading through traffic like a spaceship flying low. No, this was pure *pedal to the metal, balls to the wall, get the hell out of my way, don't care if I do hit someone*. The engine thrummed, a subtle knocking I hadn't been able to suss out yet in its high-level harmonics.

For the first time while driving this fast, I didn't try to diagnose it. No, I just leaned forward, hands on the wheel, and willed the metal to go faster. Dawn was fully broken, morning everywhere bright as a hangover and full of knife-sharp shadows, the kind of solid black you only get very early on a clear morning in the winter desert.

Luckily every street I chose was pretty lonely at this hour, and the few black-and-whites that saw me knew my car. They don't interfere when I go screaming through the streets, no matter what time of day or night it is. Sometimes, if I've called in, they even cut traffic for me. Not often—they can't keep up.

Between the scene Rosenfeld and Paloma were still probably working and this, the betting pool was going to be a-chatter this morning. I hear they have a whole system for betting on when and where I'll show up, how long before someone sees me, how many bodies at the last scene I visited. Macabre? Maybe.

But they know that when I disappear, it's time to get nervous.

Gilberto had tried to insist on coming along. I'd ignored him, told Galina to keep him under wraps. I did not want my apprentice taken too. That would leave me with too many hellbreed to kill, and having to make a choice between my duty to him and the way my entire body burned at the thought of Saul in danger, in trouble, hurt...

I did not want to make that choice. I knew what I would choose, and it would damn me in the only place that mattered—my own conscience.

Tires screaming, I jagged around a lumbering streetsweeper, cut up 182nd the wrong way between the last block of Sarvedo and Tigalle, and floored the accelerator again. Now I was in the industrial section, bouncing over railroad tracks, approaching the Monde Nuit from the edges of the block of slaughterhouses that huddled near the railyards.

The drive from Galina's to the Monde can take as long as forty-five minutes in bad traffic. Twenty at normal speeds. I made it in ten and slewed into the parking lot, tires smoking, bailing out almost before the Pontiac had come to a stop. Running, each stride taking far too long. My coat snapped and fluttered like a flag in a stiff wind.

The Monde is a long low building, crouching in a shallow depression of brackish etheric contamination. There was usually muscle at the door, Trader beefbags the size of small outhouses, with utterly illegal submachine guns. The edges of the parking lot were unpaved, and dust rose in odd swirls as the corruption creeping out in concentric circles met the tired sunlight and flinched back.

I'd probably arrived just at shift change, because there were no bouncers looming outside. I hit the wide oak double doors so hard they both flew open, the hydraulic arms atop them popping hard as they exploded. Little bits of metal and plastic rained down, but I was already through. Sparks crackled, a roaring in my ears.

"Perry!" I yelled, the scar turned into a live coal pressed in the flesh of my arm. Jolts of pain sawed up my nerves. *"Goddamn you, Perry!"*

The place was deserted. No Traders finishing up the night's games, no hellbreed at the bar, crouched on stools and hiding from the sun. The dance floor was empty, just like the stage. Dust danced in the golden shafts struggling in through keyhole skylights.

It was just like Perry to allow the sun, that great cleanser, a few fingers inside his hideout.

The only motion was at the bar, where Riverson set the bottle of vodka down with a click. His gray-filmed eyes, a little like the caretaker out at the Hill, fixed on me. But while the caretaker's gaze was mild and kind, Riverson's is just plain blind. Still, he sees a lot more than most with sight or Sight.

Behind him, bottles glowed on glass shelves. Some of them even held liquor instead of the various substances nightsiders used to give themselves a kick or two.

The vodka bottle shattered, liquid steaming as it hit dyed-russet concrete flooring. I had Riverson by the throat, dragging him over the bar. He was amazingly light, his strength only human. I don't know what he'd Traded to end up here, or how he survived night after night serving drinks to the scions of Hell.

I don't care, either. He's living on borrowed time just like the rest of them.

He flailed ineffectually. I batted one of his fists away and put the gun to his forehead. "Where?" I barked, and the word bounced back off the concrete, hurt my ears. "So help me, you helltrading blind man, I *will* kill you. *Where?*"

He choked, his face gone plummy and his filmed eyes rolling like a horse's. I realized he couldn't talk with me holding his throat like that and eased up a fraction, ready to clamp down again. I did not trust Riverson as far as I could throw him. Mikhail had come in here to pump the old man for information while I was still an apprentice. It was on one of those visits that Perry showed up at the end of the bar, dressed in pale linen and leering at me.

Misha had almost drawn down on him. Sometimes I thought it would have gone better if he had.

"—stop—" Riverson was still choking, and for a moment I struggled with the urge to close my fist and feel the little bones in his neck snap-crackle-pop. I could crush the larynx like a rotted fruit. It would take only a moment's worth of work, and it would be so worth it.

But it would not lead me to Saul.

I kept the gun to his forehead. Checked the interior of the Monde again. If Perry was upstairs in his white office, watching this on closed-circuit…but no. There was no betraying stain of a hellbreed's plucking at the fabric of reality in the whole building. Nothing but the syrupy well of etheric contamination, dark and swirling drowning-deep in some places. And Riverson's frail humanness, his pulse struggling as his face turned an even deeper plum-brick shade.

I eased up the rest of the way, though my entire body shook with the effort. "Talk fast, old man." Chill and sharp, I didn't sound like myself. I didn't sound like Mikhail, either. There was no edge of hurtful glee to my tone, either, which meant I didn't sound like Perry. Which was a blessing.

I might have shot someone, otherwise.

No, I sounded like a woman utterly prepared to kill whoever got in her way. Truth in advertising was making a comeback.

Riverson coughed, deep hacking sounds as his color eased. The colorless, nose-stinging fume of spilled vodka rose. "—*mercy*—" he managed to get out, and that was almost the last straw.

I pressed the gun to his forehead so hard I felt his skull under the thin skin, and the concrete under his head. "I am not in the business of mercy today, *old man*. Where is my Were?"

Shock softened his features. He coughed again, and even with the thick gray webbing covering his eyeballs he looked surprised and puzzled. "Huh?" Another deep racking sound, his entire body curling up like a worm on a fishhook. "What? The fuck?"

My temper almost snapped. The gun clicked, and he flinched.

"Did you miss the part where I am *not fucking around*?" The words hit a crescendo. "*Where is my Were, God damn you!*"

"I don't *know*!" Riverson yelled. "I was left here with a message! *Days* ago! *Jesus Christ Kismet don't shoot me, it's not my fault!*"

My fingers cramped with the need to squeeze the trigger. I lifted the gun, and it roared. The bullet smashed into a pile of electronic equipment on the stage. Sparks flew. Riverson screamed, the sound of a rabbit in a trap, and I pressed the smoking barrel to his forehead again. It sizzled. The scream ended on a whimper.

"Start talking." There was something in my throat. It made it hard to get the words out without a guttural growl.

The cold voice of calculation and percentage spoke up. *Don't kill him, Jill. Don't do it. Not yet.*

"It's not my fault! Perry left me here. He thought you'd be here before now, *way* before now. He's in trouble. Bad trouble."

"How exactly is that my problem?" But I had a sinking sensation in the middle of my belly, right next to the ball of unsteady rage.

"His problem *is* your problem, Kismet. They're bringing through another hellbreed. A bigger one. According to the higher-ups Perry hasn't been pulling his weight for years now. He's been fobbing them off with one excuse after another—"

I bounced his head off the concrete once. It felt good, but I didn't want to do it again. Might make it harder to question him if he got all dizzy and concussed. "Cry me a river and tell me another lie."

"No lie! *No lie!* Perry's in hiding! He needs your help! He even pulled in that Sorrows bitch—"

"Belisa." My breath hissed through the name. "Oh, I know. Where? Where is the son of a bitch? *And* that little whore too."

"I *don't know* where he is!" Screaming. Blood slicked

the left side of his face, bright red. It stank of copper, only the faintest trace of black showing he'd Traded for something. "He's got some kind of hold on her, some collar, I don't know what! He left me here—bait, and with the message for you."

"What message?" I was regretting not killing him outright. Now I was going to have to let him live, at least until I found out everything he knew. *And* separated the fiction from the truth.

Something was nagging at me. *A gift. His gift to you.* I shelved it. More immediate things to worry about.

Riverson coughed, his throat rasping. "The back room. *That* room. He left you a present. *She's* in there."

For a moment the words refused to make sense. *Oh, my fucking God.* The world snapped into a different configuration behind my eyeballs. "Alive, or dead?"

"I don't know. Jesus Christ, Kismet—"

"There's an awful lot you don't know." Cold and considering. "You're going to have to know something pretty soon, Riverson, to keep your head on your shoulders."

"I told you to stay away from him! I warned you not to come back! I did everything I could!" He didn't dare squirm. "*I did what Mikhail asked!*"

Another electric jolt through me. This was getting me nowhere. "You do not," I said, as quietly and evenly as I could, "speak my teacher's name, Riverson. The bitch is in the back room? *That* room?"

He almost nodded, caught himself when I jammed the gun against his skull again. "Y-yes. That room. Kismet, you should know something. That scar—the mark—"

"Did I ask you a question, Riverson?" I took the gun

away but still held myself ready. He had only human strength, true.

But that could have just meant that he'd Traded for something else.

"You need to know." A whisper, like he was a kid scared of the dark. The blood slicking his face was too vivid, too bright. "If I don't tell you now, I'll never get a chance. *He* was always listening. Through my ears. Through my *head*."

He. One single syllable, carrying a weight of loathing and fear. No question who he was talking about, either. I dug for handcuffs, still keeping an eye on him. "Make it quick, then. I don't have time for this shit."

"Did you ever wonder why *he* made you the bargain?"

I almost shrugged, decided not to. It might disturb my balance. The cuffs jangled, their silver coating running with sluggish blue light. "He thinks he can get something." It was a moment's work to roll Riverson over, he offered no resistance. I had him cuffed in a few seconds, tested them. Good. "You can tell him he's wrong."

"*You're* wrong." The words were muffled against the floor. Head wounds are messy; he didn't look pretty. Still, it wouldn't kill him. It would be foolish to feel any sympathy.

"Do yourself a favor and don't piss me off right now, old man." I levered myself up, restrained the urge to kick him. It would serve no purpose. "And stay there."

Riverson actually laughed. The jagged edges of that sound rubbed every inch of me the wrong way. I took a deep breath. The first priority was finding Saul, but now I had to check that back room. I set off with long swinging strides.

If Melisande Belisa was back there, I would have a few

words with her. And if it was a trap, I would spring it and find out what the fuck was happening. Either way, I won.

"He never let you do it with the lights on, did he?" Riverson yelled into the floor. His blood, slicking his face and dripping on the concrete, made the words bubble weirdly. "You never saw *his* mark, did you? Inside of the right thigh, high up, because Perry's not shy. A scar like a star."

I turned on my heel. My boot heels clicked. Three steps. Four. I reached Riverson again. Crouched, my hellbreed-strong right hand flashing out and curling in his graying hair. I dragged his face up, ignoring how the rest of his body torqued uncomfortably.

"What are you playing at?"

"Never with the lights on." His lips stretched, rubbery, around the words. "That's what he told me. Why no woman would ever see that scar. And he never wanted you to go down on—"

Cold went through me, and sick heat. The scar was a hot, hard knot on my wrist, tasting the corruption and misery filling this place. *Did he just say to me what I think he said to me?*

He *was* saying what I thought he was saying, I realized. He was intimating that my teacher had traded with Perry too.

My left hand flashed. The slap was a crack, and I dropped him. "Spread your filth elsewhere," I said softly, and Riverson sagged against the floor. A faint blubbery sound reached me.

The old man was crying. In messy gulps, like a child. My lip curled. If it was a mindfuck, it wasn't even worthy of the name. Mikhail and I had been closer than close, in bed and out of it...

...but here I was, with his Talisman again, heading back to see if his killer was waiting for me.

His *murderer*. The woman he had hidden from me. The Sorrows bitch who had killed him and stolen his treasure. He had lied to me about where he'd gone and what he'd done each time he went to hook up with her. In alleys, shitty hotel rooms, maybe even in his Mercedes. The same car I'd torched after the Weres built him a pyre to light him on his way to Valhalla.

And no, Mikhail never wanted me to go down on him. I'd been too grateful for his tact, too starry-eyed with the thought that he wanted *me*, to ever do it. It isn't the sort of thing I like, especially given where I came from.

What he rescued me from when he pulled me from that snowbank and told me *not tonight*.

He'd been a mass of scars. How could you tell one from another? Only a lover could. *I* could. But I'd never taken a look at that particular portion of his body. It just...

Oh, *shit*. Maybe it was a good mindfuck after all.

But I'd be damned if I would listen to it.

Doors in the Monde. One leads to a long corridor, rooms rented by the hour opening up on either side. Trades go down in here, meetings between the 'breed that carve up Santa Luz and occasionally test to see if I'm still on the job, various acts best hidden from daylight and even moonlight. Another leads behind the stage, to a long gallery where performers get ready before their "shows." There's one behind the bar that leads to the cellar, where the liquor and other liquids are stored.

The truly frightening one, behind a red velvet rope,

opens up on narrow stairs that lead to Perry's white-carpeted, pristine apartment. I hadn't been up there in a good long while, and the last time—

Don't think about that, Jill. Focus on the job at hand.

I took the first door. Kicked it twice, the scar pumping etheric energy through me. The iron sounded like huge gong strikes, shock jolting all the way through me. Showy, but I wanted no surprises.

On the third kick, the door crumpled like paper. If Perry wanted to find me, he probably could through the etheric force I kept recklessly drawing through the scar. I'd keep using it freely, as long as I could. It gave me an edge.

And every time I pulled on it, I hope Perry felt it like a slap to the face. Especially now.

The corridor stretched off to the side. Any place hell-breed spend a lot of time in warps a little bit. The geometry starts looking weird, angles not fitting together right. It's enough to give you a headache if you're not a hunter. If you can't see below the *twisting* and untangle the tricks of perception and illusion. My smart eye turned hot and dry, working overtime.

Nothing behind the door. But it smelled. Rot, both animal and vegetable, with the sharp copper tang of blood over it. The smell belched out over me with hot, sweaty meatbreath. My nose barely wrinkled. Of all the things about a hunter's job, the varied and disgusting stenches are not even close to the worst. You just learn to put your head down and go through.

It could be a metaphor for life, I guess.

The thought I'd been trying not to think came back with a vengeance. *His gift to you.* Who would leave an open mass grave for me? Especially one with curses that triggered into flame while someone was kidnapping my Were?

Who else? If it wasn't Perry, it was a hellbreed trying too hard.

I covered the hall with both guns. The room I was aiming for was at the very end. The door was ajar, too, a slice of ruddy light marrying with the low, ugly glow from the red bulbs marching down on either side of the hall.

"*Kismet!*" Riverson blubbered. "Don't! Get out of town! Go as far as you can! *He wants your soul!*"

Like I hadn't always known *that*. "Of course he does," I muttered. "That's nothing new." And I plunged forward into the hot close dimness.

The doors weren't staggered, and there was nothing waiting behind any of them. I went carefully, though impatience beat behind my heart, each thud of my pulse crying out for me to be doing something else. To start shooting and not stop until I'd untangled this whole mess and found my Were.

Moments ticked by. It was unbearably hot in here, but then it usually was. There's no air-conditioning in Hell.

The rooms were empty of living things. Some had beds, from narrow iron bedsteads to ornate four-posters complete with straps. A few had hard benches, or frames to strap bodies into. A few were completely empty, either tiled or carpeted on walls, floor, ceiling. All had drains in the middle of the floor and a slight slope downward from each wall, to make hosing off the night's effluvium easier.

The room at the end was normally a conference chamber, for meetings. I nudged the door open further, guns ready and nerves at the breaking point. Crimson light washed the room—the chandelier had been taken out, replaced with a festoon of cords holding bare red bulbs like poisoned fruit. The long mirror-polished table was still there, but with one long zigzag crack down the middle. The chairs, even the iron throne that sat at the head of the table, were demolished. There wasn't anything left bigger than a pinkie-fingernail sliver.

It looked like a hell of a fight had gone down in here. *What the hell?*

The wall at the end of the room, behind the ruin of the iron chair Perry settled in whenever there was a Big Meeting among the 'breed, dripped with slick metal worms. I blinked. After a moment I realized they were *chains*, and they moved slightly.

A wrongly musical clashing cut the static-laden silence. There, wrapped in orichalc-tainted chains, a slim female figure hung. Rags of deep blue silk twitched as she breathed, fitfully. Long blue-black hair, now tangled and rat-snarled. A hint of tilted catlike to the eyes in her bruised mass of a face. Her skin was a little darker than the Sorrows usually preferred, but well within canons. Her eyes, if open, would be the limitless black of the adept who has practiced for more than four cycles of their calendar; black from lid to lid, no iris or white to break the unnatural gaze. She wore delicate golden eardrops, and the bruising of Chaldean my blue eye could see in her aura was disciplined, a parasitical symbiote.

The Elder Gods give to those who serve them well, almost as often as they consume them. The Elders are hungry, and ever since the shadowy Lords of the Trees locked them away from our world they've grown hungrier. The Sorrows can't hope to undo the great sorcery the *Imdarák* worked; a whole race burned up its life to seal the Elder Gods behind a wall.

But that wall could sometimes be breached. That was Sorrows' business.

Melisande looked like she'd been worked over pretty good. There was something clasped around her neck, too. A gleam of iron, but I couldn't see it through the writhing of the silvery chains.

Last time she'd played wounded on me, too. In conjunction with Perry. A shiver of loathing threatened to rise up my spine, was repressed, died away.

I examined everything from the door. What the hell had *happened* in here? Sorrows and hellbreed don't mix. At least, they don't *usually* mix. 'Breed wanted this world for their own as well, and they don't play nice or share.

I surprised myself by stepping into the room. Hellbreed taking my Were might not lead here, but Perry was bound to be my first suspect. And just look at the interesting things I was finding. The Talisman warmed against my skin, its chain vibrating slightly.

Of course it would react to the woman who had torn it from Mikhail's chest after she slit his throat. Or it could have been my response triggering the Eye's notice. The adrenaline dumping into my bloodstream, the rage rising, the little click inside my head threatening to occur yet again. That click is the sound of a bullet loaded into a clip. It is also the sound of lifting away, breaking free, of little things like mercy and compassion closed away so you can get what needs to be done, *done*. Without counting the cost, and without hesitating.

I don't know if I am a hunter because of the click... or in spite of it.

I kicked through shattered chairs, working my way up the side of the table. Every inch of silver on me warmed and ran with blue light. I swept the room with my left-hand gun, tested the walls with every nonphysical sense I possessed. No traps.

Nothing except the soft slither of the chains moving. The scar ran with soft wet fire, tasting the misery pressing down on every exposed surface. It pulsed, silently, and the chains shivered. Their slippery clashing intensified, and Melisande Belisa's breathing body sagged against their loosening. The thing around her neck shimmered faintly, but at this distance and with the interference of the orichalc chains I couldn't tell what was going on. Her eyelids fluttered. Her breathing changed, from shallow sipping to harsh rasps. Heaving against the chains, blood-crusted blue silk moving over her ribs.

It was not the throat-cut gurgle of Mikhail's body clasped in my arms, the life leaving him in great scarlet gouts. Red as the light, his blood, with no tinge of black. But then, I bled red, too. Without a single trace of corruption.

I wasn't going to start believing Riverson's lies. Not now.

Cold sweat stood out all over me. I lowered my right-hand gun. I didn't trust myself not to shoot her.

Goddammit, Jill, put her down. She's a Sorrow. Just like a goddamn rattlesnake. Kill it now before it bites.

But shooting her now would not help me get to the bottom of this. I breathed carefully, trying to calm down and think clearly. Also trying to get in enough oxygen through the nauseating, cloying reek.

I'd been held down by orichalc-tainted chains once. A bugfuck-crazy Sorrows Grand Mother wanted to use me to incubate one of their hungry, trapped Elder Gods. Melisande had baited me into the trap, and double-crossed Perry as well. If this was his idea of a gift, like a cat leaving a mouse at its human's door—

His gift to you.

But no. *No.* It was too easy, too simple. There was a hook in this bait. And if Perry had taken Saul, all bets were off.

I could not be *absolutely* certain Perry was responsible. But who else would do something like this?

Any hellbreed who hated me. Which meant any hellbreed in Santa Luz, or at least any 'breed crazy enough to think I would not tear the city apart to find them and administer vengeance.

I took another step. Agony raced up my right arm, cramping my fingers and sawing against the nerve strings. I exhaled, hard, against the sensation. It was for all the world like a red-hot key turning in the scar, digging in, tumblers clicking.

What the—

The chains *moved*. They slid away like fat snakes, and Melisande Belisa's body fell, a limp-jointed doll. Her skull cracked against laminated wood flooring laid over concrete. I felt a nasty burst of satisfaction, quickly smothered. I weighed the advisability of taking a closer look at that iron collar she was wearing. It looked like a heavy piece of work, and thin golden light glinted on it. I shifted my weight to step forward.

Outside, in the well of the Monde, I heard movement. A high, thin giggle. And Riverson's despairing scream.

14

I just barely cleared the hall. Normally I'd want them to come at me one at a time, but Riverson was still screaming and I didn't want to be trapped with Belisa at my back, even if she was unconscious when I left her in the shattered conference room.

Four 'breed, dark-haired males. Just as many Traders, all of them frozen and snarling as I burst through the hole in the wall where the iron door used to be. One of the Traders—pale, shark's teeth, claws and joints altered strangely so he crouched like a spider—hunched over Riverson, tittering. My first shot took the titterer in the shoulder and he folded down shapelessly, a gout of black-laced crimson hanging in the air behind him as time slowed down and the mark turned into a live coal against my skin.

There's one certain way to get your ass handed to you while you're fighting hellbreed. That's to do it while distracted. Everything vanished but the fight in front of me, and it was a relief.

The Monde is familiar territory. I've fought there before, and I know its interior. I should have worked back along the wall to my left and gained the high ground of the stage. Instead I ended up in the middle of blank space, Traders circling and the 'breed hanging back, Riverson moaning like a child caught in a bad dream and twisting against the handcuffs.

I did not particularly care if he came down with a severe case of dead. I *did* care if he did so without giving me all the information he had, and I wasn't fool enough to think that he had. Yet.

When they recovered from the shock of finding me here instead of Perry, things were going to get ugly. So, I got ugly first.

Sometimes, the best defense is an attack. I put the one in front of me down with two shots, and the hole in the circling ring closed almost instantly. A half turn, another shot, but this one went wide because my instincts screamed and I threw myself aside, aiming to break for the stage. It was still my best shot, especially since all of them were focusing on me and not on the screaming blind bartender.

It just became a question of which ones were going to be in my way when I broke for it. But first I had to deal with the Trader leaping on me. The whip cracked, silver jangling.

No hunter carries a whip just because. We do it to give ourselves extra reach. It buys us those critical seconds of shock and pain, extends the circle of how far we can lay on the hurt. And this time it just might save my ass. If I could kill a few more of them.

The Trader dropped without a sound. Then they all jumped, and it became a melee.

When you're clearing a hellbreed hole, there's one good thing. You don't have to worry about where you're shooting, because every shot will get someone who deserves it. All I had to do here was avoid hitting Riverson, who technically *did* deserve it, but still.

The click inside my head sounded, and every edge and surface stood out in sharp clarity. The shining path of action and reaction unfurled inside my head, and I dropped into that state of fighter's grace where every bullet bends to your will and each one is a life taken. Hellbreed ichor splattered, I was somehow on my knees, bending back while firing, the whip curling. Then I was up again, a shutterclick of motion and I rolled sideways, gaining my feet in a convulsive leap as the body hit the concrete with a sound like a wet, rotting pumpkin tossed from an overpass. The stage was coming up fast, nobody between me and it, but any moment now one of the smarter ones might get the idea to head back toward Riverson and see if I twitched.

So I spun, heels skidding and striking sparks, and bolted straight for them again. They scattered, one of them keening in a high, unearthly wail. One more down, the blood exploding from his mouth and painting the floor in a splattering gout. I shot him again to make sure, calculations flashing through my brain. How much ammo was left in the gun, what the next move was, how far it was to Riverson, who was crawfishing wildly on the floor, trying to get out of the handcuffs. I could have used a silver-laced grenade, but the chances of fragging the person I had to question further were too high, and if I slowed down to get him behind the bar with me I might end up dead.

A copper-pale streak in the corner of my peripheral vision. *What the fu—*

The world turned over, hard. Down on the floor, trigger pulled, the 'breed on top of me snarling. It was the one with long greasy dreadlocks and a tubercular flush, cherry red lips widening and spraying me with hot acid spittle. Scrabbling, hand slapping a knife hilt and pulling it free, stabbing and twisting and had to *move* to get him *off* me, or I'd be swarmed and they would pull me limb from limb like a fly in the hands of a cruel little boy.

I shot him twice more, the silver smashing through his torso. This time I didn't have to switch to knives; the stupid bastard was lying on my guns. Crunching. Wet rasping sounds. A howl. A scream, cut short on a gurgle. I shoved the mass of decaying hellbreed off me and gained my knees—

—and stopped, staring in amazement.

Melisande Belisa, stark naked except for a heavy iron collar running with thin golden scratches, the bruising of Chaldean crawling over her skin and aura, twisted the last Trader's head in her delicate hands. The greenstick crack of a neck breaking echoed, and Riverson's screams died away. He hitched in a breath, but some instinct probably warned him to keep quiet and hope neither of us noticed him.

Those black eyes came up to mine, and under the mask of bruising on her face, the Sorrow smiled gently. Her teeth were small and white, one of the front ones jaggedly broken, and as I watched it fell out, hitting the concrete with a small definite sound. That gaptooth grin was wide, friendly, and utterly chilling. A new sliver of white broke through the bloody pink cavern in her gums.

Just like a shark, I thought. *There's always another tooth waiting.*

Broken bodies lay strewn around. The last 'breed hit the door at a good clip, tumbling out into sunlight. I stared.

The Sorrow rose fluidly from her crouch. Took two tiny staggering steps. Then her black eyes rolled up into her head and she slumped, going to her knees and keeling over. The collar ran with weird gold wires of light. She ended up curled in the fetal position, and a rumble of sorcery died away, swirling back into her bruised, coppery skin. Shadows moved, like the dappled shade of leaves on a hot day, over her flesh.

Chaldean sorcery. How many of them had she put down?

Riverson was making a soft sucking sound like a child caught in a nightmare. For a few moments I just knelt there and stared.

Then the need to get moving started deep in my bones, an itch like chickenpox. I hauled myself up and dug in my pocket for another set of handcuffs.

Perry had redecorated, but not much. Plush white carpet, a mirrored bar gleaming along one side ranked with pristine clear bottles, either empty or full of shifting gray smoke that made screaming faces when I glanced at it. The bank of television screens was there, but only the closed-circuit ones were live, showing the interior of and entrances to the Monde. The others, usually filled with news feeds, were blank and dead like gouged-out eyes.

The bed, draped with white gauze and a snowy counterpane, was there too. Belisa's nakedness lay tossed over it, shadows crawling over her skin and retreating. The

Chaldean sorcery would repair her inside and out, bringing her into perfect order soon enough. She hadn't taken nearly enough damage to put a Sorrow down.

I held the gauze down over his head wound, taped it. Didn't care if I caught his graying hair on the tape and he'd have to pull it off. Riverson shuddered. His filmy eyes blinked madly. His upper lip was slicked with snot.

At least he was still breathing.

"There." I took a deep breath. "Who were they, Riverson? Where do I start looking?" *And where is my Were?* I still couldn't rule out Perry taking him. Though I had to consider that maybe the masked 'breed could have something to do with it—but why would he, or whoever he was working for, distract me with a pile of bodies and take Saul? As an opening gambit? Why not just kill him, too?

That was an unhelpful thought. To say the least.

I glanced at the bed again, checking the Sorrow. She was out cold, or at least she looked like it.

I couldn't kill her just yet. I had to find out what she was up to.

I was beginning to wish I had access to some of those chains downstairs, though. Silver-plated handcuffs were not going to cut it for a Sorrow, though the collar looked vaguely familiar. The golden light turned out to be runes running under the surface of the metal, the queer, fluidly spiked writing of the Chaldean ceremonial alphabet.

Which was thought-provoking. The runes marched in orderly streams, like ants following formic trails.

He was shivering so hard his graying, blood-soaked hair quivered. "I. Thought. Thought we were. Dead."

"You almost were." *And you're close to it now, too.* I

stepped back, my boots leaving dark prints on the carpet. There was a trail from the door to the bed, and I kept half an eye on the closed-circuit screens. "Start talking, blind man. You're a lucky bastard, you know that? Who were they? Who do they work for? What faction wants me dead this much?" *And where the hell is Perry?*

He swallowed several times, throat working. "I . . ."

A slow singsong female purr came from the bed, the sibilants slightly slurred. "Oh, don't be shy." Melisande was awake. "Have you been telling secrets? You've been naughty, little man."

If you've ever heard a Sorrow pronounce the word *man*, you've heard the very meaning of contempt. There are two functions for males inside a Sorrows House— warrior drone or slave.

Neither has a very long life span.

Now I had to keep an eye on Belisa too, as well as the closed-circuit. Fortunately I'd settled myself against the bar at an angle where I could see everything and the door, too.

I would have bet it was right where Perry habitually stood. The thought filled me with unsteady loathing. That is, any sliver of me the red tide of rage wasn't flooding.

"Don't pay any attention to Chaldean whores, River-son." The words fell flat in the motionless air. Here in Perry's bedroom, the corruption was thick and rank, and the scar plucked wetly against my forearm. The Talis-man vibrated against my chest, a second heartbeat. "I'm all you need to worry about right now." *And boy howdy, should you be worrying.*

"I can tell you who has taken your pet, Judith." Soft and slip-sliding, she spoke as if she was in the incense-dark hush of a House. "I can tell you much more besides. I see my gift reached its destination intact. Do you like having it back?"

I was halfway to the bed without realizing it, the gun free in my hand and Riverson shrinking back against the glass and chrome of the bar. The effort of stopping made sweat spring up all over me, prickling as if each droplet was a fine hair.

That name. That goddamn name.

She'd cherry-picked it out of Mikhail's files, and it had won me the chance to slip free of the monthly visits to Perry. If Perry hadn't been so hot to use his newfound psychological leverage on me, I might have fallen neatly into his trap. Instead, I'd fallen into Belisa's.

And here she was again, mouthing the name of a dead girl. A girl with dark hair, wide, brown eyes and a bright, needy smile. A girl who had shivered on a street corner, whose ghost Mikhail had pulled out of a snowbank and *remade*.

The shadow of my right-hand gun twitched against pale carpeting. I forced the barrel down.

Careful, Jill. Be very careful. She's in cahoots with Perry. Don't do something that will damn you. There wasn't a good enough reason to kill her yet.

When she was on her feet and ready to fight back, when I knew what was going on and how she fit into it, when I had Saul back and this little situation all tied up neatly, *that* was when she could die.

But it would be so *satisfying* to blow her head off. And there she was, naked on the bed, one of her coppery haunches lifted as her body lay torqued. Her hair, tangled and sticky with dried blood and helbreed ichor, made small whispering sounds against the comforter. The bruises were fading, driven back by the leaf-dappled shadow of Chaldean. The collar was thick enough to clasp her neck and rest on her slim shoulders, and the Chaldean script on it made me uneasy.

"Funny." The word stuck in my throat. "Perry said it was from him. You two should get your stories straight."

She was wriggling over on her side to look at me. I lifted the gun again, and there was a small, definite *click*. She froze, and that was good. Because if she kept this up I really was going to empty a clip into her. And hope it worked.

And hope that killing someone when I knew I shouldn't didn't damn me enough for Perry to take out a mortgage on the parts of me he couldn't touch.

Still, one of her black eyes peeped over a fold in the coverlet. "Their little games. They always have to have their little games."

"Just like Sorrows." *Cut it short, goddammit. Something nasty is going on here, and you need to get to the bottom of it.*

"Our games are bigger, Judith."

Fury rose wine-dark inside me. The Talisman hummed. "Call me that one more time, Belisa, and I will ventilate your skull."

It didn't faze her. Then again, not much fazes them. "You haven't killed me yet. You're uncertain. I'll tell you a few things and you'll take the handcuffs *and* this damnable slave-collar off me. Then we will find your hellbreed friend, and after we bar passage to his superior we will spread his bowels upon the earth."

I wanted to shrug, but if I moved I knew I was going to squeeze the trigger. "I can do that without you."

"No, you can't. Not if they have your cat." She laughed, a sound like battered, wrongly musical wind chimes. "You don't even know what you're fighting."

"Argoth." The name made the heavy etheric bruising tighten, as if it expected a punch. Riverson shivered and moaned. It was a good guess.

She twitched, jerking. The collar ran with golden light, flaring. She laughed again, a pained rasp, and the glow settled.

Now that was interesting.

When she spoke it was a curiously atonal singsong, as if she'd memorized it. "Let's talk about something you're more interested in. Why do you think Perry has been so interested in your lineage, child? One of yours did his enemy a disservice. Now you must repay the debt." A slow blinking of the tar-black eye I could see. Like a snake's eye, actually, the lid never quite covering it. She moved, very slightly. "And how do you think the hunter of your lineage had the strength to shut away one of Hell's highest scions? He had help. He made a *bargain*."

I backed up, shot a glance at Riverson. He was so pale he was almost transparent, holding on to the minibar. The smoke in the bottles behind him flashed crystalline-blue for a moment, and I stilled. My blue eye deciphered no pulsing of ill intent.

"It's true," he said tonelessly. "Believe it or not, Kismet, it's true. Mikhail didn't tell you. I guess he didn't have time."

I couldn't help it. I glanced back at Belisa. Sourness filled my throat. There were a hell of a lot of things Mikhail hadn't told me. I suppose Riverson thought he was doing me a favor by reminding me.

The scar was flushed, obscenely full. I'd been pulling a lot of power through it, and it seemed to be getting steadily stronger, especially when I was worked up. I wondered, like I did so often, if Perry felt it. How many nights had he sat up here, possibly feeling it, while I killed things like him?

"Riverson," I whispered. "I told you not to say his name."

The gun jerked. The sound of the shot was a thunder crack.

Riverson howled, sliding off the stool. His knee was a mess of hamburger and blood, he hit the ground hard. I almost felt sorry for the old man.

Almost.

I was on him a second later, scooping him up. I carried him across the acres of white carpeting and dumped him on the bed, across Belisa. Her fingers worked like bloodless, active little maggots, twitching as she writhed against the handcuffs. I should have gagged her, but I didn't care enough to do it now.

And I didn't want to get any closer than I had to, collar or no. If I got much closer I wouldn't shoot her. I'd cut her fucking throat like she cut Mikhail's, and what I'd do afterward didn't bear mentioning.

And I would feel *good* about doing it, too. The abyss was howling my name, and this time it wasn't Perry pushing me to the edge.

Or was it?

Riverson kept screaming. I waited until he had to stop for breath. "Enjoy each other, kids. Hope the next set of 'breed finds you soon."

I knew Belisa would be out of the cuffs and on Riverson

before anyone else could happen along. You can't trust a Sorrow around a man—they're carnivorous, like praying mantises.

It wasn't a nice thing to do. But I am not a nice person.

And to find Saul, I would get a whole lot nastier.

"*Kisssssmet!*" Riverson, howling. He'd got his breath back with a vengeance. "*Kissssmet I'm telling the truuuuuuuuth!*"

"Yeah," I muttered as I turned on my heel. "Sure you are."

I got out of there.

15

The *bezoar* tugged against white silk and a spider cage of silver filaments; Galina had the cage lying around and it worked like a charm. The knife, driven through the cage, held it against the passenger-side seat like a pinned butterfly. The silver in the blade sparked in waves, spume against a rocky shore.

Tires screaming, I jagged around a corner and up Fairview. Morning traffic was just getting started, and intuition tingled along my nerves. I cut the wheel sharply just as the *bezoar* leapt, the cage yanking against the knife, and I slapped it back down. The Pontiac was an automatic, so I didn't have to worry about shifting. It was a good thing, too. Because the *bezoar* went wild, tugging and straining against the silver threads, and I had to shove the knife more firmly into the upholstery again to keep it trapped. I cut the wheel once more, tires smoking, and slewed into a turn onto 139th, the direction the *bezoar* was pulling.

Tracking with a physical link is so easy, it's frightening.

Warehouses rose around me. The industrial district simmered under a flood of sunshine, day peeking wearily through the streets, trapping dust in the air. Soon the winter frost would break and we'd get a roil of spring storms and flash floods, settling into summer's crackheat glaze.

The *bezoar* rattled and sprang, to the left this time. Intuition warned me, a sharp prickle along my entire body, and I stood on the brakes. The car slewed, I realized I was swearing low and steadily under my breath, and I narrowly missed T-boning a semi. It hove out of the way, I smashed the pedal to the floor again and was off. The subtle knocking in the engine got fractionally louder.

I penetrated the tangle of warehouses and shipping yards, following the *bezoar*'s urging. It rattled around in the cage like an angry cancer. The nearer I got to its source, the more violently it moved, fighting against the blessing on the silk and the silver's sharp gleam.

My prey probably guessed I was tracking him. He'd be stupid not to.

I finally skidded to a stop outside a shambling warehouse on 154th and Chavez. Slid the knife free of the upholstery, the *bezoar* trying futilely to knock the cage into the footwell. Grabbed the little bastard, folding the cage down around it until it hummed like an angry bumblebee in my hand. It went into my pocket, where it felt like my pager trying to get my attention.

I knew this place. Years ago it had actually been a rave joint, hopping almost every night and raided sporadically by Santa Luz's brave boys and girls in blue. Then a couple Traders got involved with slipping roofies to kids they thought wouldn't be missed and then carting them out of town to a friendly slave ring.

It happens.

One of the rules of my town is "you don't play in the under-18 pool." I came down on those Traders as hard as I could, and chased the 'breed they'd Traded with, dispatching them all in a welter of blood and screaming. Then I'd eradicated every other 'breed within the city limits who was even tangentially involved.

Hellbreed function on profit and loss. I wanted to make it so expensive for them to trade in young bodies that they gave up.

I'm still working on it.

Weathered scraps of old crime-scene tape stapled to entrances and exits fluttered in the stiff morning breeze from the river. Bleached by the constant assault of sun and weather, they made little whispering sounds. The etheric bruising swirling ripe and rank over this place would have told me I'd found what I was looking for, if the *bezoar* hadn't already been going mad in my pocket.

I watched it for a few moments. The need to go find Saul and bring him out of whatever they were doing to him itched unbearably under my skin, but I had to go carefully. Running in half blind wouldn't save him. It would just get us both in more trouble.

I was now assuming whoever took him was tied to the evocation site I'd found. If Perry wasn't involved—which I was by no means sure of—this was my next best guess. If Perry *was* involved, and had the masked 'breed running around doing dirty work while he pulled on other strings, this was going to get nastier before it got better.

The congestion tightened. Whoever was in there

could feel me approaching. Sorcery will make a hunter's apprentice a full-blown psychic before long—if they survive. It also has the benefit of helping a hunter pop up just where the filthy bastard isn't looking.

Jill. You're too distracted. You can't go in there like this.

I told the voice of reason to take a hike. If something that could lead me to Saul was in there, that's where I was going, dammit. It made little sense for anyone to mess with my Were. They had to know that taking him would only make me determined to knock down anything in my way to—

Maybe they do. Maybe they're distracting you, just like they distracted you with a pile of bodies to take him. Maybe, just maybe, you should be looking somewhere else, for something else. Like Argoth.

Hutch still needed time to sort through a mound of data. He was going as fast as he could, but I was asking him to find needles in haystacks, and do it at a distance instead of at his home with access to every text the hunters in my line had accumulated.

I breathed out softly through my nose, suddenly aware I was making an odd sound. A sort of whistling moan as I breathed. How long had I been doing that? And the shaking running through me, what was that? I was too well trained not to know that it meant I was dangerously close to running on emotion instead of calculation.

The world narrowed. I shut my eyes, my smart blue eye piercing the meat of my eyelid to show me the still-contracting bruising over the warehouse in front of me. Night after night of kids dancing and hungry Traders preying made for a messy psychic "house," and banefire wouldn't have done much good at this point. Charged atmospheres can go either way, holy or unholy.

Guess which one is more common.

I am doing this case all wrong. I should have been focusing on the bigger priority—finding out if they were, indeed, trying to bring Argoth through. And if so, the location of every evocation site—so I could get there to disrupt them in time. Any hellbreed higher-class than a *talyn* is seriously bad news, and if what Hutch had said about Argoth last time was any indication, he was *definitely* above that classification.

It was an interesting question: how did Perry's dark hints, Riverson's ravings, or Belisa's silken lies go together? Which of them to believe? Or believe none of them? If there was a deeper game being played here, I needed to get to the bottom of it.

If it was Saul's life balanced against the lives of everyone in my city in a hellbreed game...

Something inside my chest cracked a little. I was making that whistling moan again.

I swallowed it, hard. A bitter tang coated the back of my throat. *Whatever you're going to do, Jill, get cracking. Do it* now.

I set my shoulders. Drew my right-hand gun, thought about it, and kept my left hand free. I struck out for the north side of the warehouse. There was a fire escape back there that should do a little better than the front door— more cover, and kicking down the front door and yelling hadn't done a thing at the Monde. It's always been my favorite way to go.

But maybe it was time to change it up a bit.

*   *   *

Catwalks zigged back and forth inside the warehouse's cavernous sprawl. Thin fingers of daylight touched down through the holes in the roof or gaps between the boards on the windows. The day's heat had begun to creep into corners, gathering strength.

It smelled of dust, rat fur, metal, and the sick-sweet tang of hellbreed. A faint copper note of blood. But no healthy brunet spice of Were. Instead, the wet reek of danger and brooding, nasty sorcery, incense and perfect-tallow burning.

Those in the trade call it perfect-tallow, at least. The candles stink and make an ungodly psychic mess. That's because they're made from people.

Well, their bodies, anyway. How many candles would the charred bodies out by the freeway have made?

I eased along a catwalk, silence drawn over me like a cloak. Each step torturingly slow, weight spread out, toes and the ball of the foot testing before weight shifted in increments. I couldn't be sure if my heavier muscle and bone would break the rickety grating or wring a betraying groan out of the struts. My eyes roved. The shadows were too thick, sorcery lurking in their depths. The entire place breathed, dust moving oddly and the light behaving like it shouldn't, bouncing off odd corners and falling into deep black wells without a gleam or a sigh.

Another tangle of metal stretched over what had been the dance floor, a wide expanse of cracked concrete. The kids had brought in plywood, scraps of scavenged linoleum, cardboard, to make a patchwork. The cardboard and linoleum were slowly rotting, the plywood had been stolen for God knew what. It was surprising that more of the metal hadn't been scrapped, but I'd lay odds that all the copper wiring left over had been sold to the recycling plant. I wondered if any of the DJs had been back to collect their stereo equipment since the moment I'd dropped down from the ceiling and started killing Traders.

If they hadn't been back, some foolhardy asshole had probably stumbled across it. People are too inquisitive for their own goddamn good.

Especially hunters. It's one of the things that makes us, well, *us*.

A low unhealthy blot of rectangular blackness sat in the middle of the dance floor. It pulsed like an obscene heart, and I checked the moon cycle inside my head again. Dark moon was best for this, and we had a week of waxing and another two of waning before the walls between here and Hell were even close to gapping without some serious help.

So this was a secondary site? But it was further along than the one at Henderson Hill. The altar crouched like a live beast, dozing in the middle of all that empty space. My blue eye caught flashes of ill intent, nasty little tingles of sorcery and bad feeling.

The *bezoar* stilled in my pocket, tiny tremors like a frightened rabbit quivering through heavy leather. I paused, silent as cancer or a snake under a rock, weight braced and the gun low but ready.

The *bezoar* quit trembling and tugged, very faintly.

Straight down.

The catwalk screeched as I pushed off, airborne and turning. I was over the railing and dropping like a stone. Gunfire crackled, bullets spattering as the 'breed hissed up at me, leaping from a gantry below, bone claws extended and the mask fluttering at its edges.

A moment of sheer savage glee, white-hot, went through me. *You again? Oh, good. Here, have some of this aggression I've been saving up.*

Falling. Firing into him as I *twisted*, his claws tangling in my coat and shredding the leather even further. He was aiming for the *bezoar*, I realized as my foot flicked out. There was no weight behind the kick since we were both in midair, but it did jolt home and we tumbled free of each other, leather ripping. I was screaming, a rising cry of female effort tearing through the gloom with a bright razor edge.

Impact. We hit the altar squarely. No give; it was like hitting concrete. Nothing broke for once, because I spilled over to the side and rolled free, bleeding momentum. It was a good thing, too, because he was leaping for me. The gun jerked up instinctively. Fire burst from the muzzle, I hit him square in the chest and rolled, whip jerking loose. Knee up, boot grinding in anonymous dust and dirt, a shard of broken glass eating itself into smaller pieces under the steelshod heel. Striking true, the jangling end of the whip sparking with fierce blue light. He tumbled aside, soundless, black ichor spattering.

I scrambled up. Time to press my advantage. Shot him twice more, tracking him, every bullet now striking home because the world had turned into a clear crystal dish with my path mapped out in a ribbon of light.

When you fight every night, reflex takes on a whole new meaning. Sometimes, and only sometimes, you hit a fight where *everything* comes together. Your entire body dilates and compresses at the same time, and suddenly everything is easy. I've heard it called a peak experience. There's nothing peak about it—you find that out the next evening, when you've pulled a muscle or two and you roll out of bed groaning to do it all again.

But while it lasts, it's better than chocolate.

I knew where he was going to move next, and fired before he could get there. The third shot took him in the ball of the shoulder joint and he was down, flopping like a landed fish. White chips of something like bone showed in the mess of his shoulder, black silk shredding. I was on him in a heartbeat, dropping the whip and driving the knife into hellbreed flesh with a solid *tchuk!* like a solid axe sinking into dry wood. My right-hand gun slid into its holster, because I *knew* this was going to be a knife fight from here on out.

Something was wrong. It nagged at the clarity of action, but I shoved it aside because I had to concentrate *now*.

He roared and threw me off. I careened, weightless, hanging in the air a moment before hitting a tangle of metal struts with a crunch. Hot agony speared my left arm and I thrashed, falling with a thud and narrowly missing cracking my head against a sharp-sheared edge. The snap of my left humerus breaking was a red scream, but I was on my feet again in a moment, hurling myself forward to meet the hellbreed with another shattering jolt. It tore the mask halfway free, and I caught a glimpse of copper skin and an alien, gaping vertical slit of a maw before my second-biggest knife dragged through hellbreed flesh like it was water, spilling noisome reek in a heavy gush.

No wonder he doesn't talk. A fleeting thought; that orifice didn't look like it could shape a single word.

But something was definitely wrong. He didn't try to

rip my spleen out the hard way, and something about his skin nagged at me. His bony arms closed around me with a crackle like lightning. He pitched aside, inhuman muscles coiling and releasing, and a heaving, grinding sound filled the world, ending with a jarring clang.

We rolled, fetching up against steel bars with a stunning jolt. But I had my largest knife out, too. Silver sizzled, parting tainted flesh. I *twisted* it, wrist straining and arm bent oddly, the broken edges of my left humerus grinding together so hard black sparkles danced over my vision. Great heaving, sobbing breaths as my ribs flickered. The hellbreed's body jerked, corruption spilling through its tissues. The gaping, vertical maw of the mouth under the mask champed, yellow foam painting its thin lipless edges.

Shit. I hadn't meant to kill him so completely—I'd thought he was more durable. Now who was I going to question?

Wait a second, Jill. This guy's all wrong.

I struggled free of the swiftly decomposing remnants of the body, black silk sizzling a little as the ichor worked at it. The mask was a twisted rag, and his eyes were now collapsing holes. But something was wrong, very wrong, and when I raised my head, the silver still buzzing in my hair, I finally realized why he hadn't eviscerated me.

He'd been too busy knocking me into the trap.

What had seemed a random jumble of metal had fallen from the ceiling, fresh weld spots glowing with the peculiar white gleam of orichalc. Part of it fitted over the empty altar, caging it securely, and the entire thing quivered around me like it wanted to take flight. The metal had driven deep into the concrete, like fingers sinking into butter.

The body on the floor really started to stink. I froze, examining the tangle of metal now webbing us both.

An orichalc-tainted cage? What the—

A faint movement, silk against inhuman skin. I cleared leather in an instant, and the guns didn't dip as the clarity of battle left me and I began to suspect I was in deep fucking shit.

The 'breed melded out of the gloom, at the far end of the dance floor. The *bezoar* twitched in my pocket again, demonic little fingers tugging at my coat. Same compact build, same flutter of black silk, and maggot-white skin. The mask moved slightly as whatever was under it gapped its wide mouth, breathing softly.

He was *white*, not copper-skinned.

Oh, fucking hell.

I took two steps forward. It brought me closer to the crazycrack jumble of steel, and the metal moved. Runes crawled over it, visible only to my blue eye—weird, angular writing, curved only in specific spots. It glowed a sickly gold, moving like a spider's scuttle when the web is touched.

Chaldean. Just like Belisa's new necklace.

Think, Jill. Think fast. I drew back. Saw my whip handle on the other side of the bars, just barely in reach, the rest of the leather and silver jangles stretching out across the floor in a ribbon of stars. I leapt for it, because the 'breed at the other end of the dance floor twitched. If I could reach the whip I could—

POW!

My fingertips scraped concrete before I was flung away. I hit the cage on the other side, and the Chaldean struck again like a snake, tossing me down to the floor.

The screaming I heard from far away was me. My voice cracked, raging in a high unlovely torrent of obscenities.

The 'breed hissed as he twitched my whip out of the way with the tip of one slippered foot. I realized the other masked 'breed hadn't been wearing those goddamn tabi footies, either. He'd been a double.

I cursed myself for running on emotion instead of brains right before the cold concrete darkness reached up to swallow me.

16

I came back to consciousness slowly and piecemeal. Lying on my side, cheek against a rotting piece of cardboard, my entire body felt pulled apart and put back together wrong. I lay completely still, my breathing not changing as I surfaced. Hard things dug into my ribs, stomach, arms—my left arm twinged faintly, but the scar was humming with deep etheric force. Like a flash flood rumbling through an empty canyon, moments before the wall of water crashes into you.

So. I had my guns, my knives, the grenades. My arm was healed up and the scar was awake and angry. The *bezoar* was still vibrating in my pocket. I'd been taken in by that masked bastard and was now in an orichalc-tainted cage crawling with Chaldean.

Belisa. Did she know I'd leave her at the Monde? Jesus.

That's the thing with Sorrows. They are masters of the mindfuck; they make even hellbreed look simple. What was that collar on her for? I didn't know nearly enough.

And speak of the devil: "I know you're awake." A

soft whisper, still as if she was in the incense hush of a House.

I kept my eyes mostly closed. The world was a soft blur. It still smelled like the same warehouse, and I kicked myself for not realizing the tang of incense was a Sorrows blend instead of the heavy noxious reek 'breed use for their rituals. Sorrows use perfect-tallow too, it's one of the few overlaps between their different sorceries.

I could have kicked myself six ways from Sunday. Running on emotion will fuck you up big time and leave you trapped.

Slight huff of breath, a sigh like a teacher with a difficult student. "Jill. I *know* you're awake."

I couldn't pin down the location of the voice. It could be a speaker system or a very slight sorcery to misdirect. Either was a good idea, especially since I still had my guns. They might have me trapped, but I was carrying a lot of ammo. I could probably figure out something with the grenades, too, to bust myself out of this predicament.

At least she wasn't calling me a dead girl's name anymore. Small mercies.

I lay there for a few more moments. My right wrist was under me, the scar twitching in my flesh. The stench of rotting hellbreed coated the back of my throat.

No sign of Saul here. My innards whirled violently for a moment. I suppressed a retch.

Another small sigh. "Come now, child. This is not especially mature of you."

It could be a recording, filtered through different speakers so I couldn't get a lock on it. And why was she talking to me like I was one of her cursed initiates? The other Sorrows bitch—Inez—had done that, too. They probably had a file a mile thick on me. Did every female hunter have trouble with the goddamn termite queens, or just me?

That's a dangerous thought, Jill. Prioritize. You're lying here on the floor. That won't help you find Saul or stop this evocation. It doesn't matter who they're bringing through, it's your job to get to the bottom of this and stop it posthaste.

There was more, of course. Riverson had done his job well, planting a seed of doubt. I still couldn't bring myself to believe Mikhail'd had a hellbreed mark. The very thought tried to send a shudder of loathing through me. I clamped down on everything—heartbeat, respiration, blood pressure, all my training narrowing to a single point.

"I offered to tell you where your cat was," Belisa breathed, and it sounded like she was standing right over me. A faint touch of air against my cheek, spiced with incense, like a single paintbrush hair drawn along my dirty skin. I was beginning to think I'd never be clean again.

It was a trick. It *had* to be.

The pressure intensified, became metallic. As if a scalpel was gently touching me, just before a whisper of more pressure is applied and the skin splits along the razor edge. It drew itself up my cheek, over the hill of my cheekbone, and dipped down into the valley of my eyesocket.

I lunged up and away, the sensation fading like cobwebs and Melisande Belisa's genuinely amused laughter ringing all through the warehouse. I did not draw a gun, but ended up kneeling as far away from all the sides of the cage as I could. This put me at the edge of the lake of black hellbreed scrim, my boot toe touching it.

A bright idea crawled through my head. I froze, my eyes moving over every surface. Both my hands were fists, and a chill slid over me. Like I'd just been doused in cold water, or like a fever had just broken. Sweat greased my skin, and a thin tendril of it kissed the scar's pucker. The too-intense wash of hellbreed-amped senses was beginning to seem almost normal, just like every time I had the cuff off for a while.

The warehouse was dark. How long had I been out? The altar, under a mass of twisted, jagged metal, throbbed a single dissatisfied pulse. It wasn't empty now, no sir. Chalice, claw, and candles, not to mention lumps of human organs, scattered across its surface. I wondered briefly, pointlessly, how many of those organs had been in the charred bodies near the freeway, or if there was another mass grave waiting somewhere for me to find it.

The thought of being unconscious so close to the altar—not to mention while someone laid the altar, though they could have done it with sorcery, I supposed—was enough to give me the willies. If, that is, I didn't already have so many other problems that one looked like a cakewalk. Tiny sounds—chittering, nasty, whispering laughter—filled each corner. It was meant to be disorienting, but my blue eye wasn't fooled. It's disconcerting to *hear* things running for you while your eyes swear you're alone and in no danger. Even more disconcerting to feel the brushes against you, ripples of Chaldean glyphs sliding through the cage's physical structure pushing air around.

"The blind man wasn't lying," she whispered. "Mikhail did have a scar. Star-shaped, inside of the right thigh. It was full of their corruption. He was worried he would die before he could find someone to take his place *and* the corruption itself. That's how it works, my dear. Haven't you wondered why your *zilfjari'ak* watches over you so assiduously? Yours is a soul he has no intention of losing. The others, well. He could wait, and watch, for *you*."

Gee, I'm honored. Of all the things that have ever happened to me, having a Sorrow whisper sweet nothings about a hellbreed's motivations has to be one of the weirdest. And that's really saying something.

The urge to swallow hard rose. I repressed it. *Give nothing away, Jill.* Instead I turned in a full circle, examining the cage.

"Don't tell her." The second whining nasal voice was a surprise. "Let her anticipate the worst."

"Shut the fuck up, Rutger." My voice surprised me, echoed oddly against the cage. It quivered as if it wanted to clamp down on me, a gigantic veined hand with leprous-white spots. "The adults are talking."

Silence crackled. I drew my left-hand gun, holstered my right, and shook my fingers out. Took stock of myself from head to foot.

This might end up hurting a bit.

"Oh, hunter." Rutger giggled, a high mincing noise. "You and your master are both going to burn. He'll be demoted to licking boots, and you'll be dragged to Hell screaming."

"Been there. Done that. Wiped off with the T-shirt." I stretched my fingers, tendons flickering in the back of my hand as I wiggled them. *First step is getting out of here. But that one's going to be a lulu.*

"Imbecile." Belisa, very softly. "If *he* finds out you're disloyal he'll make you uncomfortable. You'd better pray your plan works." A slight scuffle, changing direction in midsound. She had to be using sorcery to disguise where she was. Rutger, however, was not. And he had just moved—away from her, it sounded like.

I stored up their words for later. Interesting. Did the stupid hellbreed not realize she was a Sorrow? You'd think he would be staying as far away from her as he could.

And where was that masked bastard? The *bezoar* was quiet in my pocket. I could still track him with it, and next time I wouldn't be so easily taken in.

At least, I hoped.

"Shut up, witch-whore. Just because I'm not the one holding your leash doesn't mean you can yap." Rutger was moving again, restless tapping sounds. He was still wearing those sharp-edged heels. I had a vivid mental image of him kicking a body on the floor, shut it away with a physical effort.

My hand relaxed. The scar chuckled to itself, a wet lip-less unsound against the flesh of my arm. Silver shifted and sparked. The Talisman pulsed once on my chest, and I considered using it for only a half second.

No. the situation wasn't that dire yet. I could still recover this. I *could*.

My fingers tingled.

"You're simply lucky I have *this* leeway to act and no more. If you weren't so useful, or if this damnable thing wasn't on me, I would…" Belisa, softly, each word coming from a different quadrant of the warehouse.

"You would what? What, exactly, would you do?" Rutger's sneer was palpable. "Pray to one of your spent, ancient masters?"

A long breath of silence, while I was doing some

praying of my own. I prayed for them to be so involved with each other they wouldn't notice what I was up to. It was hard work, the fierce relaxed concentration of sorcery when my entire body was jittering from adrenaline overload and the thought of Saul trapped somewhere, maybe in a cage as well, beating inside my brain.

The tingling in my fingers crested.

Banefire whispered. Tiny blue sparks wreathed my hand, popping free of the skin, coalescing on my fingertips. You'd think they wouldn't have left me alive, with my ammo and my guns. They were either monumentally stupid, or they had something nasty and inescapable in mind.

Since Belisa wasn't stupid, guess what my money was on. There was a third option—that they couldn't get inside the cage. They were saving me for something.

Like an evocation, perhaps? Something about the situation was off, and if I had some time to think I could tease it out. That wasn't a luxury I possessed right now.

Stop reacting and start thinking, Jill. Slow and easy, now.

"I do not need to pray to deal with an upstart *zilfjari'ak*. Even if I am currently unable to do as I like." Belisa's dulcet tone turned to a hiss. I had to admit, I liked it better that way.

"Yes, well, one of *us* put that little necklace on you. It suits you." Rutger tittered.

A susurrus of silk against unholy skin. My ears perked up. High, behind me, to my left. So the masked bastard was still here, too.

The banefire slid against itself, almost dying under the weight of corruption in the air. *Please, no. God, cut me a break on this one, please?*

Even hunters aren't immune to pleading with an uncaring god. The thing is, while we reflexively do so, we know there really isn't any point.

God's busy. It's up to us.

I kept my right hand low and close to my side, in the folds of my tattered, torn coat. The scar twinged sharply. I exhaled, a slow, soft breath. Concentration came in fits and starts, and the banefire sang a sad little dirge in a chorus of dead children's voices.

More sounds—scuffles, a wet ripping. Good news for me.

Another soft sliding of silk. How could I have been taken in by a stupid double? Because I was running blind. All someone had to do was take Saul, threaten to hurt him, and I—

The banefire blazed up. My hand jerked away from my coat, and the shadows were suddenly cutting sharp, like a photo flash, every surface the bright blue-white light fell on bleached and curling with steam. Someone yelled, a long low rumble of Helletöng, and metal screeched and tore.

I threw myself backward and cast the banefire straight at the altar in one motion. It would hit the stored-up corruption there and consume it, and then once it had a good hold it would go for the bars.

I could only hope the resultant explosion wouldn't kill *me*, too. But better to die here than at the mercy of whatever Belisa—or whoever was holding her leash—had planned.

17

The altar went up in a gout of brilliant blue, screaming faces in the twisting flames. Grasping fingers of fire caressed the cage.

Metal screamed, deafening, as if it were a living thing being tortured. The concussion knocked me back, and I had time enough for a split-second, hopeful thought— maybe the Chaldean sorcery on the bars would be spent now?

If it hadn't, I was looking at being the ball in a giant game of tennis between razor-studded rackets.

Impact. Red-black pain jolted through me. I lost consciousness briefly, stars whirling through my skull, and I wondered if I'd been too smart for my own good.

It wouldn't be the first time.

Shutterclicks of red and bright blazing blue. The banefire had a good purchase now, and was roaring. Regular orange flame was twisting, too, a clean and normal light under the black belch of smoke. The iron was curling like paper. So that was what it did to Chaldean sorcery impregnating orichalc-tainted steel. I should have Hutch write that down—

Get up, milaya. Mikhail's voice. *Get up now. Or I will hit you again.*

When he said that, he always meant it. It made me move when nothing else could.

I scrambled, my body not obeying me quite right. My left arm felt like it had broken again and I was swimming through molasses. I knew the pain would be right behind me, and I just had to move fast enough for it to stay *behind* me and not catch up.

Moving, though, would be the problem. Great chunks of burning stuff fell from the ceiling, orange and blue flame mixing in long banners. My feet went out from under me, slipping on a wash of something bubbling and foul, and it was a good thing, too. If I hadn't slipped, going heavily to my knees and almost biting a chunk out of my tongue, Rutger would have collided with me. As it was, every inch of silver on me fluoresced with blue sparks, banefire howled, and the edge of one of his sharp little shoes clocked me on the back of the head. I rolled, tucking everything in.

The pain caught up with me. Every joint, muscle, and bone in my body screamed, the scar a dumb lump of burning meat on my right wrist, and I fumbled for a gun.

The inside of the warehouse was alive with leaping blue flame. Banefire squealed and cried, the children's voices rising in a glassine chorus. And other sounds, ones I couldn't quite make out because my ears were full of something warm, trickles of fluid sliding down my neck. Even that touch of moisture couldn't cool the heat. The Eye on my chest throbbed, and it took effort I couldn't afford to quiet the thing.

Howls. Cries. Gunfire. Someone yelling my name—a human voice, young, breaking in the upper registers.

What the hell?

I floundered on the floor. *Get up. Jill, get UP.* I made it to hands and knees, coughed. An amazing jet of bright-red blood splashed on the floor. No trace or taint of black in it.

Every time I bled red it was a relief. Except there was so *much* of it.

Why was the entire warehouse burning? The banefire should have just busted the cage. It must have reacted with the Chaldean. I really needed to get Hutch on that to figure it out.

I should have been healing. The scar should have been pumping etheric energy through me. Instead, my arms almost failed, slipping on the blood and the bubbling mix of foulness coating the floor. Smoke roiled, coating the inside of my throat. A hellbreed screamed, the cry rising up to earshattering volume before it was cut short on a gurgle.

I hoped it was Rutger. But who would kill him? Belisa? *Why?*

Worry about getting up first, Jill.

Good advice. Except something dark appeared in the corner of my peripheral vision, and I threw myself back and rolled, hands going for my guns and the barrels coming up, but slow, too slow. Something was badly wrong inside my torso, darkness beating at the edges of my vision. Even my smart eye was clouding up.

The masked 'breed hung in the air over me, banefire bleaching each edge, fold, and crease of his ninja pajamas. I knew, with a sudden sickening thump, that I wasn't going to get the guns up fast enough. I knew he would come down and there would be a wet final crunch, and if I survived it I would have to go for my knives, but there was nothing in the world that would save me now. The scar was dead, not even a trickle of etheric power working up the nerve channels of my arm. He was descending from the apex of his leap, and the slow motion was not my speed working overtime but from the dragging slowness of a nightmare. One I wouldn't ever wake up from.

CRUNCH. A pale blur hit him from the side. They tumbled, and another flash of black filled up the world. The snap-crackle of flame turned into a roar, and if the fire didn't get me I was probably going to bleed to death.

The scar had finally failed me. Had Perry planned this all along? None of it made any sense. Nothing did.

That's what you always think before a case starts to jell. The thought rolled under a breaker of agony as my entire body seized up. The dumb meat thought it could get away from the pain by flopping around uselessly. I'd been relying on the scar too much. Just like any Trader, using up the bargain and spending what made me human.

Oh, Mikhail, they're lying about you. They have to be.

"*Chingada!*" someone yelled, and more gunfire spattered. Growls and yowls, almost swallowed in the fire.

"Found her!" A familiar voice, very close. Hands on me. I struck out weakly. "Holy *shi*—"

"We're trying to help!" Another voice, female, with a snarl running under the words. It was a clean sound, not the twisted groan of a hellbreed.

Weres? Here? What?

Lifted. Body bumping. Broken bones ground together. I cried out.

"Bad shape!" Theron yelled. "Move move *move!*"

What the hell is he doing here? But I couldn't get a breath in. Something was pressing on my chest. A heavy weight, hard to dislodge enough to get a breath in.

I fell back into darkness. My last thought, crystal-clear and oddly calm, danced for what seemed a very long time before unknowing swallowed it.

If the Weres came down here they're in danger. I'm going to just kill Theron.

18

Clear!" A hellbreed's voice, 'töng rubbing and squealing below its surface. "Move *back!*"

"You'd better not—"

"Get *back,* Theron! Let him!" That voice. Female, with a snap of command under its softness, so familiar. Why?

White light slammed through me. The scar lit up, finally. I might have wished it hadn't, because it sent a grinding jolt up my arm as if it was going to rip the appendage off, and I convulsed again, blood spraying slick and hot past my lips.

"Oh, you're not going yet." The hellbreed chuckled, like he was having a grand old time. I knew who it was now, and I couldn't fight. My body simply wasn't obeying any command I was giving it. The most I could manage was thrashing.

Fever-warm, inhuman fingers clamped down on my forehead. The scar keened, zapped me again. A flare of sterile light filled my head, chasing out the sound of fire and screaming.

Oh God—

Another zap. This one found every bruise, every break, every torn muscle, and filled it with acid. Broken bones twitching and melding, all the pain of healing compressed into bare seconds. Silver crackled, and Perry hissed.

"Just a little more, my darling," he whispered. "Just a very little more. Then you can rest."

I didn't believe it. Thrashed more, or tried to. Weak limbs twitching, I heard someone shapelessly moaning and knew it was me. I was saying something, over and over, the only prayer I had left.

"Saul...*Saul*..."

"Jesus," Theron said quietly. What was *he* doing here?

Then, the biggest surprise of all. I recognized the woman's voice. *What is Anya doing here? She's supposed to be over the mountains in her own territory.* "She's going to be okay, kid."

What the hell?

"*Chingada*." Gilberto's tenor, breaking at the end of the word. "What's he doing?"

"I'm repairing my investment." Perry clicked his tongue thoughtfully. "It's unpleasant work. Perhaps you should look away."

"You just better hope she keep breathing, *cabron*." Gil sounded steady enough.

"Have no fear, little boy. Our dear Kismet has not seen the last of this weary earth just yet. She has *ever* so much more to accomplish." A soft chuckle, like a razor blade against numb skin.

A silver nail ran through me from crown to soles. The world lifted up and shook me off like a flea from a dog's back. I clung desperately, fingers and toes slipping.

Rammed back into my racked, convulsing body, skin stretching, an obscene, dying scream filling my smoke-burned throat.

"This is what you get," Perry murmured. "Banefire. What next? Too impulsive by half, Kiss."

"Saul," I whispered. But the machine trained into my head clicked into life. I wasn't dead yet, and the scar settled down, humming nastily to itself while it repaired bone and stitched together muscle tissue. I coughed, retching. Blood steamed and spattered. There was a roaring, and sirens in the distance. It was a welcome sound.

It meant the cavalry was on its way. But if they got here and hellbreed were hanging around, not to mention Belisa, then I was looking at possible casualties. And where was that masked bastard? Had he survived? Why had Belisa jumped him? Or had it been her?

I jerked into full consciousness, slapping Perry's hands away. He made a small spitting sound of annoyance, and tried to grab my head again.

The gun smacked into his ribs. My fingers were slick and wet, but steady enough. "Back. Off." I coughed, spat more blood. It dribbled down my cheek, because I was flat on my back. Lying on pavement, the entire scene drenched with unholy light. The banefire had burnt itself mostly out, and now the entire warehouse was a mass of regular old orange and yellow flame. A pillar of black smoke rose, garishly underlit, and it was looking like it would involve the structures on either side too unless the fire department could do something soon. It was morning, gray light just touching the tops of the mountains. I'd lost a whole day in there, somehow.

Shit. Monty's going to have a heart attack over this one.

"A thank-you would be nice." Perry's pale hair was mussed, soot grimed into it. Under the mask of smoke and dirt, he was grinning. His eyes twinkled. "Since I did just drag you out of the dragon's maw."

Another coughing fit rasped at my throat, I pushed it down and back. The gun was steady, jammed up into his ribs, plenty of play in the trigger but that could change in a heartbeat. "Back *off*."

He moved away, gingerly. The pale linen suit was spattered with blood, hellbreed ichor, other fluids. Tarnished with smoke, and crisped in a few places. No wonder he looked like he'd had a good time. His wingtips were still glossy, though, and you could see the suit had been ironed and starched at a not-too-distant point in the past.

"Eh, *profesora*." Gil, from behind me and to my right. "Thought you was a goner."

I did too, kid. "Gilberto?" The word slurred. My mouth wasn't working correctly. The scar crawled against the flesh of my wrist. Perry's smile turning to a wolflike leer as the fire sent shadows dancing.

"Right here. *Los gatos hombres aquí*."

Well, thanks. I figured that out. "I told you. To stay at Galina's."

Slight snort. "I ain't too good at listening, *chica*."

"I got that." I found out my body would move. Shaky, like a newborn colt. My arms and legs creaked as I moved. The scar chuckled and hummed, behaving just like it normally did. A velvet tide of pleasure slid up my arm—Perry, trying to make me react.

I kept the gun trained on him as I hauled myself up. "Anya? Anya Devi?" Coughed again, spat a mouthful of something bright red.

"Here." Very quietly, also to my right. If I knew her, she had her guns trained on Perry too.

"And . . . Theron?" I had to know who *else* was here.

"We're here, Jill." A growl ran under the edge of Theron's voice. He sounded like one pissed-off Were. Galina had probably told him what was happening. Or at least about Saul, because I didn't have a clue what was happening otherwise. And if she did, she would have told me.

"Not just one beast, but dozens." Perry shrugged. "We should move from here, dear one."

"Shut. Up." *Until I figure out what the fuck you're doing here.* "Anya, what the fuck?"

"Your house, Jill." She sounded calm, and utterly certain. "Then we'll ask all the questions we need to. Perry will meet us there. With the Sorrow."

My heart gave the sort of leap usually reserved for teenage girls in horror movies, right when the bad guy bursts out of the shadows. I couldn't take my eyes off Perry, but if Belisa was around . . .

Perry heard the hike in my pulse, and his grin widened. "Don't worry." His tone was a parody of soothing, coming out of that lean, grinning face. "I don't intend on leaving her behind again to get into mischief. She served my purpose—proof of my good faith. Just like that pretty bauble you're wearing."

For a bare second I contemplated unleashing the Talisman. It would make a smoking crater out of whatever remained of the warehouse. I wasn't sure it would kill Perry, but it could make him very uncomfortable.

The fact that I was even considering it meant I wasn't thinking straight. I made a harsh, almost physical effort to prioritize, clear my head, and figure out what to do next.

Perry leaned forward, all his weight on the balls of his feet. The wingtips gleamed, incongruously clean. "After we're done, Jill, you can have the Sorrow. We can get a room. Just she and thee, and some pretty shiny blades. Won't that be nice?"

It was a relief to find out I could still tell when he was laying a trap. The guns lowered, and the scar settled down, a live coal pressed into my wrist.

I never thought I'd be glad to feel that. The strength pouring up my arm was an unhealthy glow, like a cocaine rush. It would give out soon, and the fog of fatigue would set in until I could get some other fuel in me.

I needed to be somewhere safer than the open street when that happened. This was getting me no closer to my objectives. Either Saul was dead and vengeance needed to be planned, or he was alive and needing a rescue I couldn't accomplish if I was dragging. Not to mention the fact that someone planning on bringing a big-time hellbreed through might or might not be related to the whole mess.

I'd already fucked up by running on emotion.

Perry and I studied each other. The sirens drew closer.

I thought of saying something. Like, *If you've taken him, Perry, you will die.* But it would serve no purpose. He had to already know that.

Just like he knew I wasn't going to shoot him now.

On to the next problem, Jill. "Belisa," I croaked. "Where?"

"Oh, I've put the chain on *that* little cat. She won't be selling you to my enemies again. At least, not just yet." He tipped his head back a little. My eyes didn't want to focus past him, but I saw her. She crouched, in tattered blue silk, rocking back and forth. Her black eyes were empty, and her long fall of dark hair was mussed and full of soot. My right hand jerked, the gun almost locking on her, before I forced it down.

Perry turned smartly on his heel, reached down, and picked up a length of chain from the pavement. He twitched it, and Belisa pitched forward a little, the chain jingling where it met the collar's metal gleam.

The collar positively crawled with the same golden tracery of Chaldean runes as the cage had. No glaring white spots of orichalc, though. She rose awkwardly, and I noticed that her feet were bare and horribly battered. She left dark bloody prints on the pavement as she stumbled forward.

"Little snake." Perry's half-fond tone was utterly chilling. "Did you enjoy your half freedom? Now we'll see who you betray. I expected you to do something like this, seeking to cheat me of my prize."

Oh, God. Bile crawled up into my throat.

I backed up. It was probably a bad idea. The way my legs were shaking I ran the real risk of going down in a heap. I almost ran into Theron, who closed a hand around my shoulder. I realized several other Weres were moving to surround me. Amalia—a lioness of the Norte Luz pride— had two vertical stripes of black painted down each perfect golden cheek. Some of the bird Weres had feathers in their hair; others wore variations of the paint Saul sometimes used. Red, black, white—they were dressed for battle.

And there, a mop of dark hair and a pair of bright blue eyes. Anya, in a long leather duster. Her guns were out, pointed steadily at Perry. The silver in her hair—beads instead of charms, and threaded onto small braids in the dark hanging mass—ran with blue light.

It's always a good thing to see another hunter. But if she was here, shit was about to get more complicated than it already was.

Theron's lean dark face was set. "Let's go."

"Oh, but I'm having so much *fun*." Perry twitched the chain again. The links made a tinkling, icy sound under the roar of the inferno. Belisa swayed toward him, pliant and terribly empty-eyed. "Would you like to hold her leash, Kiss? It's an experience."

Gorge rose hot and fast again. *Oh, God, what have I done?* I reeled back into the Weres. Theron was leaning forward, a snarl thrumming under his skin. Anya was still covering Perry, her strong-jawed face set as if she smelled something even more horrific than usual. Gilberto, carrying a snub-nosed .38, probably loaned from the Weres, came into view. His sallow face was alight; he looked about ready to lunge for Perry. The gun was lifting, and the savage joy in his eyes warned me.

I pitched forward, grabbed his arm, sank my fingers in. The scar gave a flare of pain, as if someone had tried to yank out the knot of corruption by its roots.

"No." I held Gilberto's gaze for a long second. He resisted, but even with every bone and muscle in my body weakened I was more than a match for his skinny human strength. "No, Gil. *No.*"

"You better not, boy." Anya's drawl, soft and clear, chill with certainty. "You fire at him, I'll be the one to knock some sense into you. Right after she finishes."

Perry giggled, a high sharp note of glee. Gil swore, and the shaking in me must have infected him, too. The sirens were almost here, and dawn was coming fast.

I let the Weres draw me away, Theron's hands gentle

and the collective rumbling from them shaking me down to my bones.

I only looked back once, but the firelit street was empty. Perry and Belisa were gone.

But I could still hear him laughing.

Saul had cleaned up a little before he'd been snatched, but my warehouse still stank of hellbreed. I went straight for the bathroom and into the shower. I couldn't stand the filth one more second. Plus, the warm water would give me another short-term burst of energy.

And I could also load up on more ammo.

It took me more time than I liked to clean up. I kept having to stop, staring at my hands, willing the shaking to go away. Stupid, stupid, *stupid*. But assuming Perry had taken Saul was reasonable, especially with the way—

Who was I kidding? Assuming is *never* reasonable. I'd lost precious time and wasted resources going off half-cocked. I'd gotten caught, trapped. My Weres and my apprentice had put themselves in danger to rescue me, and *that* was a fine kettle of fish they should never have had reason to open.

Weres don't fight hellbreed. They get hurt too badly. There is no corruption in the Weres that will allow them to outthink, track, or eradicate a 'breed. Traders are dangerous, too, but a Were has a chance against something that's basically human.

Against 'breed? No. Yet plenty of them had shown up to save my bacon. Or because one of their own was taken. Either way, they'd put themselves in danger. That wasn't their job.

It was mine. I was sucking at my *job*.

I looked up at the mirror, my bathroom wavering around me for a split second as if it was underwater. The scar twinged sharply, and the sound of cold iron chain links crashed inside my head.

Christ. Buckle up, Jill.

"*Profesora*?" Gil, in the door. He had an armful of black leather.

"I should kick your ass." I pulled the hem of the fresh T-shirt down. "You were supposed to stay at Galina's."

"An' you were gonna bring back *su marido*." He shut his mouth as soon as I half-turned and looked at him. The fall of black leather in his arms was a fresh custom-made leather trench; I'd found a new supplier who didn't balk at sewing in the ammo loops and extra pockets to my exacting specifications. I buy them in bulk, and my last supplier had been hauled in on tax evasion charges.

For once, it was completely mundane and not anything to do with me. I'd almost forgotten what that felt like.

I couldn't go off half-cocked on my apprentice for telling the truth. "Gil."

He shrugged, offered me the coat. "*Es muerto*?"

"He's not dead." I took the coat, held it up and shook it a little. Slid into it, then started slipping the contents of my old pockets into the new ones.

"How you know?"

I don't. I just refuse to believe it. "Nobody wants that much trouble from me."

"*El Diablo rubio*, he might. He don't like Saul."

"Of course he doesn't. 'Breed don't like Weres. The feeling's mutual." I looked up. A chilly silver charm touched my cheek before I tucked the curl it weighted down behind my ear. "Wait a second. Is Perry here?"

"*Si*. With the *chica* on a leash." Gil was pale under his sallowness. There were bruised-looking circles under his dark, flat eyes. "Sparring room. *La otra cazadora* is drinking some licorice shit. Says she shoulda known you'd end up like this."

"Great." I scooped up the caged *bezoar*. It quivered unhappily. If you've never taken a shower while keeping an eye on a twitching corruption-seed in a silver cage, count yourself lucky. Down it went into a padded pocket. "The Weres?"

"Some out watching the neighborhood. Others looking round your kitchen. I told 'em not to take *el gato*'s copper-bottoms." A faint smile touched the corners of his thin lips.

I found my eyeliner. Considered just leaving it, but I needed every inch of protection I could get if I was going to face down Perry again. My hands were not steady, and neither was the rest of me. The fatigue fog was creeping up quick. "Yeah, well, if they take any of his enameled cast iron either there'll be hell to pay."

The sheer unreality of it rose and walloped me sideways. I took a deep breath, grabbed the counter, and willed my body to buck up. Etheric energy trickled through the scar, coiling up my arm like ivy.

Take it one problem at a time. I focused on the most immediate thing, opened my eyes, and put on my Teacher Face. "A few of the Weres will take you back to Galina's."

His pointed chin lifted, stubborn. "I done good."

My temper almost snapped. I took a firm grip on it, and on myself. *Don't, Jill. He's just a kid. He's your apprentice, dammit.* "You disobeyed a direct order and put yourself in danger."

"Weres said I done good." Lank hair shaken back, hands curling into fists. I was not handling this right. My entire body felt heavy and pale because replacing a few pints of blood takes a lot out of you, even if you've got a hellbreed mark and the benefit of sorcerous training.

Had the mark not been working because of the bane-fire? I'd never been completely encircled by banefire before, not while I had the scar. Another thing to set Hutch working on. Sure. I could just throw that on his plate and see what he came up with.

Wonder of wonders, my pager was still working. I know because it went off then, buzzing on the counter like a small poisonous rattler.

I swayed. Closed my eyes, eyeliner in one hand, the other making a fist to match Gilberto's. Calmed my run-away pulse, breathed in deep. Shuffled priorities inside my head, and told the ball of unsteady rage inside my chest to sit back and let me *work*, goddammit. My pager cycled through the buzz and cut itself off. The Talisman grumbled against my chest.

Where is he? Are they hurting him? Whoever they are. If he's harmed I will . . .

I couldn't afford to get worked up now. I shoved the anger down into a box, slapped a lid on it, and pushed it away. As a coping mechanism, it sucked. As a short-term solution so I could *think*, it was all right. For now.

I breathed deeply, dispelling the rage. Now was the time to be cold, to use a hunter's chill calculation.

"*Profesora.*" Gil, very close. Was he about to touch me? I hoped not.

I was so not safe right now. My bitten-down fingernails scraped against the butt of a gun, and I opened my eyes. The world rushed back in, a sharp torrent of color and hard edges. I stepped away along the bathroom counter, the edge of my coat brushing the dark wood cabinets underneath. I hadn't stepped back into my boots, so my calluses rasped against the hardwood.

Gil's hand dropped back down to his side. "*Lo siento.*"

"Get my boots." The words were a harsh croak. I turned back to the mirror, leaned in, and brought the eyeliner up. I was going to lay it on thick for this. "And for the love of God don't get so close to me. I am not safe." *Not for a human, anyway. And you're still all too fragile, Gil.*

"You ain't gonna hurt me." He sounded supremely confident. "You're gonna kick the shit out of whoever took *el gato.*" But, thank God, he was moving away into my bedroom to find a pair of boots.

"Damn right I am." Still, I had an uneasy feeling.

Now I had to face Anya. And there's nothing like a fellow hunter for seeing right through any lies you tell yourself.

Gilberto had understated the case a bit. The warehouse was *full* of Weres. As soon as I stepped out of my bedroom, I had to put up with being touched no matter how unsteady I felt.

It was to reassure them, I knew. Bird Weres breathed in my face, the cat Weres brushed my shoulder or got way inside my personal space and smelled me, and there was even a hollow-eyed spider Were who walked right up and delicately laid her fingertips on my cheeks, staring at me for a few moments. She looked familiar, but her mate— smaller and slimmer than her, even—hustled her away. After trickling his fingers over the sleeve of my coat.

I suffered it. It's the way they say they're happy I'm still here, and it's also how they show they care. Gilberto was bundled off with a group of four Weres, bound for Galina's. He didn't like it, but I wasn't in a mood to argue.

I found Anya Devi perched on the breakfast bar, her steel-toed boots dangling and a modified 9 mm in her left hand. A bottle of venomous green liquor sat obediently at her right side, and I caught the whiff of licorice.

Anya believes in absinthe the way other people believe in immunization, football, or sex. It's a panacea. It was the way Mikhail had felt about vodka.

Me? I'm a firm believer in Jack Daniels. But I'll take whatever's handy.

She lifted the bottle as soon as she saw me. Her apprentice-ring, a silver claddagh, threw a hard sharp dart of light back at the overhead fixtures. Anya is built a little smaller than me, but she makes up for it with pure dangerous brains. She didn't come back from Hell at the end of her apprenticeship with anything extra, unless you count the utter crazed determination in those baby blues. She and the Weres ran herd in Sierra Cancion over the mountains, keeping the scurf population down and the hellbreed and Traders guessing.

Long nose, straight eyebrows, the faint shadow of a scar on her right cheek, a claw mark slipping down from the outside corner of her eye like a tear. The usual *bindi* above and between her eyes, this time a miniature ruby. I hear it's a subdermal piercing, but I don't ask. I'm not one to throw sartorial stones. The usual silver hoops in her ears, small ones so they don't get ripped free in the middle of a fight. A dangling carnelian rosary, its cross resting against her navel. She'd put on a little more weight, all muscle by the looks of it, and her navy-blue T-shirt was ripped and dotted with blood. Some of her leather was scorched, too.

We regarded each other for a few moments. The Weres drew away, tactfully. One of them had his head in my fridge, muttering, and there was the smell of something sweet in the oven fighting with the reek of 'breed ichor.

She tipped her chin up a fraction, finally. "Kismet."

I copied the motion. "Devi."

Another few beats of silence, the kind of quiet that rises between two old gunfighters. Then a grin spread over her face and she hopped down, landing light and lithe as a cat. "Good to see you. We've got problems."

I'll say. "I'd ask what you're doing here, but something tells me I'm going to find out." *And it's not going to be pretty or simple.*

"Oh, yeah. And I'd ask you what that hellbreed is doing with a Sorrow chained up in your sparring room, and what the hell 'breed are doing kidnapping Weres. But something tells me I'm going to find out." Her mouth firmed a little. "It's *him*, isn't it. Perry."

I nodded. My neck creaked. Her eyes dropped to my chest. If I could feel the Talisman humming sleepily along under my T-shirt, she could probably sense the etheric disturbance it created.

I hooked a finger carefully under the sharp edges of the chain, and drew the Eye out. The light changed, taking on a redder cast, and the Weres all went very still for a few seconds. "Perry brought me this. The Sorrow is Belisa. Someone's looking to bring a high-level hellspawn through, maybe with Belisa's help as she double-crosses Perry, maybe not. There were bodies controlled by a 'breed assassin, an evocation altar, and a mass grave that lit up like a goddamn bonfire when I got there. And my Were is somewhere out there at the mercy of hellbreed." I paused, running back over it. "Not sure they're connected." My pager lit up again. I dug it out and checked. The Badger, again. She was next on my list. "And my fucking pager keeps going off."

One corner of Anya's mouth lifted slightly. "Well. This should be interesting. Whoever they're trying to bring through, they started trying over in my territory. I've been chasing evocation altars for a week or so now. Hutch called me, and when I got here that blond 'breed was at Galina's. He said you were in deep shit; my Weres put the word out and we went out to find you. That new apprentice of yours is a piece of work."

"That's why I took him in." I absorbed this. Whatever was in the oven smelled really good, but the scrim of rotting 'breed over it wasn't going to win it any prizes. "They started in your territory? What are they using to fuel it?"

"Mostly hearts. Two nuns, a nineteen-year-old boy, a clutch of schoolgirls, and one old lady with a bunch of cats Balthazar just *had* had to find homes for. Apprentices." One shoulder lifted, dropped. I had a little over half a head and several pounds on her, but if we ever tangled I wasn't sure either of us would come away whole. Balthazar was her apprentice—he'd come out to keep a lid on things while I went on my honeymoon with Saul.

"You have any idea who they're trying to bring through?" *Please don't say Argoth.* But I wasn't holding out any real hope.

"Just some whispers about some asshole called Julius, maybe. Whoever *he* is, I'm told he likes virgins." She snorted. "Is he going to get a surprise, this day and age."

Wait. "Julius? You're sure?"

Her smile widened, and it wasn't nice at all. It was, in fact, the kind of smile where you wanted to take a step back and look for a wall to protect your kidneys. "I couldn't swear to it. I've just heard the name. Why?"

I don't think Anya knows she can grin like that. It makes me wonder what my own face looks like sometime. "That just means I can stop Hutch from going on a wild goose chase and possibly aim him at something more productive. He'll enjoy that."

Perry's hints about Argoth, dropped to Rutger, weren't a good enough basis to worry about it. Anya's information was. She was a hunter. It meant her word was as good as honest silver.

Of course, she wasn't sure, or she would have said so. And there was the little matter of the Trader and the pile of charred bodies. *A gift for you.* But still.

"I don't think Hutch really *enjoys* much. Have you found any evocation sites here?" She took a hit from the absinthe bottle, rolling it in her mouth like it was fine wine.

I winced. I've never liked licorice. "Two. I think the one at the warehouse was a primary." *But I'm not sure.* "You getting graves with charred bodies?"

"Yeah, they're burning them after they take the sweetmeats out. There was a site in that warehouse?" Now she looked grave.

"Yeah. And an orichalc-tainted cage." I headed for the phone. "Give me a couple minutes, okay? Then we'll powwow."

She waved her fingers over her shoulder as she turned away. The bullwhip, neatly coiled at her side, swung just like her coat. "And eat. You need it. I think we should take a peek at what that 'breed's doing to that Sorrow. Since they seem to be involved up to the hip on this."

God damn. It was good to have another hunter around.

19

Jill?" The Badger, sounding a little less than calm. Which meant severe trouble. "Thank God."

"What? More bodies?" *Not like I have time for them. Jesus.*

"No. Vanner. He's gone. Disappeared from the hospital. The trauma counselor says he's still in shock. She's afraid he'll..." The Badger's voice didn't break, but it was close.

"Tell all the black-and-whites to look for him. I'll do my best too." *Goddammit. Shit, shit, shit.* "How did he check himself out?"

"That's the weird thing. He didn't. He's just gone." Then Badger dropped the other shoe. "His uniform's still there, though. Wherever he is, he's in his hospital johnny."

"Oh, *Christ*." I tried not to sound aggravated. "Okay. Keep a surveillance on the scene he stumbled across, he might go back there. Put out an APB on him, and roust Montaigne." *Sorry, Monty.* "Tell him to get whoever he can working Vanner's trail. See if we can pull him in."

"Sully's raising Montaigne now. Anything else?"

I struggled to *think*. There was one more thing. "Call Wallace again. Give him the situation. See if he and Benito can scare up anything."

"Okay." She sounded a lot more reasonable now. Of course, nobody could ever call the Badger unreasonable. But I could hear the relief now that she had a list of things to do.

"When he shows up, have Wallace or Benito or Avery take custody. Do *not* put him in a holding cell. Got it?"

"Oh." I could hear the wheels turning as she took this in. "All right."

"Good. Have the next of kin been contacted on those bodies yet?"

She actually sounded surprised. "Not yet. Figured it was better to hold off until I heard from you again."

Meaning, she was hoping I'd call and tell her it was all right to release them. Even the Badge cavils at telling a civilian family they can't collect their violated dead. I hated to have to ask them to do it. "And Rosie and Paloma, do they have anything on the other site?"

"I checked with Rosie not a half hour ago. Not yet. Stanton's having a hissy fit over the number of bodies. Going to have to start putting them in nooks and crannies." She moved the phone a little. I could just see her at her cluttered desk.

"Stanton's always having a hissy. One more thing. Warehouse fire, 154th and Chavez. Start the paperwork for a paranormal incident, if you find any bodies buzz me again."

"Jesus *Christ*." For a moment there she sounded like Monty. "You're a busy little girl, Kismet."

"The moment the nightside slows down, I will too. Thanks, Badge. Keep me updated, and I'll keep an eye out for Vanner."

"All right." She hung up, and I stood there for a second staring at the phone. The Weres were quiet, but someone was stirring something briskly in the kitchen. The tapping of a metal whisk inside a glass mixing bowl sounded so familiar, as if Saul was standing there after a long night's work, making breakfast. Probably burritos, because nothing goes down after a night of killing hellbreed like eggs, ham, potatoes, chipotle Tabasco, cilantro, and a nice cold beer.

I shook the thought away. *Focus, Jill.* Picked up the phone, dialed again. "Galina? It's Jill. Put Hutch on."

She didn't waste time asking me what was going on. "Oh, thank goodness... *Hutch! It's Jill!*"

I heard him bitching all the way up to the phone. "Worried *sick* about you," he ended up mumbling, as Galina handed the phone over. "Jesus Christ. What?"

I could just see him standing there with pen and a pad of paper, bracing himself. Thank God he had enough sense to stay where I put him. Not like my disobedient apprentice.

"The hellbreed someone may be trying to bring through is probably named Julius." I spelled it for him. "Cross-reference it with Perry, see what you come up with. Do you have anything on the Sorrows calendar yet?"

"Nothing, we're in the Dead Time. Something interesting, though; there was a Sorrows House burned in Louisiana a week ago. Completely torched. Resident hunter out there—it's Benny Cross, by the way, he says hi—says hellfire was involved."

Louisiana. Okay. "Did he mention the spectrum?"

"I knew you'd ask. Green, shading up into blue." Hutch's tone dropped to a whisper. "Bad news."

Yeah, anything above orange on the spectrum was *incredibly* bad news. The saving grace was that the higher on the spectrum, the less likely a 'breed was to be wholly physical, which meant sorcery and banefire could be used to disrupt them.

On the other hand, I'd seen Perry produce blue hellfire. And he was all-too-disturbingly physical. This put a whole new wrinkle in the equation.

"Did Benny say anything else?"

"Just that the Sorrows are mad as hell. He's watching them go after hellbreed. Not getting in the middle of that unless they drag a civilian in, he says."

Reasonable of him. If 'breed and Sorrows were looking to off each other, it made his job easier. Mostly. "Yeah. Okay, next thing. Would banefire break the link between a Trader and a 'breed? Like, a complete encirclement of banefire, cut it off completely?"

Silence crackled over the phone line. I shoved down the impatient need to say something more while he worked it around in his head. There was a sizzle of something hitting a hot pan, and I smelled eggs. Missing Saul rose like a stone in my throat. Was he in pain? Was someone maybe torturing him?

I told that line of thought to take a hike. It just laughed at me and kept on going. That's the problem with seeing so much of the nightside. Your imagination just works too damn well, because it has a *lot* of food to keep it going.

"It's possible," Hutch finally said. "Very possible.

Banefire creates a psychic barrier as well as a physical one. What's going on, Jill?"

"Do you really want to know, Hutchinson?" I sounded more savage than usual, had to stop myself. "Look, dig up anything you can out of the theory books, okay? Check Malvern and the Breisler." I considered telling him to go through the hunter records in Galina's vault for the hell of it, but what would I tell him to look for? Evidence that Mikhail or Jack Karma had an agreement with a hellbreed?

I didn't want to believe it. But the poisonous seed of doubt was planted. God damn Perry.

Too late. He's as damned as he's going to get. You need to make sure you don't follow him.

"Breakfast in ten minutes," the Were in my kitchen said quietly, and murmurs went around. I felt their attention, though they were tactfully not listening. It felt like more had arrived, too. The fridge was going to be picked bare, and they would restock my groceries before they left.

"When you put it that way…" Hutch gave a long-suffering sigh. "Should I still keep digging for that Argoth asshole?"

Thank God for you, Hutch. I rested the phone on my shoulder, so I could check my guns. They were where they always were. I forced my hands away. "Yes. I'm not ruling that out *just* yet. Better safe than sorry."

Scratching of pencil against paper. "Okay. Look up Julius, keep working Argoth angle, cross-check with Perry, check for banefire breaking connections between 'breed and Traders. Is there anything else on this Julius character, anything at all?"

"He likes virgins." I snorted. "Does that make you feel safer, or not?"

"I went to *college*," he informed me huffily, and hung up. I laid the phone down gently, restraining the urge to slam it into the cradle and crack the plastic. The Talisman trembled on my chest, like a live thing.

It was a live thing. Now I couldn't even remember Mikhail wearing it without thinking of Perry. Or Belisa.

Sunlight strengthened in the skylights. I stood there, staring at the phone for a moment and breathing deeply. Keeping the lid on that box of rage bouncing around at the bottom of my chest.

"All done up?" Anya, at my shoulder. She was so damn *quiet*, even for a hunter. I almost twitched. "Let's get this over with, so we can eat. I'm starving."

She was always starving. No wonder she got along with Weres so well.

It was an uncharitable thought. My entire body hurt, vicious little nips of pain all over. Even my hair hurt, the charms weighing it down. "Yeah." But I stared at the phone for another couple of seconds, willing it to ring and tell me something useful.

Something like, *It's me, kitten, I'm free and coming home.*

A hand on my shoulder. This time I did twitch, but did not draw a gun. I found Anya examining me. She didn't look perplexed or concerned. There was a faint vertical crease between her eyebrows, and I saw the beginnings of crow's-feet radiating from the outside corners of those blue eyes.

There is a disconcerting directness to a hunter's gaze when they're completely focusing on you. It's a hunter's job never to look away—we bear witness, and we watch what others can't bear to.

Mikhail taught me that. He'd been old for a hunter

when I met him, but still lethal. And here was Anya—I remembered her as an apprentice, the first time Larssen brought her over to help Mikhail and me with a Black Mist infestation let loose by a circle of cannibalistic Traders. She had been quiet and watchful even then, the kind of girl who would vanish at a crowded party until you struck up a conversation and realized just how pretty and smart she really was. "Hides her light under a bushel," was Larssen's succinct sum-up.

She was getting older, too. While I looked just the same. I only *felt* old.

"Maybe breakfast first?" She actually looked hopeful.

"No." My throat was dry. "Let's get this over with."

The etheric protections on my warehouse walls were awake, tendrils of blue light sliding through the physical structure. My blue eye, and the unphysical gauze layer of Sight over the natural world, could see it clearly enough. Anya immediately moved a few steps to my left, and I knew without looking that she'd drawn one of her guns.

The sparring space was large and open, hardwood-floored, skylights everywhere filling up with gold. I could have wished for some more sunlight, but wishing never did anyone any good.

Mirrors and a ballet barre marched down one side of the room. Weapons were hung on the other three walls; at the far end, pride of place went to a long shape under a fall of amber silk. The spear quivered gently, sensing a current of bloodlust in the air. Between the lance and the Talisman humming sleepily on my chest, I could probably handle Perry if I had to.

It was a comforting thought. For a certain value of comforting, I guess. The fact that I would rather not lay a hand on the spear unless I *had* to was incidental. Wasn't it?

In the middle of the open space, Melisande Belisa knelt, her battered feet still bleeding a little on the hardwood. Her silks were torn, and she reeked of smoke. The iron collar clasped her delicate neck, laid against her shoulders like a yoke, and thin threads of blood slid down from where it rubbed against her skin. The Chaldean marks on it ran with diseased gold. Her black eyes were completely blank.

The chain crawled with those same golden runes. They unraveled halfway up its length. *Now that's interesting.* I hadn't asked Hutch about collars for a Sorrow. I was going to have to do that.

He was really earning every single moment's worth of effort I'd spent on getting him back home without federal charges.

Perry crouched in front of the Sorrow. He was immaculate again, and I wondered where he'd cleaned up. The pit of my stomach turned over hard, thinking of him in any of my bathrooms. Or, maybe worse, not having to—just stepping out of the grime and smoke tarnish and somehow becoming his usual self.

They were both moving slightly. Perry would lean forward a little, shifting his weight, and Belisa would lean back just as infinitesimally. Then he would relax, rocking back, and she would go back to her slump-shouldered kneeling.

He was making a slight crooning sound, too, like a child trying to entice a reluctant dog.

A nasty, sociopathic little child.

My gorge rose. I swallowed bitterness. "Pericles." It
had all the snap of command I was used to putting into
it. "Answers."

He was silent for fractionally longer than was polite.
At least it stopped that goddamn crooning. "Hello, darling." Soft, reasonable, bland. "Do you like her? She's so
wonderfully *decorative*. And so predictable, too. Always
treacherous. You appreciate that in a woman after a
while. Constancy of its own sort."

I kept my hand away from my guns with an effort.
"Tell me about Julius, Perry."

He was still for a whole long-ticking fifteen seconds.
Utterly, eerily still—not the stillness of a hunter, which
contains little bits of motion in its own way. No, this was
as if he'd turned into an inanimate object. The scar was
full of soft fire, little brushes against it like the wet rasp
of a cherry-red, scaled tongue.

When he did move, it was to slowly straighten, his legs
stretching out. He made a queer little twitch with his head.
Something inside his neck crackled a little. "There are other
things I'd rather tell you about." He didn't turn to face us,
and Anya drifted another few steps, stepping soundlessly.

It was a comfort to have another hunter in the room.

"Start with Julius, Perry. Save the rest of it."

"Oh, but you'll want to hear this. It seems my lackey
was rather a naughty boy. He gave you a gift I had no
intention of giving just yet, but I can't begrudge it to you.
Tell me, how does it feel to know your teacher bore the
same cross you do?"

A gift for you. For a moment I thought he'd meant the
bodies near the freeway, and bile rose in my throat. Then
the meaning hit home.

My jaw set so hard my teeth ached. Basic healing sorcery means they don't shatter or fall out very easily. Still, there was something creaking in my mouth. The creaking slid down my neck, and the scar was soft velvet. Wet pleasure slid up the nerve channels, touching my shoulder like a lover's hand.

It was just like being in the room off his white bedroom, the one with the tiles and the iron rack and him fiddling with the scar, trying to make me react. Trying to make me jump the way he wanted me to.

Anya glanced at me. The silver in her hair slid soundlessly. Her eyebrows were up, her lips slightly parted as if she wanted to say something. Her leather duster whispered slightly as she moved again, covering Perry from another angle that would mean she could shoot clear of Belisa.

I wanted to tell her not to bother. The sooner that snake's head was chopped off, the better.

Then why didn't you do it, Jill?

Because doing it for the wrong reason would damn me. Even more thoroughly than a hunter could be said to be damned in the first place. Even if nobody else knew the difference, *I* would, and that was all that mattered. Knowing that difference and doing it anyway would make me no better than the things I hunted.

And then Perry's little smile would turn into a sawtooth grin, and I would pay for every single insult I'd ever offered him.

That would keep him busy for a long, long while. And he'd make sure I was awake for all of it.

Oh, I knew. I'd known since the beginning. I'd realized it the moment he'd made the offer, that cherry-red tongue flickering out to touch his bloodless lips. Perry and I were playing this game for different reasons. I wanted the power to keep cleansing the night.

He wanted something else. Something that would end with me even worse than a Trader.

"I know Riverson told you." Silken, even, each word just so. "I regret I wasn't there to see your face. Such an interesting shade of white. Almost as pale as you are now."

"Julius." I managed the one word, found I could use others. "Your immediate superior?"

"I? I *have* no superior, my darling. And certainly no equal, in this world or in Hell." Now he turned on one elegant heel, and though his suit was perfectly clean and his hair neatly arranged, his face was still streaked with smoke. It glared at me, that mask of banality, the even regular features unassuming except for the shadow of twisting under them, like a knife under a blanket. His eyes burned blue, a sterile inferno as far away from Anya's clear steady gaze as it was possible to get.

"Hellspawn," the other hunter said, softly but with an edge of incredible disdain. "Answer the question."

"Little human hunter." He didn't look away from me. "You're interfering with business not your own."

"Ooooh, scary." Her tone said very clearly that she wasn't impressed. "Kismet?"

It took two tries to make my throat work. Fortunately the words came out just right—bored, with an edge of menace. "Julius, Perry. Your immediate superior, coming through to ask you a few questions. Belisa playing both sides against the middle again. You should have learned not to mess with Sorrows last time."

The snarl drifting over his bland face was a balm. It

disturbed the mask of humanity for a critical half second. Now I was in control of myself, and I slid the gun free of the holster.

Anya exhaled softly. But her pulse was even and steady, marching along. Mikhail was always on me about my pulse. My heart cracked, but no expression reached my face. "One more time, Pericles. Julius. Rutger planning on moving you aside, since Shen didn't manage?"

He considered me. Lifted one hand, tapped a finger to his smoke-grimed lips. "Don't you ever wonder why your teacher sought out his death at the hands of a Sorrows whore?"

"That's none of your business." I raised the gun. "The next time you sass me, Pericles, it's going to be a bullet. Start talking about Julius."

"It started with Jack Karma. The first one, dear, not the pale copy. I'd been looking for a hunter lineage with certain...peculiar qualities, and I finally found one. The Karma children have always had such charming personalities. A fault line right down the middle, hair-thin but so vulnerable."

I'll admit it. I lost my temper. Two steps forward, Anya drifting with me, and my finger tightened on the trigger. "Julius, Perry! Start fucking talking."

He actually smirked, the bastard. "Language, Kiss. Such indelicate—"

I took another step forward, but Anya was quicker. The knife blurred, parting the air with a low sweet sound, and sank into his throat. He folded down, making a very undignified choking sound, and I stood and stared like a civilian.

Anya glanced at me. "You didn't know? How could

you *not* know?" She now had both guns out, and pointed at Perry while he keeled over onto the floor with a far-too-heavy thump.

The world shifted underneath me. Just a few inches, but that was enough.

Riverson I didn't have to believe. But Anya was hunter, and hunters don't lie. Not to each other.

We *can't*.

I actually swayed, half-turning and staring at her. My mouth dropped open, but no sound came out. The .45 almost slid free of my fingers; they spasmed shut at the last moment.

I found my voice, a harsh croak that didn't sound like me at all. "What?"

"I thought you just didn't talk about it." Her coat whispered as she stepped aside again, to make sure her angle of fire was still clear. "Jesus, Kismet. How could you not know?"

"I..."

Perry gurgled. He reached up, fingers closing around the knife hilt. Worked it back and forth. An obscene squishing sound came from the unholy flesh while black ichor welled up sluggishly. She'd pegged him right in the larynx, missing the arteries neatly. A double-bladed dagger with a plain black hilt, just the thing for shutting up sassy-ass hellbreed.

He choked, writhing, working the blade back and forth in the wound. The squishing sounds got worse.

"Mikhail had a bargain with this piece of garbage, too. I don't know about either Karma, though. You seriously didn't..." Something occurred to her then. She considered me, blue eyes gone cold. "Huh."

"Breakfast!" a Were yelled from the other room. A ripple of appreciative sound went through the rest of the warehouse, a counterpoint to Perry's gagging. The knife slid free on a gush of black ichor with a weird, opalescent sheen.

Perry was still grinning. His mouth worked, but he didn't speak. The hole in his throat, his shell breached by the blessed silver loading the blade, would be slow to heal. But he still looked like a cat full of canary.

My stomach curled up against itself. "Mikhail." I sounded like I'd been punched.

"We've got other problems." Her chin jutted forward a little, indicating the hellbreed on the floor. Melisande Belisa still crouched. The pool of ichor almost touched her knees. "Like what the fuck he's doing with a Sorrow."

"He..." I swallowed hard, again. My stomach closed up even tighter, as if it would throw the mouthful of spit right back out. The Talisman rumbled unhappily on my chest, almost like Saul's purr. Except Saul would comfort me, and this unsteady deep thrum wasn't comforting at all. It was like the whine of a jet engine before something goes terribly wrong and the plane rediscovers gravity in a big way. "Met her before. A while ago." A horrible supposition rose inside me like bad gas in a mine shaft.

"I'll just bet." The corner of Anya's mouth lifted slightly. "Kismet..."

Perry knew Belisa from that case, the one with the bugfuck-crazy Sorrows Grand Mother and her job to shove a Chaldean Elder God into my resisting body. But what if, just *what if*, he'd known her before?

How had Mikhail met Belisa? I'd often wondered. Usually in the long, dark watches of the night, while I patrolled the city looking for trouble. I used to come back to it like peeling at a scab, until time had given me other things to think about.

Pieces of the puzzle slid together inside my head. I inhaled sharply, and Anya actually yelled as I leapt.

I was on Perry in a heartbeat, pistol-whipping him. His head bounced. Bone cracked, black fluid spraying, and even though he had a hole torn in his throat the hellbreed was making a queer chuffing noise that I realized was *laughter*.

He was *laughing* at me.

The world turned red. I was not flailing wildly. No, the instinct and expertise of years of murderous combat every night was filling me in an ice-burning torrent, and I hit to kill.

Chaos, the world turning over. Bright stars flashed across the red sheet my vision had become.

Someone had just punched me.

I hit the floor and wrestled with them. Whoever it was, they were unholy quick and strong, and they didn't move like a 'breed. No claws, and someone was yelling my name. Someone I should recognize.

But first I had to kill *him*. They had my left hand locked, arm twisted bruising-hard, someone supple and dangerous as a python in my grasp. Suddenly more hands were clamping down on me, hard but not with the hurtful prick of hellbreed claws. I heard someone screaming obscenities in a ragged, cracked, unlovely voice, and realized it was me.

I also realized I was under a pile of Weres, and they were having trouble holding me down. Anya had dragged me off of Perry. I'd been trying to kill him by pistol-whipping him. Or with my bare hands.

Oh, shit. I'd lost it.

He'd finally found a way to make me react. Only it hadn't been Perry, it had been her.

If she said it, it had to be true.

Oh, God. A wrecked scream rose up inside me, was throttled, died with a whining, hurt sound.

I struggled, but not with the hands holding me down. With *myself.* The scar was a brand, pressed into scorching flesh, laughing in a low, nasty whisper nobody else could hear. The abyss howled, and I pulled myself back from it with an effort that bowed me up into a hoop, every muscle locking down and my throat on fire, trying to scramble back from the howling madness opening up inside my head, inside my chest, inside everything that made me myself.

I made it. Just barely. Closer than I'd ever been.

I went limp. They sagged down on me, and I hoped I hadn't hurt someone. "Anya?" I whispered. "OhGod. God, oh God."

"God*dam*mit." I heard the click of silver-plated handcuffs. "Is she all right?"

"We can't sedate a hunter." It sounded like Amalia. "She'll burn right through—"

The very suggestion of sedation made me heave up from the floor again, struggling madly. They bore down, a tangle of arms and legs and more-than-human weight.

"Jill! Goddammit, Jill, calm down!" Anya, the snap of command under her sweet high-pitched voice. "*Calm down or I will make you, hunter!*"

She probably used that tone on her apprentices. It worked. I lay still as death. My eyes squeezed shut so hard tracers fired geometric shapes and whorls in the darkness behind my lids. The glow of the living beings on top of me poured in through the dumb meat of my left eyelid, my smart eye piercing the veils. Even when I tried to shut it out, I could not look away.

"Kismet." Still with the crisp bite of authority. "Are you reasonable?"

No, I am not reasonable. This is not reasonable. I made some sort of noise, whether affirmation or denial I couldn't tell, but it was apparently good enough.

One by one the Weres flowed away. They were all lionesses, their tawny hair falling in beautiful ripples and their eyes lambent. One of them was Amalia, and she leaned down, offering her hand. Muscle stood out under the bare, burnished skin of her upper arms. Her mouth was drawn tight, though, and her entire face was set and paler than a Were had any right to be.

I reached up as if drowning. Her warm fingers threaded through mine, and she hauled me to my feet. As soon as I had my balance she was away, stepping with the peculiar soft-footed glide of a cat Were, and a longing to see Saul shook me right down to my bootsoles.

Anya had Perry handcuffed on the floor. He was a mess. The urge to cross the intervening space and start kicking him with my own steel-toed boots rose, was repressed. Did not die away. The Talisman made a thin keening sound, and a curl of smoke rose to my nose. My aura crackled restlessly. Every piece of silver on me was warm and running with blue light.

"Jill." Anya, very carefully. "Are you reasonable?"

I cleared my throat. Swallowed twice. Stared at the hamburger mess of Perry's face. The grin was still there, white teeth flashing through meat and a chortling gurgle far back in his throat.

He had finally, after all this time, made me react.

"Jill." Anya, again.

Hunters do not lie to each other. We can't. It's too dangerous. Not only that, but each hunter has descended into Hell at the end of their apprenticeship, trusting their teacher to hold the line and bring them out alive. If you ask an apprentice what the line's made of, you'll get varying theoretical answers. If you ask a hunter, you'll only get one. It's why we don't even shade the truth.

It's so simple, really. You can't lie to someone else who has been loved like that. Loved so hard it pulls you out of Hell itself.

Mikhail. Bitter acid filled my mouth. "No." The word stung my throat. "I am very fucking far from reasonable, Anya Devi." Was that water on my cheeks? I was crying?

Why? God, why *cry* at a time like this? It had to be blood. I was bleeding salt and water from the knowledge.

"It's true." Was there a rock caught in her throat, too? Did she have to pull every word out of that raw bleeding place inside that makes us what we are? "I swear it's true. I thought you knew."

Idiots, Mikhail said. *They think we do this for them. There is only one reason for to do what we do,* milaya. *It is for to quiet screaming in our own heads.*

Hearing him in my head used to be a double-edged comfort. Now it tore at everything I'd ever believed about him.

"Is there anything else?" My hands were fists. I had no idea where my gun had gone, and that was bad. A hunter doesn't lose track of something like that. I licked my scorch-dry lips. "Is there any fucking thing else someone *forgot* to tell me?"

"He must have had his rea—" She shut up as I looked at her. My blue eye was burning, and I knew there would be a pinprick of red in the depths of my pupil.

And I honestly do not know what I would have done if the loud, clanging chime of my doorbell hadn't rung. It cut the tension like a knife, and every Were in the building tensed. Intuition hit me with a sick thump, right in the solar plexus.

I turned on my heel and ran for the door.

20

The envelope, heavy cream-colored linen paper, stank of hellbreed. The sweet candy sickness mixed with rotting ichor, cinnamon rolls, and breakfast smells, as well as the spice and healthy fur tang of Weres. There were no obvious traps or tingles of sorcery on it.

Someone had spent some effort to get it delivered right to my door. Whoever it was had evaded the watch the Weres had set, and they all looked grave about that. It didn't stop them from queuing up for breakfast, though. I sank down on the couch—an old orange Naugahyde monster Saul had slipcovered. It was about the first thing he'd done when he moved in. Other than throwing out all my kitchen gear and starting afresh. It was a good thing I had municipal funding; he'd about wiped me out when it came to pots and pans.

Stop stalling, Jill.

Anya stood at the end of the coffee table, watching me. Like she expected me to go bugshit again at any moment. She had her absinthe bottle out and took a swig as she stared at me.

I tore the envelope open. Two photographs and an 8½-by-11 sheet of the same expensive linen paper. The writing was copperplate script, the ink rusty and watery, scratched on with what I'd bet was an iron nib.

The first picture. Black-and-white, glossy, high quality. I stared at it for a few moments, my pulse pounding in my ears. Handed it to Anya.

It was Saul, whole and unharmed, lying on the floor of an iron cage. Taken between bars, it focused on his profile. His eyes were open, but he had curled up, one arm under his head. Grace in every line of his long, lean body, his boots and fringed jacket gone but the rest of his clothing there. He looked a little disarranged, and the paint on his cheeks was drying and flaking off. The cage was square, and as far as I could tell there was no Chaldean scoring on the bars.

They would have other ways of keeping a Were quiescent. He was obviously not dead.

Anything could happen, though.

The second picture was taken with a telephoto lens. A slight figure, hunching his shoulders as he went through Galina's front door. A nose that could have come from an Aztec codex, pitted cheeks, and his lank hair.

Gilberto.

I handed that photograph over, too. It quivered a little bit in my fingers.

The note was short and to the point.

Via Dolorosa, at dawn tomorrow. Come to the middle of the bridge and wait.

It was signed with a twisted little sketch—a glyph that looked like a crying mouth behind clawed fingers. That was the closest the little bastards could get to writing Helletöng down. It was a name-mark, and a huge break. I could get it to Hutch and find out who was working to bring this Julius, or whoever, through. That was just one short step to serving justice on him, her, or it.

Justice? No. *Vengeance.* Screaming, bone-breaking, blood-spattering vengeance.

Via Dolorosa had to be Wailer Memorial Bridge, lifting up from downtown and flying over the river, leading to the highway that ran under the bluffs. There wasn't much room for anything but freight yards and a sad shantytown or two. Every morning you could see some of the homeless trudging across the bridge toward the better pickings of the city's beating heart.

I handed the letter to Anya. It fluttered like a bird in my unsteady fingers. And I wondered just where Rutger and that goddamn 'breed in black pajamas were. I hadn't seen their bodies, so they were possibly still alive.

And "possibly" will bite you on the ass at every opportunity, when you're dealing with hellbreed.

"It's a trap," she said immediately. "Probably set by that son of a bitch in there or one of his vassals. There's no cover on that bridge. Bet you anything it's being watched now, too."

"Yes." I nodded. Silver chimed. I took my hand away from a gun butt when she gave me a meaningful stare. "Exactly."

"You're not going to do it." Flat and final.

I couldn't lie, so I just stared at the paper. *Her* hands were steady. There was a scrape on her right knuckles, thin threads of healing sorcery sunk into the skin and binding everything together. If I didn't have the scar, I'd be a mass of healing sorcery by this point too. I probably wouldn't have tried banefire in that cage, either.

There were so many things I couldn't have survived or done without the mark of Perry's lips on my wrist. I'd never caught the smell of sicksweet corruption on Mikhail... but then, after Perry had given me the mark and my enhanced senses, had Mikhail's mark vanished?

No, because Belisa had seen it. Or was that another lie? Did the scar remain even if the bargain was cleared?

I shuddered at the thought.

Anya dropped the letter on the coffee table. It fell as if it was heavier than it had any right to be. Leather creaked as she folded her arms, the cape of her duster moving as her shoulders came up. "Jill. You're *not* going to do it. Not without me."

I searched for a reasonable answer. Finally found one. "You have to shut down those other evocation sites. The Weres can't do it; it takes a hunter. There might be other mass graves lying around, too."

"How are we going to—" She caught on. "No. No *way*. Jill, for Christ's sake. You go in there like this, he'll eat you alive."

She had a point. "He hasn't yet." I clasped my hands, my apprentice-ring glinting sharply. I remembered Mikhail fitting it on my third left finger, a small strange smile on his aquiline face. *There, little snake. Honest silver, on vein to heart. You are apprentice. Now it begins.* And his eyes, bluer and paler than Anya's, cool and considering. Weighing me. "What else didn't Mikhail tell me?"

She spread her hands. "I don't know."

The smell of food was drowning out everything else, and I didn't know whether to be happy or revolted about that. It was just masking the hellbreed stink now. Just putting a pretty face on it.

I sank back into the couch. Stared at the ceiling. The skylights were full of thin hot winter gold now. I'd lost a lot of time knocked out in that warehouse, behind bars running with Chaldean runes. It was small comfort that Rutger or Belisa hadn't pulled off whatever they were attempting. The more fools they, leaving me in there with my weapons...

...but could I take anything about the whole episode for granted? I couldn't.

Whatever was going on, Perry was playing for keeps. There might be others working at cross-purposes; God knows hellbreed don't cooperate. It had all the makings of a clusterfuck in progress, and not much in the way of stopping it unless I put on my big-girl panties and started getting some shit *done*.

When I brought my chin back down, I found Anya watching me. There was also a plate of breakfast—eggs, pancakes, hash browns, and cut-up cantaloupe that Saul had been planning on using for a fruit salad as soon as he could get by the farmer's market—held at eye level by a somber Theron. He wore a Trixies T-shirt, jeans, and the expression of an unhappy but determined Were.

My heart wrung down on itself.

"Gilberto." My lips were numb. "They might grab him outside Galina's."

"We've already sent more Weres." Theron's mouth was set in a thin line.

"Hellbreed—" I began.

"Shut up." He shoved the plate in my face again. "And eat. No, we don't go up against hellbreed. We can buy him some time to get to Sanctuary, maybe. Make it harder for them to steal him away. But *you* need to eat."

I grabbed the plate, because otherwise he would have pushed it right up my nose. "Theron, goddammit—"

"You're about to do that Lone Ranger shit, Jill. It never ends well." He gave me a level, dark glare, then turned on his heel and stalked away.

Jesus. Taken down a peg by a *Were*. And not a word about Saul. Of course, it would be tactless to say anything about it, wouldn't it? They were the soul of tact.

And if he was dead, they wouldn't speak his name. They have some funny ideas about that. Ancestor-worshipping people usually do.

I set the plate down on the coffee table. A young bird Were, brown feathers tied fluttering in his sleek dark bowl cut, handed another plate to Anya, holding a fork against the side with his thumb. They were going to have to break out the paper plates and picnic cutlery in a bit; I didn't have nearly enough china for the crowd in here.

"He's right. You get stupid now, we'll lose a hunter. And quite possibly more Weres." Anya crouched, setting down her absinthe bottle. She started shoveling in the food as if it was oatmeal, neatly and ferociously. She hunched a little, too, the way you do in juvie or prison.

Just like Gil. It had taken me forever to learn to eat like a civilian. I'd done it for Saul, mostly. He was big on manners.

I stood up. Anya tensed, her fork in midair. "What the hell do you think—"

"I am going to take those two somewhere else." Brittle calm enveloped me. "You round up the Weres and get out of here. I want you to kill every evocation site you can find and liaise with Montaigne in case there are more bodies. I'll question Perry and leave any information I get with Hutch."

She shook her head, vigorously. "Bad idea. *Bad* idea."

"They'll come for me, here or wherever I am, before dawn tomorrow. Meeting on the bridge is just a ploy. There's another game being played here, and I want to find out what it is before it gets any deeper *or* another hellbreed comes through to wipe my city off the map." My fingers ran lightly over weapons—guns, knives, my bullwhip, my full pockets, everything stowed away. "They won't give me a whole day to get my feet under me and make plans. I don't want the Weres catching any *more* flak. And Perry will answer every one of my questions." *Every single one. God help us both. But especially me.*

She didn't think much of that idea, either. "You can't trust him not to—"

"Anya. I've been playing Perry for years now. Since before Mikhail . . . left." *Died, Jill. Call it what it is. That Sorrows bitch that cut his throat is in there, and you haven't killed her yet. Do you know what you're doing?* I told that little worried voice to take a hike. Checked my ammo again, the equivalent of a nervous tic for a hunter. "I haven't done too badly."

Meaning: *I'm not damned yet.*

"If you didn't even know that he—" She shut up when I stepped away, leaving the plate on the coffee table. Saul had thrown away the ruins of the box and its silver bow, too, probably with fistfuls of salt. He knew what precautions to take, now.

Too bad it hadn't saved him.

Had they meant to kidnap him here? Should I have asked him to go straight to Galina's? Were they tracking him even as he left the cemetery?

I brought myself back to the present with a jerk. My aura wasn't crackling anymore, and that was good. The Talisman was a sleeping weight on my chest, heavy and warm. Like a consoling hand. "No matter what I knew, or know, or should have known, Mikhail's dead and my city's in danger. My best bet is getting that fucking hell-breed to a place where I can deal with him. With you and the Weres getting those evocation sites shut down, I have a chance of getting Saul out of this alive and my city another few days of rolling along. Do it, Anya."

"Jill? *Jill!* You're not going to—"

I walked away.

21

I figured the Monde Nuit was the last place anyone would expect me to go at this point. Shafts of sunlight pierced the gloom, because the lights downstairs were all turned off now. The entire place looked like a stage set, dusty and disused, every angle subtly off and placed that way for show.

Perry was trussed up like a Christmas goose, double pairs of silver-plated handcuffs doing their duty at wrists and ankles, the larger sizes around his elbows and knees. Anya had gagged him, too. His eyes were closed; the gaping hole in his throat was closed but not completely healed. He mercifully didn't even try to squawk. He was heavy deadweight, and I checked the cuffs every time I set him down.

Belisa obeyed every time the chain was twitched, stumbling around as if she was blind. She'd follow verbal directions, too, and I wondered if she was playing dumb or if the chain had something to do with it. With just the collar on she'd been pretty peppy, and obviously she couldn't take it off.

Another mystery to solve.

Still, I heaved a sigh of relief when I got them both up the stairs and into the office. The chain pulsed obscenely in my hand, Chaldean runes flinching away from my fingers. The metal was warm; it almost felt alive.

The white bed was torn to shreds, the bar a ruin of glass and mirror shards. Riverson was nowhere in sight. But the closed-circuit cameras were still working. I put Belisa in a corner facing the wall, like the bad little girl she was. It was work to haul Perry's unresisting weight along the floor, but getting him up the stairs had been the hard part. The scar was burning, the feeling working deeper and deeper, as if it would hit bone soon. It never had yet—but still.

The small room leading off his office/bedroom was glaring white tile on all four walls and the floor. An iron rack stood off-center, closer to the far wall than the door. The ceiling was a blank pane of fluorescents, their harsh glare bouncing off the table set to the right along the wall.

A rosewood case, its gold latches unbuckled, sat in the precise middle of the table. As if waiting for me. My skin turned cold and tight, except for the hard little pinprick bumps of gooseflesh.

Perry didn't struggle as I got him fastened into the iron rack. His eyes were still closed, lips moving slightly around the leather strap of the gag. Spread-eagled, slumping from his arms, the front of his shirt blackened and his suit spattered. I made sure he was fastened in securely, testing each strap twice. His fingers moved like little white spider legs, and he didn't help or hinder. I popped the gag, and his mouth gave it up without complaint. It was slick and wet, but I stuffed it in a pocket anyway.

When I stepped back, his eyes opened slowly. For a moment he looked half blind, indigo threading through the whites like veins and sending questing tendrils into his glowing irises. His lips still moved, writhing obscenely, and a faint rumble of Helletöng rattled away from him in concentric rings.

I waved an admonishing finger. "Now, now. None of that."

The 'töng bled away, like a freight train vanishing in the distance. He stared at me, and the indigo retreated from his irises. Finally, he licked his lips, and his voice was a hoarse ruin of itself. "We were always going to come to this, Kiss. *Always.*"

Careful, Jill. Make this his mistake, not yours. "Let's start with Saul, Perry. Who has him?"

"Perhaps I did take your cat." He grinned through a mask of rotting ichor. "Perhaps not. What are you going to do now?"

It wasn't time to play the biggest card I had, yet. Instead, I reached up and touched the Talisman. It arched up under my fingers, cool metal that somehow conveyed the impression of faraway flame, a heat not quite felt against my skin. "Who has him now?"

The strap across his forehead was as tight as it would go. He tried to move his head, couldn't, and rolled his eyes, still grinning. "Now why would I tell you that? With him out of the way, you're so much more amenable. So much more *pliant.*"

That's what you think. I turned away. Headed for the table. The rosewood was slick and satiny as I opened the case.

The flechettes lay arranged neatly against dark-blue

velvet, each one a razor gleam. There were tiny ones that
fit over the fingertips, curved and straight ones as long as
my hand, other assorted shapes and sizes. The largest was
as long as my forearm, its cutting edge curved slightly
and a blood-groove scoring down its fluid length.

"Ohhhhhhh…" Perry sighed. "How much will you hurt
me, Kiss? You see what a *good* little hellspawn I am. I take
things from your hand I would take from no other."

Don't tempt me. But it was too late for that. I took my
time, running my fingers over the flechette handles, considering each and every one.

I'd used them all. Before Perry had welshed on his
end of the deal by playing with Sorrows, I'd been in
here every month. More often than not he had me strap
him into the frame and start cutting. Sometimes it was a
beating, and he grinned each time I broke his pale, hard
hellbreed shell. Once he lounged in his bed, narrow pale
hairless chest exposed, and toyed with a dish of strawberries while he asked me questions. What my favorite color
was. What I wanted to be when I grew up. What I thought
of politics.

All a game, to get me to respond. Gathering up little
bits of psychology, storing it up for the day I stepped over
that hairline crack and into his world.

The day I was damned. The day he owned me.

*It might end up being today, if you let it. Careful,
Jill.*

I picked up the largest flechette. The metal handle,
scored for traction like a gun butt, was ice-cold. The scar
chilled, too, a warning.

My face settled against itself. My pulse dropped, as if
I was waiting on a rooftop for a target to show. I wasn't

as calm as I could be. For one thing, the skin of my right cheek was twitching as if a seamstress was plucking at it with a needle.

For another, the Talisman was rumbling too. Louder than the Helletöng, the subsonics striking the tiled walls and reverberating. The Eye's song swallowed the unmusical nastiness of Helletöng, turning each limping broken hiss and groaning curse on its head, blending it into an even greater theme.

Something about that helped, though I don't know why. I let out a sharp breath and was suddenly, mostly, back in control of myself.

Except for another worried little thought. Why would Perry give it back to me?

When I turned, I found Perry considering me. The indigo had bled out of his eyes, and they were bright, glowing blue around the too-dark pupil. The border between pupil and iris shifted, each an amorphous blob of darkness with a red spark buried in its depths.

He'd never done *that* before.

The tip of his tongue crept out, wet cherry-red, and touched the corner of his mouth. "You look lovely."

I felt the smile pull up my mouth, baring my teeth. An animal's grimace as I crossed the room. "Why, Perry. Thank you." The tip of the flechette caressed his cheek. I considered it, drew it up his smoke-tarnished skin to the corner of his left eye. "How would you like to be blind?"

Not a twitch of uneasiness, but he was so very still. "You can't."

"I can put silver in the holes once I've dug your baby blues out." I cocked my head. "Wouldn't that be interesting."

His expression—interested, avid—didn't change. "Then I could no longer see your beauty, Kiss. I would miss that."

The tip dug in a little. There was nothing human under that shell, but I was fairly sure if I twisted my wrist and scooped, the eye would pop out. I knew the blade was sharp enough to cut him, whatever metal it was. No silver, because it didn't fire with blue sparks when it got near him.

"Last chance, Pericles." The calm descended on me. "Saul. Who has him?"

He grinned. Like a skull.

And then he told me. I didn't even have to cut him once.

22

I gunned the engine. Beside me in the passenger seat, buckled in like an unresisting doll, Melisande Belisa swayed. I wanted to keep an eye on her. And leaving her with Perry seemed...wrong.

For all I knew, Perry was still strapped in that rack. God alone knew how he got unstrapped at the end of our long-ago monthly sessions, but then he'd had flunkies. There was nobody in the building to come get him out.

I hoped he'd stay there for a while. Long enough for me to get this done and figure out a way to deal with him.

The tires squealed as the car spun, a roostertail of golden dust rising. The car leapt forward obediently. The day was well underway, noon past and the sun sinking from its apex. The chain hanging from Belisa's collar clanked as I hit the corner coming out of the Monde's parking lot and stepped on the gas. There wouldn't be many people on the street, but—

My pager buzzed. I dug it out, one hand on the wheel

and the pedal to the floor. Intuition tingled along my nerves. I hit the brakes and narrowly avoided a pickup truck running a stop sign on Soledad Street. The driver was obviously drunk, careening away in a flash with ranchero music blaring.

One look at the number on my pager convinced me to pull over. There was a phone booth at Soledad and 168th. I cut the wheel hard and Belisa slumped in the seat. The chain jingled musically, a queerly wrong clashing, and I wondered where Riverson had got himself to. If, that is, Belisa had left him alive.

One more of those questions I had no time to answer. I pulled over, hit the parking brake, and took the keys with me.

Galina's phone rang twice before Hutch picked up. "Jill?"

"It's me. Is Gilberto there?"

"I thought he was with you. Anya Devi came through, she's looking for you. But there's something else. Listen, Jill—"

I cursed. Considered putting my fist through the plastic shell of the booth. Stared at the car. Belisa was deathly still, slumped against the window, and the Chaldean running through the chain flickered gold.

Yes, I parked where I could keep an eye on her. Just because she hadn't been any trouble so far was no indication.

"Shut up." Hutch actually snapped at me. I shut my mouth. "Listen, Jill. This Julius, the hellbreed? Likes virgins, looks like a manlier version of Buster Keaton, according to the description—"

"Cute," I muttered. "What about him?"

"He's already out. He surfaced two and a half weeks ago. In Louisiana."

There was a glimmer inside my car, a foxfire glow fighting with the sunlight. It was the golden glyphs, brightening. Was she struggling against the chain?

I should kill her. It would be so easy. Just a moment's worth of work and I could be done with the whole thing.

Then what Hutch had said hit home. "Oh, shit," I whispered.

"Yeah. I called Benny Cross again, on a hunch. He's madder than a wet hen, there's a full-scale war between the Sorrows and Julius's henchmen spilling over onto civilians. Julius is nowhere to be found. Benny says to be fucking careful."

"Hutch." I struggled to breathe. "What kind of chain binds a Sorrow? What does it look like?"

He was silent for a full five seconds. "Meteorite iron, I guess. It has to be bloodworked and runed; they use them for the *Pas'zhuruk*, where they eat their own. Expensive, it'd cost you an arm and a leg to get one, assuming you could pry it out of a House. Regular pin and lock on the collar, and once the collar's on the Sorrow's a slave, but has some agency. Add a chain of the same stuff and they're catatonic."

Pas'zhuruk. "Isn't that where they sacrifice a Grand Mother to one of the Elders?"

"Yeah. Um, listen. Gilberto's not here. Thought he was with you."

Fuck. "Any Weres showed up yet?"

"No, none of them either. What the fuck is—no, scratch that. I don't want to know. What do you want me to do?"

Wise man. "Call my house, see if you can raise Anya. Or get her pager. If all else fails, she'll check in with you." I shuffled priorities. Evocation altars meant they were planning on bringing *someone* through. It was too expensive a ploy to waste just to keep me chasing my tail...or maybe not. Still, I couldn't take that chance. "Tell her to evacuate my house pronto, and that Gil's been snatched, unless he shows up with the Weres. Tell her not to send any more Weres to Galina's or after me, that I have a line on Saul, and that Julius is out and making trouble. Tell her to find and burn those evocation sites as fast as she can. I don't have locations."

He was scratching furiously on a pad of paper again. "Anything else?"

"Call the Badger. Have her check every John Doe homicide in the last three weeks for anything funky. And *do not step foot outside.* I don't want to rescue you, too."

"Oh, for fuck's—come on, Jill. I don't go outside when you tell me to stay in. I just *don't.*"

"Good. Make sure Galina stays undercover too. And keep digging—cross-reference for any other hellbreed with a link to Perry that would need or just like virgin flesh to break out of Hell."

"You got it. Anything—"

"No. Stay inside." *And pray for me.* I didn't add that. He didn't need the stress. I did hang up, and leaned inside the pay phone for a moment, watching my car.

Belisa was helpless. It was the best shot I'd get. And she killed Mikhail.

I turned my right wrist over, looked at the scar. It was just the same—the print of Perry's lips, now flushed because of the etheric energy humming through it.

Mikhail.

"I don't care." My voice took me by surprise. "He must have had his reasons. He *had* to have his reasons."

Had Belisa killed him before he could find the way to tell me?

It doesn't fucking matter. Perry's out of the way for the moment. You've got a line on Saul. Go get him, then you can get to the bottom of the rest of this. And when it's over, you're going to seriously consider killing Perry. I don't care if the scar is useful, this is Too Far.

The nasty little idea that this was just what Perry would want me to think so he could damn me—or so he could help me damn myself—just wouldn't go away. So I ignored it.

Big mistake.

23

It was just as Perry said—a nice three-story in Greenlea, never my favorite part of Santa Luz.

Greenlea is just north of downtown, in the shopping district. If you're really looking, you can sometimes catch a glimpse of the granite Jesus on top of Sisters of Mercy, glowering at the financial district. But Greenlea's organic froufrou boutiques and pretty little restaurants don't like seeing it. Sometimes I think it's an act of will that keeps that particular landmark obscured from certain places in the city, especially around downtown.

The last time I'd been down here, I'd been tracking down a voodoo queen's rage before it could unleash a hellbreed's idea of a circus on my town. *That* would have been unpleasant, and Perry had been up to his eyebrows in it as well.

Crackerbox houses, postage-stamp yards, yuppies and the upwardly mobile jealously watching for any sign of weakness in their neighbors. The bitch who used to live out here—Lorelei—had made quite a living for herself from their petty squabbles, for a *very* long time.

Her bakery and coffee shop was now a place claiming to sell vegan Thai and Indian food. I shuddered at the mere notion, and Saul had looked puzzled when he saw the sign.

You can't explain vegan ethnic to a carnivore. You just *can't*.

The entire neighborhood—centered around one street with two high-end bookstores, vegan eateries, a coffee shop, and a couple of kitschy-klatch places selling overpriced junk—was quiet. There's a few antique stores down at one end, and a fancy bakery and two pricey bars at the other. This particular house was at Seventh and Mariposa, a high wooden fence around its tiny yard and every window glazed with venetian blinds. Everyone was at work, looking to afford the property taxes, and the main shopping drag was two blocks over. The street was quiet, but it wouldn't stay that way when quitting time arrived and the hipsters came home.

I parked two blocks away behind a closed-down whole-foods warehouse just to be sure, then pushed Belisa into the backseat and laid her down, making sure the pin holding the collar closed was secure. The chain rattled. She sighed. Her flayed feet were healing. Long tangled dark hair, and if she closed her eyes you could see where she would be pretty. The exotic sort of woman a man would look twice at on the street.

But those black eyes were holes into another place. She didn't close them. I had to watch for a few seconds to make sure she was blinking.

My right hand moved. The gun was out of its holster in a hot heartbeat, barrel pressed against her forehead. It would be so *easy*, and the mess in the backseat wouldn't be the worst thing I've ever cleaned up.

No, Jill. Don't do it.

She blinked again. Utterly helpless. Revulsion twisted my stomach.

Not this way. If you kill her, make it clean. Don't be like what you hunt.

You don't live long as a hunter if you're not willing to just get the fucking job done, with whatever means are to hand. But there is a line you cannot cross, and the only guide for where that line is rests inside your skull. You could call it conscience, I guess. It's not your teacher or your lover, it's not even God. Because you can fool all of them, some of the time. When it counts.

The only person you take accounting with as a hunter is *yourself.* And I knew as surely as I was breathing, if I pulled the trigger on Melisande Belisa right now, I would be damning myself. It would be easy for Perry to own me after that step.

I breathed out a soft curse. I was wet with sweat, the way I never am unless I've been fighting hard. The clammy-cold film reeked of adrenaline and a bitter copper tang.

Fear.

It was a struggle to put the gun away. My arm actually physically resisted, muscles locking. I tipped my head back and swore, and finally got the .45 back in its dark little home.

I closed Belisa in the car and left her there. It would get hot with the thin winter sun beating down, but I found I didn't care.

I shimmied up over the board fence from the house next door and dropped down cat-soft. Drew my right-hand gun again, surveyed the backyard. The grass hadn't been cut, and the entire house was a brackish bruise of etheric contamination.

Oh yeah. We've got hellbreed. Hang on, Saul. I'm coming.

No cover. It was bare as a bone except for metallic trash cans clustered near the high wooden gate to the front. Coming over that way might have caused a racket.

Three concrete steps up to the back door. My blue eye caught no betraying quiver of ill intent, nothing to suggest there were hellbreed here beyond the thick etheric bruising. No hint of Saul.

But then, they would want to keep him well hidden. In a basement, probably, since the picture had shown him on concrete.

Hold on, baby. I'm on my way.

A thin high horsetail cloud scudded in front of the sun, the light darkening a bit. It was a bad omen, but it was still daylight.

The doorknob was ice-cold. I exhaled softly between my teeth, sorcery tingling in my fingers. The scar tensed, sensing something it was akin to. I wondered if Perry had managed to get out of the iron rack yet, banished the thought. Sorcery requires fierce, relaxed concentration, and if I kept thinking about Perry and what he'd told me I was going to be anything but relaxed.

The deadbolt eased free with a *snick*. I winced, waited. No sound. It was child's play to undo the other lock, and I twisted the knob a little at a time. It eased free.

I shoved it open, stepping to the side in case they opened fire, then stepped back and dove through, rolling to come up in a crouch. It was a hall that had been turned into a utility room, a washer and dryer standing to attention and a little bamboo-mat thing to clean your shoes.

Dead silence, sunlight falling through windows. The gun tracked, every inch of me alert and quivering, ready for all hell to break loose.

Nothing. Not a peep. A tang of hellbreed corruption, sick-sweet, and a fading ghost of dark spice and clean fur, familiar to me as my own breath.

Saul.

Nothing. No betraying creaks or little whispers, no sense of breathing habitation houses get when someone's around. I braced my back against the wall, drawing my other gun. My stomach turned over hard as I gapped my mouth, tasting the air. There was another smell under the perfume of supernatural. It was the gassy note of mortal death.

No.

The kitchen was as empty as a dry well, all the cabinets closed and the sinks clear. Whoever lived here was a big believer in minimalism. Either that or they spent so much money affording the house they couldn't buy more than a cheap round table and two scavenged chairs.

There was the door that probably led to the cellar, open just a crack. Nothing but darkness beyond. I ghosted up to it through two bars of wintry sun, toed it until it swung wide and disclosed wooden stairs going down into absolute darkness. There was a light switch, difficult to flip with my elbow but I managed it. The little sound it made was loud in the thick silence.

I was suspecting there weren't any hellbreed in the house. If there weren't...

The stairs were solid, at least. I hate going down cellar stairs, they're often open and something reaching through to grab you isn't just for horror movies. So I went down fast, easier to keep my balance *and* gave me an edge if anything was waiting to trip me up.

But there was nothing. I reached the bottom, slid along the wall, and ended up in a defensible corner.

The cellar was empty. The concrete floor was cracked and uneven in places, but I could see the marks where something very heavy had been scraped around.

There were other marks, too. A smear of something that was red paint, a different color from the faint bloodstains. And something else. A shapeless lump of material. Suede, its fringes lying dead and discarded.

Hot bile whipped the back of my throat. It was a good thing I *hadn't* eaten. I would have spread every bite of it over the concrete floor.

A faint whispering sound. My head jerked up, tracking it. A rushing, like water. My blue eye pierced the etheric bruising for a second; I saw the geometric shapes of a hellbreed curse sparking and flowing in an intricate pattern.

The Talisman sang, a high piercing note. I immediately bolted for the steps, and that was probably what saved me. Because I smelled smoke, and the house overhead exploded with a dry *wump* that sucked a draft of cool air past me. I made the kitchen just in time to dive for the utility room as a wall of orange flame with blue wires at its edges burst through from the living room. The curse had triggered up on the top floor and moved down, probably to catch me like a rat in a rain barrel.

Another trap. I'd walked right into it, and I had a sneaking suspicion the owners of this place would be among the dead near the freeway.

And the hellbreed had moved Saul.

*   *   *

I dove out the back door a bare fraction of a second before the wall of hell-fueled fire coughed free. Rolled, came up and swept the yard with both guns. Nothing but the pale glare of fire in sunlight, sweeping up the brick like great, grasping, throb-veined hands, the flames oily and edged with blue. The heat was monstrous, crisping the grass as I skipped back. The board fence was smoldering.

Holy shit. I ran up against the boards, not quite believing what I was seeing. Survival took over, the guns were stowed, and I was on top of the fence in a heartbeat, balanced like a tightrope walker.

Something exploded. The concussion blew me off the fence. I flew, weightless, hit another fence hard, wood splintering in great jagged pieces. Glass shattered—the shock wave blew out windows in neighboring houses. I hit something else with a snapping *crunch* and found myself in the ruins of a kid's swing set. The cheap metal had twisted and bent instead of breaking, or I'd have been wearing some of it *through* me.

It was broad fucking daylight. Next would come sirens and attention. I swore internally, struggled to my feet, and vanished.

24

The sun was sinking fast when my pager buzzed. I picked a sliver of glass out of my hair and sighed. Belisa sighed too, in the backseat.

I didn't like that.

Of the four locations Perry had given me, three had evidence of Saul's presence...and traps. I was now certain—the kind of cold certainty that settles on me halfway through a case—that the people who had lived in each place were all resting in the morgue.

The fourth locale, a dun-painted McMansion on the edge of the suburbs, had the carpet yanked up in the empty master bedroom, marks on the floor where a huge heavy object had been placed, probably brought in through the French doors. There were *also* five little guard-breed—little yappy things that looked like Lhasa Apsos with burning-red eyes. One of them had sunk vicious, needle-sharp teeth into my calf before I could break its neck. I would have worried about the sound of gunfire, except the mansion's neighbors were far enough away that it didn't matter.

Goddamn little dogs. Of course, if they were as large as German shepherds they'd be much more dangerous. They were just a demonic *annoyance*, especially if you had other 'breed or Traders to worry about.

But there hadn't been anything bigger. I was chasing my own tail, goddammit.

I dug the pager out. They had to be moving Saul every few hours. I should have known they would, especially if Perry had any notion of where he was likely to be held. Now I was wishing I *had* cut him, and cut him deep.

That wouldn't have led you to Saul. Of course, this isn't doing a whole hell of a lot, either.

I found a Circle K and pulled into the lot. Glanced back at Belisa, made sure the collar was still snugly on. Here I was ferrying around a woman I should have killed on sight. God had a sick, sick sense of humor.

But I knew that. I'd known it since I was five years old.

"No sense," I whispered to the pager's glow. "This makes no fucking sense. As usual."

But I was not quite being honest with myself. I had a bad bad feeling, down deep in my gut.

I dialed, it rang twice and she picked up. "Jill."

"Hey, Badge. What do you have for me?"

She got right down to business. "You wanted to know about funky John Does in the last three weeks?"

"Yeah?" I tried not to feel like a bloodhound straining at the leash.

"Rosie and I have been digging all day. The short answer is, there's none. But there's something else."

"Like what?" Her sense of the weird was almost as finely tuned as Carper's had been. I shut my eyes at the thought of Carp, sleeping under a counterpane of green.

"Like disappearances up twenty percent. Rosie crunched some numbers. Adult disappearances are holding steady. It's the kid ones that are accounting for the bump."

"Huh." If it was summer, the numbers might make sense. Kids get into trouble when school's out, here as well as everywhere else.

But a spike of twenty percent? That was something. In winter too. "When did it start?"

"Let's see...two weeks ago, missing persons reports did a sudden jump. Among kids too young to be runaways. We took a look at unsolved numbers in the last two weeks compared to unsolved over the last three years, and allowed for a certain percentage of retrievals—"

"Badge, you're a wonder." The sun slid below the horizon, and Santa Luz took its regular nightly breath before the plunge.

"Don't I know it. And they're up twenty percent, even accounting for variables in weather and unemployment. Does that help?"

Kind of. It tells me we are *looking at a new high-level hellbreed in town, a hungry one. What were those evocation altars for? Just to keep me chasing my tail? To bring through someone else?*

A sudden, blinding thought occurred to me. The victims I'd taken the *bezoar* from had to have been virgins, but it might have been a fluke or a crime of opportunity. In Anya's territory, the virgin flesh might have been just to create extra punch in doing an evocation while the moon was wrong. Nothing pierces the walls of Hell like innocent flesh—and if they were attempting an evocation out of phase to bring someone *else* through, they'd need all the help they could get.

The pattern showed itself for a blinding moment. The scar buzzed on my wrist, etheric energy jolting up my arm. The *bezoar*, securely caged, twitched madly in my pocket as if someone was yanking at my coat. I looked up, and every sorcerous sense I had informed me shit was about to get ugly.

I didn't need intuition to tell me that. All I had to do was look at the creeping dusklit shadows clustering up to my car. Those shadows had eyes like flat russet coins, and teeth that sparked with phosphorescence. They hunched and lunged through the shadows with the peculiar, crippled speed of the damned.

"Jill?" Badger said cautiously. "You still there?"

"Gotta go. Keep digging, give my best to Rosie. And thanks." I hung up, drew my guns. One of the low twisted things leapt up on the trunk of the Pontiac, and the car's springs groaned as it growled. Its muzzle twisted up, showing ancient, yellowed teeth. Its front paws were shaped like hands except for the two or three extra fingers, enlarged knuckles, and tarnished ivory claws. It dented the metal, and irrationally, all I could think of was the paint job.

"Son of a *bitch*," I yelled, and launched myself forward. They melded out of the gathering dark, four of them, and spread out. *Oh, this is gonna be fun.*

At least I was sure I'd been poking around in the right way. They wouldn't send *rongeurdos*—bonedogs—after me if I hadn't been wandering around closer and closer to the truth.

The first one coiled down on its haunches, sprang with a deadly scraping of claws on concrete. I faded to the side, hit it twice at the top of its leap. It fell with a thump,

steaming and scrabbling as blessed silver punched a hole
in its shell and fragmented, filling it with poison.

The worst thing about the bonedogs is that they hunt in
packs. The best thing? They die and *stay* down when you
breach them with silver shot. And they never run by day.

Of course, that didn't do me any good now.

As soon as I put that one down, another was leaping for
me. I heard the little *ding* as the Circle K's door opened,
and I hoped nobody was coming out to take a look at the
ruckus. You'd think even in the suburbs they would know
to stay indoors when they hear gunshots.

My own leap was reflex, like a cat jumping back from
a striking snake. I landed hard, already pitching to my
right to draw them away from the convenience store's
entrance and whoever was stupid enough to be walking
in or out. My boot flashed out, and the crunching shock
of it meeting a *ronguerdo*'s face jolted all the way up to
my hip, but I was already turning and shooting the other
one with both guns. *Pushing* off, arms pulled close and
angular momentum conserved enough to give me a spin.
When I faced the other two my left hand held my whip
instead of a gun, and I felt much more sanguine about the
situation. The whip jingled as I shook it, assuring myself
of free play. "All right, you sonsabitches." My voice, a
bright thread over the deep twisting Helletöng-accented
growls. "Come get some."

The Talisman thumped on my chest, its song of
destruction hiking up a notch.

One hung back as the other slunk forward, head down
and lips lifted over a slavering snarl. Yellow foam spattered, writhing into cracks in the pavement in long oily
ropes.

I was bracing myself for the one in front to leap when the one behind flung its head up and howled.

The howl was answered. Eastward, another cry lifted into the night. Then, to the south, another one.

Oh, fuck. Kill them quick, Jill.

I swung forward. Hip leading for the whip work, the force uncoiling through me and flinging out through my hand, gun speaking at the same moment as the bonedog jerked aside to avoid jingling razor-sharp silver. The second, his duty done, leapt too, but I'd gotten the first right through his broad canine skull. He dropped like a stone and I had the last one to worry about.

The last one was the smartest. He looked at me, those eyes widening and turning bright crimson instead of a low punky russet glow. The sky was indigo now. In winter, night falls quick and hard in the desert.

The thing scrabbled backward, turned tail, and ran.

I leapt for my car. Fast as I am, I can't follow a bonedog on foot. With a V8 under me, though, I can track it as far as possible.

If the *bezoar* was reacting, I could track it even farther. That masked son of a bitch might have survived, but he wouldn't survive what I was about to do to him. I could find out who he was really working for as a bonus.

But I thought I knew. And the knowledge chilled me all the way down to the bone.

You've gone too fucking far this time, you son of a bitch.

I piled into the car. She roused with a purr, and her tires smoked as I spun the wheel. I let off the brake and peeled out. There was an *oof* from the backseat, but I couldn't do more than glance in the rearview and get a jumble of shadowy impressions, a flash of pale-copper flesh and the chain jingling. A merry, Christmas-like sound, but if you knew the real story behind Santa Claus you'd probably never want to hear sleigh bells again.

Hellbreed aren't the only things that like tender little children. And don't even get me started on the Tooth Fairy.

The bonedog was just visible down the street, nipping smartly around to the right. I gunned the engine and the Pontiac leapt for it, happy to be going fast again. The knocking in the upper registers of the engine's roar was even *more* pronounced, I was really going to have to nail that down—

I checked the rearview again. Shadows ran like ink on wet paper. Little spots of red in the distance, loping along two by two.

More bonedogs.

The accelerator was already jammed against the floor.

Now it was a race.

25

$\mathcal{A}$ long, looping trail of rubber came to an abrupt stop. Something had blown in the engine. It didn't matter—I bailed out, not caring that Belisa had rolled forward and was now half on the floor in the back.

She could stay there. I'd settle her hash after I settled Perry's, when this was done.

The gates were shaking like epileptic hands. They banged together, and Henderson Hill rose behind them.

But something was wrong. It should have been a starlit sky, the waxing moon already risen like a yellow-silver coin. Instead, the vault of heaven was black, the stars blotted out and an unnatural dark covering my city like an old, veined hand.

Oh, this isn't going to be fun.

I timed it just right, plunged between the gates. The Hill closed around me, I didn't have time to slow down and see if it was going to try to make things tricky. Besides, something *else* was wrong—the bath of ice-cold prickles was much weaker than it should have been. I should have been hopping one step ahead of Henderson Hill's voices, sparking off the thick sludge of etheric bruising.

Instead, the ghosts rushed at me in rotting cheesecloth veils. Their mouths were open in distorted screams. They poured through and past as if I was an empty door, splashing against the threshold where the bonedogs pulled up short, snarling.

The *bezoar* went nuts inside my pocket, straining against the silver cage and the leather. Buzzing like an angry bumblebee. A really big one.

One of the bonedogs put a paw over the threshold and snatched it back with a Helletöng-laden squeal, like metal rubbing against itself in an empty, echoing stadium. The Hill's ghosts trembled on the edge of visibility, twisting together in boneless contortions to make a weird flowing screen.

A long black smear was the remains of the bonedog I'd chased in here. It bubbled, the eyes rolling free like weird crystalline fruits, the nerve roots decaying strings of quartz.

Now that's weird. Back here again, just like a bad dream. And why does it feel so strange, Jill? Oh, this is great. Just fucking great.

I didn't stop to ask myself why the Hill's ghosts would be holding the bonedogs back. I just dug in my pocket for the *bezoar* while lengthening my stride, and bolted for the lowering bulk of Henderson Hill.

The sky was still featurelessly black. I kicked in a boarded-up door, the *bezoar* rattling and straining when I shoved it back in my pocket. I found myself staring at a hall with a slight upward slope. This was the building on the north side of the quad, a huge brooding monstrosity. It vibrated with agony and fear, but something was muting the force of the Hill's terrible cold unlife.

The doors marching down the hall jerked and shuddered. Normally they'd be opening and closing hungrily, and the entire hall would stretch to infinity, a trick of light and shade. There was a long smear on the floor, some dark weeping fluid, and I hopped over it. *Making a lot of noise. They have to know I'm coming.*

That's okay, an iron voice inside me replied. *Get Saul, kick their asses, and close up whatever door they're opening to Hell. One two three, easy as can be.*

I should have checked the entire Hill for a secondary evocation site. Either that or they'd come back, since this was too good a snack to resist for whoever they were bringing through. But goddammit, physical 'breed didn't come up here!

Unless the reward—or the threat by their master on the other side of the walls separating worlds—was greater than the cost.

Up the hall, avoiding the heavy doors as they sluggishly swung wide to catch at the unwary, the *bezoar* straining against the leather of my coat and sending up a thin keening sound. I smelled smoke, the Talisman rumbling against my chest, and when I reached the top of the slope and the circular hall around the huge operating theater opened up, I was prepared for the crosscurrent, a psychic torrent raging around the still, horrible eye of where a great many of the old Hill's worst excesses had gone down.

I was so braced for it, as a matter of fact, that I almost

fell over when it didn't show up. I actually stopped for a moment, braced in the threshold.

The hall should have been alive with screaming faces, weird noises, and a strong current of not-quite air pushing against every surface. Instead, it was a dingy, institutional hallway, curving out of sight on either end. My breath still puffed out in a freezing cloud, and my hair still stirred on a not-quite breeze.

But the roaring weirdness was gone.

Shit, shit shit—I hooked around the corner, running for the secondary door to the operating theater.

The one they used to wheel the bodies out through.

There were windows, long narrow strips of chicken-wire-laced glass up too high for anyone to peer through them. Maybe they were psychological. They ran with diseased blue light, the corners dripping fat little blobs of it to sizzle against the chipped layers of yellow paint. The scar sent a jolt of agonizing pain up my arm, but my hand didn't waver, freighted with the gun. My boot soles pounded on the water-damaged linoleum. Each step seemed to take a lifetime, but I knew I was moving much faster than an ordinary human—or even an ordinary hunter.

I skidded, turning, and hit the secondary door with megaton force. The Talisman's thrumming went up a full octave, and my aura began to sparkle with little sea-urchin specks of light. The door exploded, steel flying as shrapnel—

—and I was through, rolling, coming up with both guns and taking in the lay of the land.

The operating theater was concave, with two or three concrete terraces that used to hold audiences back in the days of electroshock and experimentation. The space at the bottom of the bowl was wide enough for two iron cages, one of them twisted and battered a bit, and an altar. The fluorescent glare of the lights blinked and buzzed, and the entire place was just *full* of robed, cowled hellbreed.

I shot the first one and didn't have time to check the cages. Because between them, right where the central operating table would have sat, was an evocation altar—a pulsing blot of blackness and corruption. And atop it was a pale spinning oval of light.

It was an egg, and if they kept feeding it etheric force it would crack, and when it did the walls between here and elsewhere would gap just a little, and *something* would slip through.

Something old and hungry that Jack Karma had sent back to Hell during a firestorm in Dresden, decades ago.

The 'breed exploded into motion. I'd already put down two of them, one with a head shot and another with a glancing blow. Now all I had to do was stay one step ahead of them, and not shoot whoever was in the cages.

One of the hellbreed screamed, Helletöng like metal and glass buildings rubbing each other during an earthquake, and the curse hit me squarely. Right in the gut. The world turned over, I flew up toward the ceiling, but that was okay—twisting in midair, shaking the remains of the 'breed's curse like so much water from a duck's back, still firing. The fragments of hellbreed nastiness flew free, flapping their leathery wings, so many pieces of shadow careening through space. Momentum bled, etheric force crystallizing around me, and I hit the ceiling a glancing blow. Old warped glass fixtures shattered.

Falling, then. I was going to hit hard, braced myself, still firing. By the time I crunched into one of the concrete terraces with a terrible snapping sound, I had my whip free. It slithered, hit the floor, and my ribs ran with agonizing pain. The scar burned, burrowing into my flesh like acid, and the 'breed leapt for me, hanging in the air with his robe and cowl fluttering, arms up, claws extended, and his legs drawn up like a spider flicked into a candle flame.

Split-second reflex was all I had. The whip's end was airborne, my side giving a hot flare of spiked agony as muscles pulled against broken ribs. I caught him as he was already heading down from the apex of his leap, the other 'breed hanging back for some reason, and that was bad news.

He was slight and dark, with a handsome bladed face the flechettes tore across with a smart crackling jingle. Skipping aside, reaching the next terraced step up and my legs bending and tensing, flung up with a leap that was half instinct and half desperation. If they were avoiding me, waiting for this guy to finish me off, he was probably a Big Cheese. I had never seen him before, which meant he wasn't local.

Which, ten to one, told me I was looking at Perry's boss, the one trying to bring Argoth through. He did look kind of like a handsomer Buster Keaton, right down to the pouting lips.

And since Perry could produce hellfire in the blue spectrum, his boss was likely to be more badass than one tired hunter could handle.

For a brief moment I thought of unleashing the Talisman. But with the spinning egg over the evocation altar hungrily grabbing at all the power it could find, that was a monumentally bad idea.

Dammit.

Julius howled, and the windows shattered, blown outward. I gained my footing on the uppermost tier of concrete, a few busted wooden seats to my left and clear running room to my right. Shook the whip free as my ribs fused together with heavy red pain, the scar like hot lead whittling deeper and deeper as I aimed. *One shot, God, come on, one shot, give me a good shot here—*

I pointed and squeezed, praying.

I hit him. I knew I hit him, too—his sleek head snapped back and black ichor flew.

But then his chin came down, the hurt sealing itself over and the hard carapace of a hellbreed flowing like so much molten sugar, and he hissed at me, baring his pearly, shark-sharp teeth.

I heard a high nasty giggle from one of the watching 'breed, and braced myself. This was going to hurt, and I was down to four shots left in the extended clip.

Goddammit.

The lights—and who the hell changed the bulbs in here, anyway?—flickered. Glass rained down, and the bits of curse flapped in lethargic circles. The scar gave an agonizing wet crunch of pain, and I hissed in a breath, broken ribs twitching with pain. Every hellbreed in the operating room crouched except Julius, whose blue eyes widened—

—before more glass shattered. Perry resolved out of thin air and knocked him on his ass. The screen of bland normality over Perry had dropped, and for a heartbeat or two I saw *underneath*—the thing that inhabited his shell snarled and crouched before leaping down toward the altar, on a trajectory that would take him right to where Julius was landing.

Go figure. I was actually not unhappy to see him. Despite the fact that he was playing me and his boss off against each other for some reason.

My fingers moved mechanically, tucking the whip and reloading. I was almost able to aim again before one of the other 'breed decided to take care of what the boss couldn't, and as I threw myself away toward the wooden chair, I saw the mask fluttering over the lower half of his wax-white face and knew who I was facing.

Oh yeah. This just keeps getting better.

26

Rule number two of fighting 'breed: *keep moving*. Even if your ribs are broken and your entire body feels like it's been passed through a meat grinder, don't slow down. Slowing down means dying.

What little I could see of the masked 'breed's face was a ruin of scar tissue. Guess Belisa hadn't put him down for good, but it wasn't for lack of trying. I bounced like a jackrabbit, whip uncurling, knew he'd dodge, and swung back, my leg flashing out to kick a lean dark cowled 'breed in the face. The shock jolted all the way through me, but it did knock the son of a bitch away and into a snarling mass of 'breed vying to take Perry's guts out the hard way. Including Julius, but Perry seemed to be doing all right and I had all I could handle in front of me.

I landed on the twisted cage to the right and snapped a glance down. It took a moment for it to register, because I immediately had to hop aside, my whip flying out again and my gun speaking with a sharp crackling roar. The recoil grated in my shoulder. The scar writhed on my wrist like a live thing. I landed on the other cage, and the roaring of the thrashing hellbreed kicked up a notch. They hit the altar squarely, and the pale egg of etheric force began to spin.

That's not good. So not good. But I couldn't worry about that, because the masked 'breed was stalking me again, and this time I was sure he wasn't a copy. He was just too goddamn fast, and he had his little tabi booties on, the bastard.

And to top it all off, the cages were empty.

What the hell? But I had no time, because Perry was thrown back like a meteorite, a streak of black ichor and the incandescence of pure unholy rage trailing him. He hit the concrete so hard he dented it, and the *crack* was loud enough to drown out everything else.

Julius snarled and leapt on him, I shot the masked 'breed twice, and began to think of how I could get out of here while Perry was still ass-deep in angry 'breed. If Saul and Gilberto weren't here—but there was that pale egg of light needing to be dealt with, and the evocation altar too. Good luck calling up banefire while dealing with the Great Masked Ninja in Pajamas.

There was only one thing to do.

This is going to hurt.

Tensing, stupid body bracing itself for a hit it knew was coming, I leapt from the top of the cage, my boots skidding on the slick iron. Falling, right for the pale egg. The silver I carried, not to mention my hard thick exorcist-trained aura, would disrupt it. I'd be thrown like popcorn, again. I'd been doing a lot of that lately.

I might also lose an arm or a leg. Or more. Details,

details. But I'd slam the door closed on the toes of the 'breed trying to come through, and that was worth the risk.

It's always worth the risk.

I hung in the air for a long crystalline second. The body was still flinching, like that was going to change the outcome. The rest of me kept firing, the masked 'breed having realized what I was going to do and spitting a stream of curses like rancid lasers at me. They were too slow. I was going to make it.

But the world paused, the way it will do when something truly significant happens. There, in the door I'd kicked in, a pair of familiar figures: one male, one female. The female had a vacant smile, her black eyes wide and hungry as collapsed neutron stars. The collar around her slim neck had rubbed through her skin, biting into her shoulders as well, and blood slid down her tattered blue silk. The Chaldean wasn't healing her fast enough.

The other was the caretaker, his filmed eyes wide and the clarity around him brighter than the fluorescents. He reached up, slowly, and his clever thin fingers touched the locking pin holding the chain to the collar. Hellbreed hung in the air, their motion arrested, and I saw—No, I thought I saw...

No, I *saw*. I saw the light shining through the caretaker's façade of mute blind scarring, his hair turning a feathery gold—and the things behind him, reaching up in spires of snowy white, what were they? Wings, but not of any terrestrial bird. Glowing, in a way that seemed oddly tip-of-the-tongue familiar.

My blue eye *burned*, a twinge of acid fire spearing back into my brain. I could not look away from the light, dear God, the *light* pouring through him like dawn breaking, a dawn that was not tired or old...

What the hell?

The pin holding the chain to the collar clicked free. The chain slithered, clashing all the way down, but the collar stayed put. Melisande Belisa inhaled sharply, and hurtful intelligence came back into her black eyes. She looked across the confused jumble of 'breed doing their best to kill each other, and I swear to God I saw an awful sanity in her gaze.

The caretaker's lips were moving. He whispered in her ear, his eyes unfilmed for a long terrible moment, piercing blue casting shadows against her face. The shadows of Chaldean moving over her aura flinched back from that blue glow.

The chain finished hitting the floor with a slither, and she was already moving. Time made a snapping sound, like a huge rubber band breaking, and the noise of an almighty huge fight broke over me like a wave. My hair blew back on a breeze from nowhere, my coat flapped, and something out of the ordinary had indeed happened.

Because instead of falling into the oval of light and cutting off the door between here and Hell, I landed with bonecracking force in *front* of the altar, a short howl escaping my abused lips. And the masked 'breed was on me in a heartbeat. I shot him twice, but he was too close.

Now it was time for knife work.

He tried to grab my head and slam it into the altar's base. I wriggled away, and he'd taken so much damage he was moving slowly, at least for him. I jerked my leg up, the bony part of my knee sinking into what passed for his groin and meeting something weirdly squishy. That was only a distraction, though, because my largest knife had sunk in to the hilt, only the crossguard stopping it from vanishing into his belly. I wrenched it back and forth, the reek of hellbreed guts spilling free assaulting me. Hot noisome fluids bathed my hand.

The noise was incredible. Now I knew what happened when a Sorrow went up against a 'breed. It wasn't pretty. But between her and Perry, Julius might have a lot of trouble, and if I could just get *up*—

The assassin slumped atop me, corruption racing through his tissues. His fingers flexed, and I half-swallowed a scream. His claws grated between my ribs, and I was losing yet more blood. The scarring on his coppery face cracked apart, fine noxious dust bleeding out.

That meant he was dying. Thank God. I'd worry about the next 'breed to step up and start committing assassinations when I survived this.

If I survived this.

Get up, Jill.

But there was a problem with that. My body would not obey me. I blinked warm wetness out of my eyes, every muscle tensing and the scar a cicatrice of fierce heat on my wrist. There was a horrible *draining* sensation, worse than any blood loss I'd ever felt. A warm lassitude spread up my ankles.

I stared up at the pale egg. It was spinning now, filaments of it reaching out and snagging the flying bits of curse as they got too close. Each little bat-flapping thing went into the hungry maw. That was where most of the nasty psychic force of the Hill had gone, too. A nice snack for whoever was waiting under Hell's dry screaming skies, probably impatiently tapping a clawed and twisted foot.

He would have to step through to claim that snack, though.

And he can't do that if you get up and stop him. So DO it!

Swearing at myself didn't work. But my body twitched. Something hit the floor next to me—a hellbreed claw, ripped free of its owner's body and smoking with corruption. It twisted and flexed, wet, rancid dust pouring out of it in veined streams.

Will and life roared back into me. There was an odd ringing in my ears. My body suddenly obeyed, jerking up off the floor. A split second later, something huge barreled for me and I leapt aside instinctively, knife in one hand and my whip flashing out. It hit the bleeding mass of Julius squarely, and his resultant roar was a wall of warm air pushing me back. My boots slipped in greasy crud—bits of hellbreed rained down, plopping obscenely and still twitching as they hit.

A blue blur streaked by. Belisa, her battered feet slapping the stone and her mouth a rictus of effort, leapt with fluid effortless authority onto Julius. She clawed at him, screaming in the heavy consonant-laden mess of Chaldean, the bruising of the parasite on her aura turned as dark and sonorous as mountain thunder. Perry, just as battered and wearing a mad death's-head grin, was right behind her. They descended on the hapless 'breed, and I snapped a glance up.

The room that had been full of Hell's citizens was now an abattoir. Rotting bits of 'breed were *everywhere*. My breath came in short, hard sobs; the scar went back to chuckling as it tasted the death and misery riding the air. It sent a jolt up my arm, and the terrible draining sensation swirled away.

Julius howled. Both of them were ripping at him, like a pair of wolves at a carcass. His head smashed against the altar, right where mine had been a few seconds ago. Bile burned the back of my throat, I retched silently and pointlessly. Belisa made a guttural noise, the chanting in Chaldean hitting a vicious peak and the collar flashing with deep gold, and she finally grabbed Julius's head in her strong slender hands.

I was expecting a quick movement and the green-stick crack of a breaking neck. But no. Her flexible thumbs dug and gripped, and she popped his eyes like two over-ripe grapes. The 'breed's spine arced up into a hoop, his heels drumming the concrete, and corruption raced through his tissues.

If I'd eaten lately, it would have come up in a tasteless rush. As it was, I retched again and stumbled back, slip-ping and sliding. The floor was awash.

Perry was suddenly there, resolving out of thin air with a sound like nasty laughter trailing him. "Enjoying the show, my dear?" His ribs heaved, but he didn't sound at all out of breath. "What a pleasant little interlude. I've waited to do that for *so long*."

"P-P-P—" My lips refused to shape his name. I wasn't looking at him. I was looking *past* him, at the spinning egg. A hairline crack had appeared in its center, a thin line of darkness.

Melisande Belisa threw back her head and howled. It was an animal's cry, except for the all-too-human rage tinting it.

The hairline crack widened. My right hand swept

down, sheathed my largest knife, and was heading for my gun when Perry grabbed my wrist and squeezed, grinding the small bones together. "Oh, no you don't. She's expendable, my darling. I still have plans for—"

My left fist, braced with the whip handle, got him in the belly. It was a good solid punch, and that did make him lose all his air. My other fist crashed into his face and his head snapped back. I kicked him, too, and the Talisman made a rustling, roaring sound.

I hadn't used it, had I? No, if I'd used it this whole place would be a crater and the door to Hell would be busted wide open. And yet...

Perry went down. He slid back along the floor, fetching up against concrete with another stunning sound.

And the pale, spinning oval over the altar...

Cracked.

27

Belisa howled, a guttural, abused scream. A hairline crack, darker than the pit of a black hole, zigzagged through the spinning egg of light. It widened, just a little, and something white showed.

The Sorrow rose. She cast a glance back over her shoulder, her face slack and terribly graven. Bruises crawled over her skin, the shadows of Chaldean sorcery doing what they could to ameliorate the damage. But she was in bad shape, bleeding all over, her tangled hair smoking at each knot.

Each inch of silver on me ran with blue flame. My head was full of screaming noise.

"*Kill,*" Perry hissed, from where I'd kicked him. "*Kill it now!*"

I lifted my gun slowly. It was a terrible dream, fighting through syrup, my muscles full of lead.

Belisa's chin dipped wearily. She pitched forward just as the egg stopped spinning.

The thing that slid its malformed hand through the

barrier between this world and Hell twitched. I heard myself screaming, sanity shuddering aside from the sight. They do not dress when they are at home, and when they come through and take on a semblance of flesh it's enough to drive any ordinary person mad. Wet salt trickles slid down from my eyes, slid from my nose and ears.

They were not tears.

There was a rushing, the physical fabric of our world terribly assaulted, ripping and stretching. My screams, terrible enough to make the Hill shudder all the way down to its misery-soaked foundations. Perry, hissing in squealgroan Helletöng, and under it all, so quiet and so final, Mikhail's voice from across a gulf of years. Long nights spent turning over everything about his death, remembering him, all folding aside and compressing into what he would say if he was here. Or maybe just the only defense my psyche had against the *thing* struggling to birth itself completely.

Now, Mikhail said. *Kill now,* milaya. *Do not hesitate.*

My teacher's killer was in the way.

The scar crunched on my wrist. I squeezed the trigger. *Both* triggers, and I saw the booming trail of shock waves as the bullets cut air. Belisa's fingers had turned to claws, Chaldean spiking the soup of noise, and she tore at the not-quite-substantial flesh of the thing. Blue light crawled over her as if she wore silver, the same blue that the caretaker's eyes had flashed. The shadows of the Chaldean parasite flinched aside, for some incomprehensible reason.

I was still screaming as the bullets tore through her and the egg as well. The collar made a zinging, popping noise, the golden runes shutterclicks of racing, diseased light. Her body shook and juddered as she forced the thing behind the rip in the world *back*, and the physical fabric of the place humans call home snapped shut with a sound like a heavy iron door slamming. The bristling, misshapen appendage thumped down to the floor.

Belisa's fingers, human again, plucked weakly at the collar. She was a servant of the gods who were here long before demons, the inimical forces the shadowy Lords of the Trees trapped in another place long ago. It was a Pyrrhic victory; the *Imdarák* didn't survive, either. And the Sorrows are always looking to bring their masters back. The 'breed? Well, they're always looking to bring more of their kind. It's like two different conventions fighting over the same hotel.

If anyone could have slammed a door between here and Hell shut, it was a Sorrow.

But *why*? And the caretaker, what was he—

My knees folded. I hit the ground. Henderson Hill whispered around me like the end of a bell's tolling, reverberations dying in glue-thick air.

Oh, no.

Belisa folded over. I'd emptied a clip. Sorrows can heal amazingly fast, but she was probably exhausted after all the fun and games.

Her knees hit the concrete in front of the altar. Blood flowered, spattered on the floor. She shook her head, tangled hair swaying. The golden runes on the collar snuffed out, one by one.

"Ahhhhh." It was a long satisfied sigh, escaping Perry's bleeding lips. "Oh, yes. *Yessssssssss.*"

The scar drew up on my wrist and began to ache. This wasn't the usual burning as I yanked etheric energy through it. I tore my eyes from Belisa's slumped form and turned my right wrist up.

The print of Perry's lips was not a scar, now. It was *black*, as if the flesh itself was rotting, and it pulsed obscenely. As I watched the edges frayed, little blue vein-maps crawling under the surface of my flesh.

And I knew why. I could have shot around her.

But I'd chosen not to.

Melisande Belisa's body hit the floor too, next to the swiftly rotting hellbreed appendage. The last rune on the collar winked out. There was a terrible mortal stench—even a Sorrow's sphincter relaxes when death takes them. The blood spread out from her body in little tendrils. Soon it would make a pool. A lake.

The tendrils made a screaming face for a moment, traced on the cracked and blackened floor, before a wash of bright-red blood poured over and obscured it. I sagged, my mouth open and the gun falling out of my right hand.

"At last." Perry, on his feet now. He danced a little capering jig, and I saw one of his shoes had been lost somewhere. His sock was pale cream, and absolutely filthy. "A hunter of my very own. My darling one, my Kiss, we are going to—"

I don't know why he forgot I had another gun in my left hand. I raised it, and the shot took him right in the chest.

The scar shrieked with agony. But each time he'd fiddled with it over the years, each time he'd used it to fuck with my nervous system, he was training me to disregard it. My right hand curled up into a seizure-lock, but the left was fine. I got him twice more in the chest before he snarled and was on me, knocking the gun away. His free hand closed around my throat, and my back hit the floor. He snarled into my face, his breath an exhalation of spoiled honey, and I heard the buzz of dead metallic flies in a chlorine-painted bottle, bashing at the sides as they tried to escape.

I fought for leverage, but he was too quick and I was exhausted. And damned besides. The knowledge beat inside my head like a drum, robbing me of the clarity of a hunter's reactions. All I had left was...

...what?

Saul. It was like breaking water and taking a breath. "You. *You* have him. All the time, *it was you.*"

He'd played both me *and* Julius. The rest of the pattern came clear now. He hadn't been trying to bring a higher-up hellbreed through; he'd been stringing along the other 'breed trying to bring Argoth out. And Perry had set out to kill his immediate superior with my help as well—or with Belisa's. The whisper of Argoth was to keep me chasing my tail while he worked me into a corner—with the Talisman to knock me off balance and the revelation of Mikhail's bargain to keep me there. It was all a game, every set of obstacles balanced against the others and working at cross-purposes.

The prize wasn't any power or position game among 'breed. He wasn't playing to get any higher in the hierarchy.

No. *I* was the prize. And I'd fallen right into his trap.

He'd won. At last.

"Oh, darling. Not personally, of course." He leaned in and sniffed, taking a good lungful. It couldn't be pleasant—reek of hellbreed death, blood and human death, corruption and whatever foulness was spread all over me. "This has been so entertaining. And there's more to come." He grinned, a terrible grimace. "Via Dolorosa, my darling. At dawn. Don't disobey—or that black rot will start to spread. You won't like it."

I heaved up, but he shoved me back down. The extra strength from the scar had deserted me now. I was only weakly human, hunter or no, and my body started reminding me I'd been abusing it far past the norm, even for me.

Perry leaned forward. His tongue snaked between his bloodless lips, wet and cherry-red. A drop of clear liquid hung trembling at the tip. Little bits of blue hellfire danced and dazzled in whatever that liquid was, and I was suddenly very certain I didn't want it touching my skin.

The drop slid back up his tongue, hellfire crackling in the spaces between the scales. The rough tongue tip touched my cheek, flicking along the skin. It caressed my jawbone, slid down to touch the pulse beating a frantic tattoo in my throat. Rasping, dryly.

It reeled back up between his lips with a snap. The Hill shuddered again, and I exhaled. My right hand was still cramped up, my fingers an absurd claw.

But my left curled around a knife hilt. I braced myself slowly, tensing muscle by recalcitrant muscle.

"Come see me at dawn, my darling." He breathed in my face again, a hot dry draft from a desert of powdered bones. "I've waited for this *so* long. Best savored, don't you agree?"

I exploded into motion, slashing. But he was already gone, glass shattering and his footsteps a rapid light beat.

The Hill shuddered, settling in itself, and little sparkles began as my aura pushed against the psychic soup spilling into the nerve center of the hill like wine into a glass. The force that had been gathered, held to open a gap and feed a fresh hungry 'breed, was exploding out from confinement.

I had to get out of here.

I rolled to one side. Pushed myself up. A single drop of blood fell from my nose. It hit the concrete, flowered into a star.

I looked at the black traceries defiling the clean red. Melisande Belisa's body still slumped, the bruising of Chaldean settling in to do its work of erasing her from the world. They were dead the moment they took vows. Most of them had no choice, they were born into the Houses—a Mother impregnated by a soldier drone, bred like cattle.

Had I been aiming at her?

Why do you ask, Jill? You know you were.

Scrambled to my feet. My right hand relaxed slightly, fingers shaking out. I felt a plucking at the scar, but nothing else. No etheric energy swelled through it to mend my body, nothing. It might as well have been a rotting lump of flesh.

That's exactly what it is, Jill. The truth of what I'd done hit home. I'd solved two problems at once, but it hadn't been clean vengeance. I'd killed her because the entire time she'd been in the car, she'd been wearing on my nerves. It didn't matter that she was Perry's servant in all this.

I had killed her while she was helping to seal the rip in the world. And I'd done it not because she was a threat, but because I couldn't stand to have Mikhail's killer breathing one more moment.

I had damned myself.

The Talisman was a warm weight on my chest. It hadn't turned on me yet. How long would it last?

Just long enough, I promised myself.

My left hand could still make a base for the banefire. I concentrated, *hard*, as the flaming blue wisps fought me in a way they never had before. But they came, moaning and crying, and they *burned*. Bubbling, blistering the skin.

That sacred fire burned me.

I cast the banefire. It hit the altar and roared up in a sheet of cleansing flame. I could have stayed and let it take me too.

But I had things to do.

28

The sky had cleared, bright diamond points of stars glaring through the bowl of night.

The warehouse was echoingly empty. The Weres had cleaned up and restocked the fridge. The food probably wouldn't go bad—they'd gather here afterward for Saul, if I succeeded.

Not if, Jill. When. You're just damned, not out. But then I would move, and the leather cuff on my right wrist would rub against the blackened scar. A jolt of sick pain would go through me, and I would almost flinch.

I walked from room to room, stashing ammo, touching things. I'd never noticed how bare and drafty the entire place had looked before Saul moved in. The weapons and the clothes were mine. Everything else ... well.

The sheets were still tangled from the last time we'd rolled out of bed to catch Trevor Watling. Saul had slip-covered the old orange Naugahyde couch in pale linen, stocked the kitchen with cooking gadgets, arranged little things on shelves and even hung an ailing wandering Jew up in the living room, in a fantastically knotted macramé holder complete with orange beads and the faint smell of reefer—a thrift-store find he'd been so proud of. The laundry room was arranged the way he liked it, the detergent within easy reach and the eight different kinds of fabric softener sheets ranked neatly on top of the dryer.

Everywhere I looked, there was something he'd touched. I opened the kitchen cabinets, ran my knuckles over the fridge's cool white glow. The dishwasher had finished running, and it was full. The drying rack was full of the last load of pots and pans from breakfast, not arranged the way he would have, but still.

I filled up on ammo. Loaded a couple more clips. Considering writing a note. Decided it was a cliché. Anya would piece it together, one way or another.

Before I left, I stood for a long time in our bedroom door, looking at the peaks and valleys of the sheets and thin blankets. He ran warm, and I never needed much in the way of covers. We slept during the day, the bed set out in the middle of the floor so I could see anything creeping up on me.

The low hurt sound I was making shocked me back into myself. There were still other things to do. I'd just meant to come here to get some ammo, and...

The Eye twitched on my chest, a tiny dissatisfied movement. I wiped my cheeks and touched it with a tentative, tear-wet finger. No crackle of electricity. It wasn't going to get rid of me just yet.

But under the cuff, the blue veining was spreading from the blackened lip print. Up my arm, in tiny increments.

"God," I whispered. "You bastard."

I wasn't sure who I was talking to. Mikhail? Perry? God Himself?

I didn't have nearly enough time with him.

But I couldn't bitch about it. There was nobody else to blame. I'd damned myself.

The clock next to the bed showed the time in pitiless little red numbers. My car was dead, and I had to get to Via Dolorosa. I ached all over, healing sorcery crackling through me in little blue threads. It didn't burn like banefire, but it was probably only a matter of time.

Only human strength and healing.

It would have to be enough.

I made sure I had enough ammo. Stalked into the weapons room, stared at the long slim shape under its fall of amber silk. I couldn't take the spear—it was just asking for trouble. The sunsword might help, but one look at me and Galina would know there was something wrong. Plus, why drag more trouble to her door? She and Hutch were safe, and that was where I wanted them.

After all, I'd sucked at protecting Gil and Saul. Now every innocent in my city was going to be at risk. Perry had to have more of a plan, and without me to keep him in check…

Goddammit. There isn't any way out. There hasn't ever been.

I couldn't even blame God. *I'd* done it.

I came back to myself with a jolt. The clock read five minutes later. I'd just checked out, like a CD skip.

Can't afford to do that. Something left to do, Jill. Then you know what's going to happen.

I turned on one steel-shod heel. My coat flared out. I realized I was running my fingers over gun butts, checking each knife hilt, my hands roaming over my body like I was in a music video or something. I dropped them with an effort just as my pager went off.

I fished it out, gingerly. It was Badger again.

She could wait. Dawn was coming soon.

The cab let me off at the end of the Wailer Bridge, made a neat three-point, and drove away maybe a little faster than was necessary. The driver wasn't Paloulian—it was a big, thick good ol' boy in a flannel shirt and greasy jeans, with a ponytail under his bald spot and the radio tuned to AM talk.

It just goes to show you can get a cab to anywhere, even Hell. If you know how.

The eastern horizon was paling, scudding clouds over the mountains breaking up in cottony streamers. A faint glow of pink showed where the sun would crown and push itself up.

A long, long night was ending.

The bridge is a concrete monstrosity with high gothic pillars, built during the big public works binge of the thirties to try and keep Santa Luz from bleeding to death. Every once in a while someone would make noise about renovation, and about whose job it was anyway to pay for said renovation, and on and on. Then there would be a big public outcry about the homeless who lived under the bridge's glower on the river's banks, especially the ones you could see trudging over every morning, heading for downtown. They shuffled like the hopeless, and sometimes one of them would go over the side and into the water's uncaring embrace.

They were mine just like everyone else in Santa Luz. There were predators even here, and I'd chased cases over on this side of the river before.

Today, though, the Wailer stood empty. There wasn't even a stream of traffic for the industrial park and docks on the other side. I kept thinking that someday they were going to zone in some residential and spread up into the canyons like Los Angeles. But no, why do that and worry about landslides during spring downpours when you had the rest of the desert stretching away from the river's artery to fill up? There were a couple retreat mansions up there, mostly people with more money than sense, but nothing else.

Four lanes. A yellow line down the middle. The city really needed some dividers out here, but they were engaged with a running fight with county over who was going to pay for *that*. It's the oldest story of bureaucracy—who's going to foot the bill?

Except I knew who was going to be paying on this bridge today. It was yours truly.

I went slowly, looking for traps. Nothing on this side of the bridge, but it made an odd sound—humming a little, as if it was cables instead of concrete. The water underneath, and the rebar inside, would make it an excellent psychic conductor.

I stopped halfway, scanning with every sense I owned. Having the scar gone was like being blind; I hadn't realized how much I depended on hyperacute senses and jacked-up healing. I was back to being an ordinary hunter—about as far away from a normal person as possible, but still. I was used to so much more.

Nothing. Even my blue eye was oddly clouded.

The wind came off the river, ruffling my hair. I wondered what would happen when the silver started to burn my skin.

You've got a while, Jill. Use it.

This could have been just another ploy. But I didn't think it was. The glyph on the letter, tucked safely in one of my pockets, had to be Perry's name in their language. Or another lie—maybe Julius's. Perry had neatly double-crossed Julius as well. That's the thing about 'breed—they can't even trust each other.

What, after all, do you think Hell is?

The image of Belisa's body, slumped in front of the altar under a pall of bruise-dark Chaldean, rose up in front of me in vivid detail. I could have counted each of her tangled dark hairs and named every bruise and cut. Memory is a curse.

I'd known as soon as I fired that I'd done something wrong.

What the—

I whirled. Footsteps. Lots of them, and the sky was darker than it had any right to be. Dawn wasn't far off—but the closer to dawn, the harder the fight. And if what I was hearing wasn't just a trick of sound bouncing off the waters, I was in even deeper shit.

They massed at either end of the bridge. Hellbreed and Traders, a crowd of them. Bright eyes, painted lips, curve of hips and glimmer of dewy skin, the beauty of the damned on display. On the city side of the river, shapes appeared. I had to blink a couple times before they resolved into a coherent picture behind my eyes.

Crosses. They were carrying two twelve-foot crosses. A slight figure on one, a heavier male figure with silver in his hair in the other. My blue eye turned hot and dry, and I did not let out the breath I was holding until I could focus . . . and saw the glow of living creatures around both of them.

Gilberto slumped against whatever was holding him to the rough wood. Saul's head was down, his hair hanging. I saw lashings, instead of nails. They were only *tied* to the things.

The mockery made my stomach turn over hard. I swallowed hard, and almost wished I hadn't.

The Talisman made a low angry noise against my chest. A curl of smoke drifted up, tickled my nose. I eased my right-hand gun out. My hand might cramp up again if Perry wanted to play a little game, but I still had my left. Which closed around the bullwhip's handle, and I set my feet against the bridge's surface.

If a semi comes along, it's going to ruin this lovely picture. All of them coming out to see the hunter get hers. They're going to enjoy this.

"*Behold!*" someone screamed from above. I snapped a glance up—hellbreed, crawling on the bridge. Like maggots in a wound, seething. Except maggots actually did something useful by cleaning up dead flesh. "*The sacrifice!*"

Oh, honey, if you're talking about me, you'd best be warned. I'm not a good sacrifice. I tend to stick in the craw when you try to eat me. I bit back a murderous, contemptuous little laugh. The world narrowed down, became basic.

The only thing that mattered was getting Gilberto and Saul off those crosses. Saul might still be able to run, Gilberto was a chancier proposition, but either of them would stand a better chance if I could somehow get them free.

Where are you, you son of a bitch?

The scar crunched with sick pain, all the way down my cramping fingers. I blew out between my teeth.

There was Perry in a pale linen suit, capering in front
of the mob of hellbreed on the city side. His legs moving
in ways no biped's should, he cracked his heels together
and danced. The throng of 'breed and Traders were humming, a weird subsonic note with the squealing groan of
Helletöng underneath it, rubbing against the fabric of the
physical until it frayed.

They were about to bring the crosses onto the bridge.
Some of them were dancing too, little jig steps. Behind
Perry, to his left, Rutger minced. I could even hear the
tip-tapping of his ridiculous shoes against the road.

So, Rutger had been playing according to Perry's dic-
tates all along. Color me unsurprised.

"Thou Who has given me to fight evil," I whispered, my
lips barely shaping the words, "keep me from harm."

It was useless, just like everything else.

Now, Jill. Do some good.

I launched myself toward death. Without the scar's
eerie stuttering speed, but still—I was hunter enough to
move pretty damn fast. My heels struck sparks as my
stride lengthened, and a cry went up from the hellbreed on
the mountain side of the bridge. The entire structure reverberated, and the Talisman warmed against my skin. Like a
lover's hand, fingers trailing down between my breasts.

I needed my breath for running, but I heard a cry of
rising effort anyway. It was too high to be male, and it
echoed oddly. The crowd broke, streaming past Perry
and leaping for me. The crosses dipped crazily, and I
suddenly understood they were going to throw my Were
and apprentice over the side just to be assholes.

Well, it wasn't surprising. It even had a kind of mad
hellish poetry to it, just what you'd expect from Perry.

The scar was dead, but I pulled on it anyway. A thin trickle of etheric force slid through it, a wire of nasty heat up my arm. Perry stopped in mid-caper, his eyes blazing infernos. The thing that wore his human shell rippled through pale skin, and his grin was a shark's.

Gunfire. But I hadn't shot anyone yet. I was still just out of optimal range, and—

There was a commotion behind the screen of 'breed and Traders. Then the screaming started, and I was within range. I leapt as I reached the first of them, my own gun speaking. Howls and screams lifted—that's one thing about facing a crowd of Hell's citizens.

You don't have to watch where you shoot as much. And with the only two people who mattered to me up on the crosses, I didn't have to worry about hitting them.

My right hand seized up, the scar fighting for control. I could *feel* it, thin little tendrils of corruption yanking on muscles and nerves. But nightly murder will make shooting more than a habit. It will burn it so deep into your hands you don't have to think—if you're breathing you're fighting, and the scar wasn't deep enough yet to reach that yet.

It was a losing fight. But then, it always was. The tide of Hell is so broad, so deep, we can't hope to do more than hold it a little while.

I cannot hold back the tide forever. Another misdirection, a good one because it held the seed of truth. Perry hadn't wanted Argoth to come through and come gunning for me. He just wanted me to damn myself, and he'd worked it so I could. It had taken him years, but he'd done it.

The entire bridge shuddered, and I heard something

familiar. *Very* familiar. When Anya fights, she cusses almost as much as I do. I saw her, breaking through the hellbreed like an avenging angel, firing with both hands and moving inhumanly fast. Hunter-fast, as fast as I was moving now.

Behind her, there was a roil of struggling figures. Weres, more than I'd ever seen in one place before. They were swarming the Traders and trying like hell to stay out of the way of the 'breed. The 'breed were concentrating on Anya, but she was giving them so much trouble it was going to take a while.

And up on the top of one of the crosses, Saul raised his silver-starred head.

29

Crunch.

The whip snapped and Rutger danced back. Perry snarled. The scar boiling with agony on my wrist, I was too slow because I had to fight it. Its tendrils were all the way up to my elbow now, twisting and yanking.

I was screaming. My only battle cry now.

"Saul! Saul! Saul!" His name, over and over again, while the Weres clustered the Traders holding the crosses. Lionesses leapt, and if you haven't seen the Norte or Sud Luz pack lionesses work together to take down a kill, you've missed one of the most amazing sights on earth.

The huge splintered things jerked and danced crazily; Gilberto's head flopping and Saul moving, looking around. I couldn't watch, I had my hands full; Rutger skipped toe-tapping aside and Perry leapt for me. I faded to my left, firing, how I was going to reload with a cramping hand and the whip keeping them back was an open question. Perry darted in, took a shot in the shoulder, and snarled. My wrist bloomed with hot acid pain, and he wasn't bleeding the way he should have been.

That was worrying. If I'd had time to worry, that is.

I was still screaming Saul's name when Anya appeared, her arms up, the sunsword's silver length rising forever from her hands. Shock jolted through me.

She can't use that without a—

The Eye dilated on my chest, singing a long high sustained note of power.

This is why two hunters can take on an army of hellbreed. Because it never occurs to 'breed to give, or to help each other. Each one of them is out for himself, plain and simple, in any melee. None of them ever thinks to *share*.

You can't use a sunsword without a key. But I *reached*, an unphysical movement from the Eye on my chest toward the blade's hilt, a hand held out in thin air. A red glimmer showed in the empty space trapped in the sunsword's hilt, whirling as it strengthened.

I might have been damned, but I was still hunter enough to help her. She'd expected me to understand and use the Eye as the key, both of us working in tandem to hold back the tide.

Anya caught hold, strong slim mental fingers in mine. The silver in her hair crackled with blue sparks, and the sun was almost up over the horizon. If we could last long enough for it to break free, we might have a chance.

Flame blossomed against the sunsword's razor-silver edge. The Eye twitched on my chest, and the fire deepened golden-orange. A thin wire of white ran through the blade's center, the red gleam in the hilt suddenly a small star, and the fire coughed as it exploded free.

Dawn was early today. The light drenched the bridge,

and the leaping sinuous forms of the bonedogs howled and cowered. Rutger screamed, falling in slow motion, as the sword descended.

The scar fought, clawing at the meat of my arm, for control. I shot Perry again, but I was too slow, the world dragging me down and my body refusing to put up with one more damn thing. He collided with me, a huge snapping crunch that turned the world over, I flew. Hit the concrete bridge railing, more things breaking inside me, and a warm gout of blood exploded between my lips.

The crosses swayed, but the Traders had broken and were fleeing. The 'breed hanging in the bridge's spires slid away like oil, hissing at the terrible light spreading from the sunsword. Anya screamed, a hawk's cry, and stabbed down. The blade slid through Rutger's chest as if through soft butter, sinking into the concrete below just as effortlessly. Pavement scorched, and the 'breed's dying scream was lost in the inferno roar as the sunsword burned, cleansing the corruption.

Don't let go, Jill. Whatever happened to me, I had to keep the sunsword going. The Eye was a warm weight on my chest, humming along happily as something burned.

Don't you dare let go.

I tried to get up. My chest was broken, a fragile eggshell in pieces. The warmth between my lips was blood, I coughed up more. Perry bore down on me, his face avid with terrible glee, each footstep making the bridge sway like tall grass in a high wind.

The crosses were down now, Weres crowding them. They were cutting the leather straps free, and as I rolled my head painfully to get a better look, charms digging through my hair and into my skull, I saw two of them lift Saul tenderly between them. Perry's footsteps drew closer, each one like the heartbeat of some huge monstrous thing.

Relief burst inside me. I turned my head back. Looked up at him.

The sunsword's light etched lines on his face, eating at the shell of seeming he wore. I coughed again, fresh blood welling up. The scar jolted with sick heat, etheric force like a mass of red-hot wires sliding up the nerve channels and fusing flesh and bone back together. Healing me, probably so he could do more damage. And the corruption from the scar was spreading up to my shoulder.

I cried out, scrabbling weakly, a small sound lost in the chaos.

He loomed over me, his lips shaping words I didn't want to hear. Just two of them, really.

You're mine.

Helpless, I just lay and watched. *Get up, Jill. Get up and kick his ass.*

But Saul was safe, and the Weres had Gilberto too. There was nothing left to do but hold the sunsword's fire steady, the Eye burning as my blood touched it—

"Goddamn motherfucking sonofabitch, get the fuck away from her!"

Anya. The sunsword's light turned fierce white, the glare of full noon as the sun lifted its first limb over the rim of the mountains, and the world was lost in that brilliance. The light filled my eyes, my mouth, my nose, all the way down to my toes. I held the sunsword in sight as long as I could, realizing the hopeless broken cawing sounds I was hearing as quiet fell on the bridge were my own screams, my voice ruined.

The shadow that was Perry flinched aside from the assault of light. He was really such a small thing, that shadow.

I blacked out briefly, surfaced still holding the line to the sunsword. Nothing mattered but that line, etheric force thundering through it, and the cleansing light. If I was lucky, it would burn me to ash too, and—

"Let it go, Jill!" Anya yelled. "Let it *go*, or you'll melt the bridge! *Let go, hunter!*"

Again, that snap of command.

So I did, my mental fingers loosening. The white-hot glare receded, bit by bit, and the Eye hummed softly. The sense of pressure building inside the Talisman had bled off significantly. Like the spear hanging in my weapons room, it needed to be drained every once in a while, or it would get dangerous.

Even more dangerous than it usually was, that is. I had to tell Gilberto about it. So many things I had to do.

I lay there. There was a crackle, and a warm bath of sensation. It was healing sorcery, and if Anya was doing that, it meant the fight was over. I shut my eyes and let her work.

If I wasn't dead, I had to be able to walk for what I had to do next. But for the moment I just lay there on the bridge, listening as the Weres spoke softly and the sounds of hellbreed and Traders fleeing retreated in the distance.

30

Galina freed the stethescope's earbuds with a practiced motion. "He'll be fine," she said quietly. Her eyes glowed green, and the sunlight pouring through the window made her skin luminous. "A little bit of shock. They starved him. No sign of beatings or other abuse."

My fists refused to unclench. For once, I didn't try to hide it. "You promise? You *swear?*"

"Of course." She gave me an odd look, her necklace flashing against her white throat. "Are you all right?"

In other words: *What the fuck, Jill? You never doubted me before.*

"I just want to be sure," I mumbled. Stared at Saul's sleeping face. He was gaunt, and the yellow tint to his copper skin was new. His fingers were too thin, bony knobs.

Their metabolisms run a lot faster than regular humans'. It's one reason why Weres are all about the munchies.

I wanted to lie down on the bed next to him. Put my arms around him and whisper, *It's all okay, you're safe now*. But the scar was still burning. The corruption had been driven back, healing sorcery pushing it away as thin blue threads settled in and bound bone back together, repaired blood vessels and muscles, swirled through me and made every inch of silver on me glow softly. My right hand cramped, fingers squeezing down as if I held Perry's throat between them.

"Gilberto?" I whispered.

Galina sighed. But she was smiling wistfully. "Young. He'll bounce back. I gather he gave them quite a time. Doesn't know when to quit, that boy."

Sanctuaries are gentle souls. It's really terrible that so few people pass their entrance exams. The world could do with a few more.

"No, he doesn't." *It's part of being a hunter.*

Theron knocked at the door. The smell smoked off him in waves, an unhappy cat Were sending out a musk of aggression and combat readiness. "Kid's awake. Asking for you."

I nodded. "The altars?"

"We found four of them. Devi spiked them all. We had just enough time to get to the bridge. You okay?"

"Fine," I lied. It left my lips easily, a preparation for the other lies I was going to have to tell today. "Galina, can you give me a minute?"

"Sure. I should mix up some boneset for Gil anyway." She gave me another curious look, her eyes darkening before they cleared, and I had to work to keep my face set. "Are you sure you're all right, Jill?"

"Peachy. Just, you know. Tired." I exhaled sharply. "I'm getting too old for this shit."

"Pshaw. Mikhail said that all the time." She grinned,

slipped past me, and I saw her brush against Theron's arm as she left. He looked down, a private smile curling his lips, and my heart swelled up, lodged in my throat. They'd been dancing around each other for a while.

What else did Mikhail say to you, Galina? I didn't ask. What could she tell me? A big fat nothing, that's what.

Nothing that could save me.

She went down the hall to her spare bedroom. I heard Hutch ask her a question, her soft reply. It was like listening through cotton wool, I didn't have the scar jacking me up into redline sensitivity.

I never thought I'd miss that.

"Jill?" Theron sounded uneasy. I dragged my attention away from Saul's gaunt, yellow face.

"Tell him I love him." I didn't sound like myself. Who was the woman using my voice? It was a thin, colorless murmur. "Do you hear me, Theron? When he wakes up, you tell him that."

"You're going to tell him yourself." A crease appeared between his eyebrows. I hoped my face wasn't betraying me. "Right?"

"Yes." Another lie. Really racking them up. What did it matter? "Of course. But I want you to tell him as soon as he opens his eyes, Theron. It has to be the first thing he hears. Promise me."

He examined me, top to toe, for a long moment. I was covered in gunk, I hadn't even washed my face yet. Normally I like at least my cheeks and forehead clean, if nothing else. But this time I'd left the grime. I already felt filthy all the way down inside where soap couldn't reach. No washcloth was going to help.

"Theron." I tried not to sound like I was pleading. Failed miserably. "Please."

He nodded once, his dark sleek head dipping. "I promise. It will be the first thing he hears."

"Good." I did not look at the bed again. Closed the sight of Saul's face against the crisp, white pillowcase away, deep in my chest where the pain was already beginning. Took the first step away.

The steps got easier. I brushed past Theron, who took a deep breath. I was hoping the smell of the Eye, its forest-fire burning, would cover up everything else. He didn't move, just stood stock still as the ribbon-flayed edge of my coat brushed his leg.

"Jill?"

I paused, between one step and the next. If he asked me . . . "Huh?"

"Don't do anything stupid." He stared at the bed, that line still between his eyebrows, his profile clean and classic. They're all so *beautiful*, the human flaws burnished away.

It's enough to make you sick.

I found something closer to my regular tone. "I'm a *hunter*, Theron. It's part of the job description. See you."

I didn't precisely hurry out of there and down the stairs, but I didn't take my time either.

Past the kitchen, where Weres congregated, speaking softly. I made it up the ladder, quietly but not *too* quietly, as if I just wanted a moment alone or to check on the sunsword. I reached the greenhouse, climbing up through the trapdoor, and found my escape path blocked.

I should have known Anya would be waiting for me.

She held a cup of coffee, the venomous-green absinthe

bottle set on the table where the sunsword glittered. It drank in the morning light, no glimmer of red in the empty space its hilt curled around. Its clawed finials twitched a little, like the paw of a dreaming cat. That was all.

Anya studied me. Half her face was bruised, the swelling visibly retreating under the fine thin blue lines of healing sorcery. I looked back at her.

Silver glittered in her hair and at her throat, her apprentice-ring sending a hard dart of light into a corner as she lifted her coffee cup. It paused on the way to her lips. She lowered it, set it on the table.

Silence stretched between us. Her clear blue gaze, no quarter asked or given.

I'd thought I could lie even to a fellow hunter now. I was wrong.

I reached down with my left hand, slowly. Pushed my right sleeve up, heavy leather dried stiff with blood and other things. Unsnapped the buckle. Dropped the cuff on the floor, and turned my wrist so she could see.

The air left her all in a rush, as if she'd taken a good hard sucker punch. "Jesus," she finally whispered, the sibilants lasting a long time. "Jill—"

"This stays between us." I was now back to sounding like myself, clear and brassy. All hail Jill Kismet, the great pretender. "I'm going to take care of it."

She didn't disbelieve me, not precisely. "How the hell are you going to do that?"

I shrugged.

She read it on my face, and another sharp exhale left her. "And if..."

I suppose I should have been grateful that she couldn't bring herself to ask the question. So I answered it anyway.

"If it doesn't work, Anya, you will have to hunt me down. No pity, no mercy, no *nothing*. Kill me before I'm a danger to my city. Kill Perry too. Burn him, scatter the ashes as far as you can. Clear?"

She grabbed the absinthe bottle. Tipped it up, took a good long healthy draft, her throat working. "Shit."

"Promise me, Anya Devi. Give me your word." Now I just sounded weary. My cheek twitched, a muscle in it committing rebellion. The scar cringed under the assault of sunlight, I kept it out. The pain was a balm.

She lowered the bottle. Wiped the back of her mouth with one hand. "You have my word." Quietly.

I dropped my right hand. With my left, I pulled the Talisman up. Freed the sharp links from my hair, gently. It was hard to do one-handed, but I managed. I took six steps, laid the Eye on the table. The sunsword quivered. "For Gilberto. Will you . . ."

"You don't even have to ask. I'll train him."

Then she offered me the bottle.

Tears rose hot and prickling. I pushed them down. Took a swallow, the licorice tang turning my stomach over and my cracked lips stinging. When I handed it back to her, she didn't wipe the mouth of the bottle. Instead, her gaze holding mine, she lifted it to her lips too.

I bit the inside of my cheek. Hard, so hard I tasted blood. The thought that it would be tinged with black made my stomach revolve again. There were so many things I wanted to say. Things like *thank you*, or even *I love you*.

Because I do. We are lonely creatures, we hunters. We have to love each other. We are the only ones who understand, the only ones who will.

Except I wasn't a hunter anymore, was I.

"I need a car," I croaked. "It won't be coming back."

"Shit." It was a pale attempt at a joke, and neither of us smiled. She dug in her pocket and fished out two keys on a keychain that also held a cast-silver wishbone. "Here's my spares. Take them."

I nodded. Tweezed them delicately out of her fingers, but she was quick—she caught my wrist. Warm human skin against mine, and she tugged a little. We stood under the flood of clean yellow light.

She licked her lips. "Mikhail was a good hunter." As if daring me to disagree.

It was hard to get anything out, around the lump in my throat. "One of the best."

"So are you." Her mouth set. "You do what you have to, Jill. I'll take care of everything here."

My face crumpled. I squeezed my left hand into a fist around the keys, sharp edges digging into my palm. The scar burbled unhappily, and the thin creeping tendrils of corruption slid another few millimeters up my arm.

Just like gangrene.

She let go of me, a centimeter at a time. I stepped away, set my shoulders. The protections on Galina's walls shimmered.

"I'm parked west of here, around the corner." Anya's hand fell back to her side. She held the absinthe bottle like a lifeline. "*Vaya con Dios*, Kismet."

"*Y tú tambien*, Devi." I half-turned and headed for the door. By the time Galina realized I was leaving, I'd already be out.

My cheeks were hot and slick with saltwater. By the time I hit the door, I was running.

31

The closest freeway on-ramp took me north and slightly west, toward the fierce heart of the desert. Anya's car was a newer Ford Escort, fire-engine red and with no pickup at all. A cheap plastic glow-in-the-dark rosary hung from the mirror, and she had four bobblehead hula girls stuck to the dash, one of them with cropped punk hair. They bobbed and swayed, their gentle vacuous smiles faintly creepy.

The thing barely went seventy. Still, it was wheels. I drove all afternoon, the windows down and sheer golden sunlight parting in shimmering veils. Past the city signs, out to where the road met the horizon. That's the thing about America—you get to some places and there's so much space. It's amazing and faintly nauseating that people pack themselves into cities, living on top of each other like rats in a warren.

If it was summer the tar on the road would have been sticky. As it was, it was one of those rare winter days that's almost balmy, a cloudless pale sky and the sun like a white coin. It's the kind of weather snowbirds come down for, to bake all the aches out of their bones.

When the shadows started lengthening I checked the map, found a handy access road, and slowed down in time to catch it. The car bounced and juddered over wash-board ruts, and it was a good thing Anya wasn't expecting her car back. The suspension probably wouldn't survive this.

I saw an outcropping I recognized, guesstimated the distance, and turned the wheel hard. There was no ditch, so the car immediately bounced and wallowed in sandy soil. I worked the accelerator—the brake will make you fishtail worse than anything in sand or snow. At least Anya understood about keeping her car in reasonably good condition. Leon Budge, out Ridgefield way, seemed to keep his truck going with spit and baling wire.

The rocks in the distance were a little farther away than I'd thought, and the sun was touching the horizon by the time I skidded to a stop, a roostertail of dust hanging in the evening air. This far out there was no breath of the river, just the smell of heat and the peculiar flat-iron tang of bone-dry air in winter. The desert smells of minerals, like dried blood without the rust.

My right arm hung limp. I made sure the windows were rolled up, got out of the car, and stretched.

I thought I'd remembered this place correctly, and of course I was right. The outcropping was marked on sur-vey maps, at the edge of a lunar landscape dotted with other rocks, some bigger than houses, others bigger than skyscrapers. Other than that, it seems empty. There's life everywhere in the desert if you know where to look, but in late afternoon it appears barren as an alien planet.

I stepped onto fine sand, into the mouth of a pile of black stone. The semicircle of stacked black rock was glossy, a type that didn't belong in this area. Heaven alone knew what had dropped it here. Inside, the sand was fine and thick, blown in by a wind that somehow avoided sending trash or tumbleweeds along. It was sterile and clean, and I picked the edge farthest inside.

Thirst stung my throat. I hadn't brought a drop of water, and my stupid stomach growled loudly, thinking it was time to get some chow since the bad part was past.

The flesh is always so weak, no matter how hard you train it. I didn't have the heart to explain to my stupid body that the worst was coming.

Outside, the wind moaned against sharp glassy edges. I slid out my left-hand gun and settled down cross-legged, my back to the stone's cup but not touching it, leaving me a good three or four feet of room. Etheric force hummed sleepily through this rock, and the air was a few degrees cooler than outside. I checked the ammo, a trick to do one-handed, and settled the gun in my lap.

I waited.

The sun sank by degrees. I had to pee. It was an urge just like hunger, and I ignored it. Drew the hunter's cloak of silence over me. Peeled my right sleeve up a little, looked at the inside of my wrist.

The mark was hard and cancerous now, the skin swollen and hot. The thin unhealthy threads of corruption spreading were now hard and black as well, a shiny crackglaze on my skin. My entire arm felt numb up to the ball of my shoulder, occasional pins and needles jabbing and tingling.

Night falls quick out in the desert. I breathed deep,

brought my pulse down. As soon as the sun touched the horizon, I concentrated on my left hand.

Not long now. Not long at all.

The banefire hurt. It *burned*. Blisters rose on my left hand, and silver shifted uneasily in my hair, rattling. The silver chain of my ruby necklace, the apprentice-ring on my third left finger, all warmed dangerously. But the twisting blue flames came, bubbling and boiling. I flicked my fingers, and the banefire leapt. It obeyed, snaking in a ragged circle from one curve of rock to the other. I was tucked safely inside here, and as soon as the circle of banefire closed there was a not-quite-physical *snap*.

My right arm cramped, curling up as if the triceps had been cut. The ball of my right fist struck my shoulder, and I made a small hurt sound.

"This won't do any good." Perry melded out of the shadows.

He was immaculate. White linen suit, wine-red tie, but snakeskin boots instead of the usual polished wingtips. His hair was longer, and messy. Instead of his usual blandness, his face had morphed into sharp, severe handsomeness. The bladed curves of his cheekbones could have gotten him a modeling contract, even if the photographer could have caught a glimpse of what lay below.

He took a mincing step forward, but the rock creaked and groaned. Banefire leapt and he froze, staring at me.

Thank you, God. My left-hand fingers found a knife hilt. I drew the blade free. Shifted a little bit, careful to keep the gun in my lap. "How long have you been working on this, Perry?"

"Longer than you can imagine." He was utterly still, but his mouth twitched into a wide, mad, hungry grin.

"One must be careful, don't you find? When one has a plan, one must be very exquisitely careful. Everything must be just so."

"You never intended to let Julius live, but he distracted everyone nicely. If Argoth would have come through, you would have bargained with me to send him back." My chin dipped, I nodded wearily. "If he didn't you were sure I'd damn myself with Belisa. Or, if not, I'd trade myself for Saul's safety. Any way you sliced it, you won."

"I traded some rather large favors to acquire the collar and chain. Then it was only a matter of finding the Sorrow to go into it. Simpler than I thought, too. She never managed to go very far from you, darling. You fascinated her."

Not anymore. I tried forcing my right arm to uncurl. It didn't want to. I struggled, sweating, and the banefire hissed. It cast weird leaping shadows all over the rock, turned Perry's face into a caricature of handsomeness. He moved slightly, shifting his weight, and the banefire leapt again.

Mikhail had brought me out to these rocks once. It's good to know where places of power are, even if they're a day's drive from your territory. You just never know. The humming force inside the stones fueled the banefire nicely, and as long as I concentrated . . .

He watched as I uncurled my arm, inch by inch. His lips parted slightly, avid, and the red flash of his scaled tongue flicked once, twice. "A deal's a deal."

I set the knifeblade against the meat of my right hand, drew it across with a butterfly kiss. It stung, and flesh parted. Red welled up.

I stared at it in the shifting light. The tracery of black at its edges mocked me.

I drove the knife into the sand next to me. Picked up the gun. Hefted it, and looked at him.

If his grin got any wider, the top of his head would flip open.

I pointed the gun at him and smiled. The expression sat oddly on my face. He hissed, Helletöng rumbling in the back of his throat.

I almost understood the words, too. A shiver raced down my spine.

"You can't escape me." The rock groaned as his voice lashed at it, little glassy bits flaking away. They plopped down on the sand with odd ringing sounds. "The fire won't last forever, my darling. Then I'll step over your line in the sand, and you'll find out what it means to be mine."

"Think again." I bent my left arm. Fitted the gun's barrel inside my mouth. My eyes were dry, my body tensing against the inevitable.

Comprehension hit. Perry snarled and lunged at the banefire. It roared up, a sheet of blue flame. Twisting faces writhed in its smokeless glow, their mouths open as they whisper-screamed.

I glanced down at the slice on my palm. Still bleeding. It was hard to tell if the black traceries were still there. For a moment, I wondered.

Then I brought myself back to the thing I had to do. Stupid body, getting all worked up. What the will demands, the body will do—but it also tries to wriggle, sometimes.

Not this time.

"*Kiss!*" he howled. "*You're mine! MINE! You cannot escape me!*"

I saw Saul's face, yellow and exhausted, against the white pillow. I smelled him, the musk and fur of a healthy cat Were. I saw Galina's wide green eyes and marcel waves, Hutch's shy smile, Gilberto's fierce, glittering dark gaze. I saw them all, saw my city perched on the river's edge, its skyscrapers throwing back dusk's last light with a vengeance before the dark things crawled out of their holes. I saw Anya perched on Galina's roof with her green bottle, staring down at the street and wondering if I had the strength to do this. Wondering if she would have to hunt me down, if I failed here.

And I heard Mikhail. *There, little snake. Honest silver, on vein to heart. You are apprentice. Now it begins.*

I love you, I thought. *I love you all.*

"*You cannot escape!*" Perry screamed, throwing himself at the banefire again. It sizzled and roared, and the rocks around me begin to ring like a crystal wineglass stroked just right. If this kept up they might shatter.

Wouldn't *that* be a sight.

"*Do you hear me, hunter? You cannot escape me!*"

Watch me, I thought, and squeezed both eyes shut. The banefire roared as he tried again to get through, actually thrusting a hand through its wall, snatching it back with a shattering howl as the skin blackened and curled. It was now or never.

I pulled the trig—

To Be Continued

Glossary

Arkeus: A roaming corruptor escaped from Hell.

Banefire: A cleansing sorcerous flame.

Black Mist: A roaming psychic contagion; a symbiotic parasite inhabiting the host's nervous system and bloodstream.

Chutsharak: Chaldean obscenity, loosely translated as "oh, *fuck*."

Demon: Term loosely used to designate any nonhuman predator with sorcerous ability or a connection to Hell.

Exorcism: Tearing loose a psychic parasite from its host.

Hellbreed: Blanket term for a wide array of demons, half demons, or other species escaped or sent from Hell.

Helletöng: The language of the damned.

Hellfire: The spectrum of sorcerous flame employed by hellbreed for a variety of uses.

Hunter: A trained human who keeps the balance between the nightside and regular humans; extrahuman law enforcement.

Imdarák: Shadowy former race who drove the Elder Gods from the physical plane, also called the Lords of the Trees.

Martindale Squad: The FBI division responsible for tracking nightside crime across state lines and at the federal level; mostly staffed with hunters and Weres.

Middle Way: Worshippers of Chaos, Middle Way adepts are usually sociopathic and sorcerous loners. Occasionally covens of Middle Way adepts will come together to control a territory or for a specific purpose.

OtherSight: Second sight; the ability to see sorcerous energy. Can also mean precognition.

Possessor: An insubstantial, low-class demon specializing in occupying and controlling humans; the prime reason for exorcists.

Scurf: Also called *nosferatim,* a semipsychic viral infection responsible for legends of blood-hungry corpses, vampires, or nosferatu. Also, someone infected by the scurf virus.

Sorrow: A worshipper of the Chaldean Elder Gods.

Sorrows House: A House inhabited by Sorrows, with a vault for invocation or evocation of Elder Gods.

Sorrows Mother: A high-ranking female of a Sorrows House.

Talyn: A hellbreed, higher in rank than an *arkeus* or a Possessor, usually insubstantial due to the nature of the physical world.

Trader: A human who makes a deal with a hellbreed, usually for worldly gain or power.

Utt'huruk: A bird-headed demon.

Were: Blanket term for several species who shapeshift into animal (for example, cougar, wolf, or spider) or half animal (wererat or *khentauri*) form.

extras

orbit

meet the author

LILITH SAINTCROW was born in New Mexico, bounced around the world as an Air Force brat, and fell in love with writing when she was ten years old. She currently lives in Vancouver, Washington.

Find her on the web at: www.lilithsaintcrow.com.

introducing

If you enjoyed HEAVEN'S SPITE,
look out for

ANGEL TOWN

The final volume of the Jill Kismet series
by Lilith Saintcrow

In the shifting wood of suicides that borders the cold rivers of Hell, what is one tree more or less?

They are every color, those trees. Every shade of the rainbow, and colors humans cannot see. Every color except one, but that has changed.

There is one white tree. It is a slender shape, like a birch, and instead of a screaming face hidden in the bark, there is a sleeping woman's features carved with swift strokes. Eyes closed, mouth relaxed, she is a peaceful white pillar amid the shifting.

Hell is cold. The trees shake their leaves, a roaring filling their branches.

Under the spinning-nausea sky full of the dry stars of an alien geometry, something new happens.

Pinpricks of light settle into the white tree's naked branches. She has not even been here long enough to grow the dark, tumescent leaves every other tree shakes now. The screaming of their distress mounts, for these trees are conscious. They do not sleep as she does. Their bloodshot eyes are always open, their distended mouths always moving.

The pinpricks move like fireflies on a summer evening, each one a semaphore gracefully unconnected to the whole. They crown the tree with light, weaving tiny trails of phosphorescence in the gasping-cold fluid that passes for air in this place. They tangle the streamers, and the storm is very close.

Hell has noticed this intrusion. And Hell is not pleased.

The streams and trails of light form a complex net. The other trees thrash. Takemetakemetakemetakeme, *they scream, a rising chorus of the damned. Their roots hold them fast, sunk deep in metallic burning ash. The river rises, white streaks of foam like clutching, clawed hands on its oil-sheen surface. Leaves splatter, torn free, and their stinking blood makes great splotches on the ash. A cloud of buzzing black rises from each splotch, feeding greedily on the glistening fluid.*

The net is almost complete. Almost. Hell's skies are whipped with fury, the storm breaking over the first edge of the wood with screaming thunder. Malformed, maggot-white lightning scorches. The pale net over the white tree draws close, like a woman pulling her hair back.

Long dark hair, spangled with silver.

The storm descends, ripping trees apart. The souls of the damned explode with screams that would turn the world to bleeding ice, if the world heard. And the ashes of their destruction will sink into the carpet on the floor of the woods, each separate particle growing another tree.

For there is always more agony in Hell.

The net collapses, silvery filaments winding themselves in. It shrinks to a point of brilliance, and the shadows that light casts are somehow cleansed. They etch themselves on the ash, and under the wrack of the storm is a sound like a soft sigh.

The light... winks out.

A few tiny, crystalline-white feathers fall, but they snuff themselves out before they reach the heaving ground.

The white tree no longer stands. It is gone.

And Hell itself shakes.

Buzzing. In my head. All around me. Creeping in.

No, not a buzzing. A rattling roar, filling my skull. Crawling into my teeth, sticky little insect feet all over my face, feelers probing at my lips. They move, hot and pinprick-tiny, and that sound was enough to drag me screaming out of...

... where?

Dark. It was *dark,* and there was no air. Sand filled my mouth, but the little things crawling on me weren't sand. They were *alive*, and they were droning loud enough to drown out everything but the sounds I was making. Terrifying sounds. Suffocating, it was in my mouth and my nose, too, stopping everything, lungs starved, heart suddenly a pounding drum.

Scrabbling through sand, dirt everywhere, the buzzing

turning into a roar as they lifted off me. The insects didn't sting; they just made that horrible sound and flew in disturbed little circles.

I exploded out of the shallow grave, my screams barely piercing the rumbling roar. The little bits of flying things buzzed angrily, flashing lights struck me like hammers and I fell, scrabbling, the wasps still crawling and buzzing and trying to probe through my mouth and nose and ears and eyes and hands and feet and belly.

They were still eating, because it had rotted.

I had rotted.

I scrubbed at myself as the train lumbered past. That was the light and the roaring. My back hit something solid and I jolted to a stop. The wasps crawled over me, and when I forced air out through my nose it blew slimy chunks of snot-laced sand into the night air.

I collapsed against the low retaining wall, breath sobbing in and out. My head rang like a gong, I bent over and vomited up a mass of dark writhing liquid.

The stench was awesome, titanic, a living thing. It crawled on the breeze, pressed against me, and I vomited again. This time it was long strands of gooey white, splatting. Coming from nowhere and passing through me, landing in twisting runnels.

Just like cotton candy! a gleeful, hateful voice crowed inside my head. The eggwhite was all over me, a loathsome slime turning the sand into a rasping dampness.

I squeezed my knees together, bent over, and whooped in a deep breath. The wasps crawled, and other bits of insect life clung to me. Maggots. Other things. Of course—out here in the desert, the bugs get to you after a little while. Especially in a shallow grave, when there's been trauma to the tissues.

I grabbed my head. The sound was immense, filling me up, the roaring swallowing my scream. Gobbets of rotting flesh fell away, the wasps angrily swarming, and the train rumbled away into the distance.

Leaving me alone. In the night.

I tore at the rotting flesh cloaking me. It peeled away in noisome strips, and under it I was whole, slick with slime. I retched again, a huge tearing coming all the way up from my toes, and produced an amazing gout of that slippery egg-white stuff again.

Ectoplasm? But—The thought floated away as the pain came down on me, laid me open. Head cracked open, bones twisting, everything in me cracking and creaking and re-forming. My knees refused to give; my short-bitten nails dug through the cloak of rotting and found my own skin underneath.

I scrambled along the retaining wall. The grave yawned, leering, crawling with disturbed insect life. I fell on sand, grubbed up handfuls of it, and scrubbed at myself. I didn't care if it stripped skin off and left me bleeding, didn't care if it went down to bone—I just wanted the rot *away*.

Under the mess of decaying flesh was a torn T-shirt, rags of what had been leather pants. At least I had some clothes. I was barefoot.

I collapsed to my knees on the sand, looked up.

A full moon hung grinning in the sky, bloated cheese-yellow. The hard, clear points of stars glittered, and steam slid free of my skin.

Whole skin. Clear, unblemished, scraped in places. But not rotting.

The pain retreated abruptly. My questing fingers

found filthy hair, stiff with sand and God knew what else. The wasps were sluggish—it gets cold out here at night. Everything else was burrowing.

My skull was still there. Hard curves of bone, tender at the back. I let out a sob. Held my hands out, flipped them palm-up. They shook like palsied things.

Branches. Like branches.

But the image mercifully fled as soon as it arrived. My forearms were pale under the screen of filth. On my right wrist, just above the softest part, something glittered. Hard, like a diamond. It caught the moonlight and sent back a dart of it, straight through my aching skull. The sight filled me with unsteady loathing, and I shut my eyes.

Start with the obvious first. Who am I?

The train's rumble receded.

Who am I?

I tilted my head back and screamed, a lonely curlew cry.

Because I didn't know.